NIGHT

at the

OPERA

STACY HENRIE

Mirror Press

Interior Design by Cora Johnson
Edited by Kelsey Down and Lisa Shepherd
Cover design by Rachael Anderson
Cover Image Credit: Arcangel

Published by Mirror Press, LLC
ISBN-13: 978-1-947152-39-7

Chapter 1

The late afternoon sun poured through the open carriage window like a weary traveler anxious for a chance to rest his aching feet. Gwen Barton could relate. Her left foot throbbed inside her shoe after standing in place too long, but she felt no resentment. Not even the sticky heat outside could upset her mood. A full day of helping at Heartwell House always left her feeling tired but happy.

She brushed her errant black curls away from her dampened forehead. If her mother were here, Cornelia would insist the window shades be drawn down. But Gwen relished the slightly cooler air moving across her flushed cheeks as the carriage navigated its way toward the Bartons' brownstone.

From the window, Gwen watched businessmen striding purposefully down the sidewalks, while clusters of women walked more sedately beneath their summer parasols, none of them with a limp. She shifted against the leather seat as the carriage turned a corner. A small boy stood there, a beggar's cup in hand and a crutch tucked under his arm.

"Stop the carriage, please," she called out the window. The wheels rolled forward another few yards, then the vehicle settled to a stop.

1

The driver appeared at her door moments later to help her out. "I'll be right back, Jenkins. Though it's possible we may have to return to the orphanage before continuing toward home."

"It's quite all right, Miss Barton," the gray-haired man said, his eyes twinkling with understanding.

Gwen kept her steps slow, as much to disguise her limp as to avoid adding to the ache in her foot, and crossed the short distance from the carriage to the boy. "Hello there."

"Spare a penny, miss?" He held up his cup.

Crouching down, she did her best to ignore the curious and disapproving glances she sensed from those streaming past them. "What's your name?"

"Don't got one," the boy said with a shrug. He couldn't be more than six years old, though the dirt smudges on his cheeks made it difficult to tell.

"What do your parents call you?"

He eyed her suspiciously. "Don't got those neither. Who's askin'?"

"I'm Gwen Barton," she said, touching the lacy bodice of her dress with her gloved hand. "And I'd like to help you."

Some of the toughness faded from his expression. "How?"

"My cousin runs a home near here for orphaned children."

"I ain't going to no orphanage."

Giving him a nod, she straightened. "I understand. If you change your mind, though, you can earn three meals a day and a bed all to yourself at this orphanage, in exchange for doing your daily chores and some trade work."

"Three meals?" The longing on his face squeezed at her heart. "But what could I do with this bum leg?" He jiggled the leg favoring the crutch.

Swallowing the lump in her throat, Gwen leaned close to whisper, "Quite a lot, actually. I myself have a bum foot."

"You do?" He appeared more surprised than skeptical.

Gwen lifted the hem of her skirt an inch or so, just enough for the boy to see the crooked twist of her left foot. "There's still a lot we can do, especially with two good hands."

She meant the words each and every time she thought or spoke them, though they didn't always succeed in squelching her own moments of doubt. Moments when she also wondered at what she could contribute to the world and how much more that might be if her foot hadn't been injured, or had healed properly. But her injury wasn't void of purpose. Without it, Gwen would not have discovered her calling to aid God's injured and orphaned lambs, nor would she have gained the compassion that flowed through her as she regarded this small boy before her.

"What do you say? I can take you to Heartwell House right now in my carriage. Dinner will be served in about an hour."

The boy smacked his lips together as if he could smell the freshly baked bread the girls apprenticing in the kitchen had made that morning. "All righty."

Smiling, Gwen held out her hand. He plopped his dirty palm in hers, and together they walked slowly to the waiting carriage. Jenkins didn't bat an eye at the newcomer. Instead he assisted both Gwen and the boy inside the vehicle. His kindness, and loyal discretion, had long endeared him to Gwen.

"Back to Heartwell House, please, Jenkins."

"Right away, Miss Barton."

As the man shut the carriage door, the boy stared wide-eyed at the fine leather interior. "Are you rich, miss?" he half whispered, his voice tinged with awe.

"My father is."

Although next year, if she was still unmarried at the age of twenty-one, Gwen would inherit a large sum from her fortune. And she knew exactly where the majority of it would go. She'd promised her cousin Dean Griffin and his wife, Amie, the owners of Heartwell House, that she would provide the needed funds to build another wing and employ a doctor who specialized in the treatment of childhood injuries and illnesses. Not unlike the renowned Dr. William Smithfield in London. Gwen had read every article her cousin had saved about the man's remarkable work with restoring mobility in previously injured limbs. Hopefully she and the Griffins would be able to find someone like him here in America.

Gwen asked the boy about his family as the carriage turned around and headed back in the direction she'd come. He had been left to fend for himself after the death of his older brother the year before and couldn't remember much about his parents. Unlike Gwen's injury, which had been the result of a carriage accident, his had come after getting his leg caught beneath the wheel of an automobile two years ago. He thought he remembered a doctor coming by. But Gwen guessed that with little to no money, the boy and his brother had likely been left to their own devices as far as helping the leg to heal.

When they reached the orphanage, Jenkins helped them from the carriage. Gwen led the way to the front door. "You ready?" she asked, her hand on the doorknob.

"Teddy."

"Pardon?"

The boy shot her a hesitant smile. "My brother called me Teddy. Said I had the makings of bein' a president. Just like that Teddy fellow."

"Teddy. I like it." Gwen returned his smile. "And I have a feeling your brother was right."

The boy's entire face lit with happiness, restoring the lump of emotion to Gwen's throat. She gave Teddy's shoulder a gentle squeeze before opening the door. "Dean? Amie?" she called as she ushered the boy into the foyer.

"Did you forget something, Gwen?" Dean's voice floated out from the small office to the left.

She moved to stand in the open doorway. "More like I found something." She motioned for Teddy to come stand beside her. "This is my new friend, Teddy. Teddy, this is Mr. Griffin. As you can see, Dean, the boy is a lot like me, but he's also confident that he can earn his keep here."

Dean circled his desk and squatted before the boy. "Would you like to live and work at Heartwell House, Teddy?"

The boy glanced up at Gwen, then back at the man. "Yes, sir."

"Then I'll have my wife show you to your room before you wash up for dinner." Dean rose to his feet. "I think peach pie is on the menu for dessert."

The boy's eyes bugged out, making Gwen laugh. "I ain't never had peach pie."

"You will tonight," Gwen said. "I have to go now, Teddy. But I'll see you tomorrow."

"All righty. Bye, then . . . Miss Gwen." He grinned at his little rhyme, and the gesture was almost carefree.

"You're going to be late for your own dinner," Dean murmured with a hint of humor as he trailed her to the main door.

"I know, I know."

"How much longer will she indulge your work here?" Her cousin followed her out the door and onto the front step.

Gwen didn't need to ask who he meant. "Hopefully, for a very long time. I think my mother has—blessedly—given up on my ever marrying. Especially since there are no bachelors in New York who don't already know about my limp."

With a shrug, she spread her arms wide as if in surrender. "My guess is she's trying to find contentment over having only one of her two children married."

Gwen's only sibling and older brother, Charlie, had wed the heiress of an old New York family the year before. But even that hadn't elevated the family to the elite status among American aristocracy that Cornelia Barton greatly desired.

"Aren't you still heading to Newport this week, though?"

"Yes, but only because that's what we do every summer—not because she hopes I'll make a suitable match."

While the Bartons might not be American aristocrats, they did follow the dictates of high society, which included summering in Rhode Island. To Cornelia's dismay, Gwen had been as unsuccessful in securing a husband in Newport as she had in New York.

"I'm confident my mother won't care how or where I spend my time once we return to the city in September."

Dean smiled as he pocketed his hands. "I hope you're right, Gwen. Amie and I greatly appreciate your help."

With a wave goodbye, Gwen moved as quickly as her foot would allow, and with Jenkins's help, scrambled back inside the carriage. Her tardiness would likely result in a thorough scolding. After all, married or unattached, she was still expected to conduct herself as a lady, which meant being prompt. Even the inevitability of a tongue lashing, though, couldn't dampen her spirits. Not when she'd been able to offer real help to another human being as she had with Teddy just now. It was why she loved coming to the orphanage as often as she could. And why she would keep coming.

The only other thing that would seal this day's perfection would be reading a new romance novel. But last night she'd finished the most recent one loaned to her by her best friend, Syble. Which meant no new book to escape into tonight. No new story that would allow Gwen to believe, if only for a time, that she too was as flawless in form as the young heroine and would soon be loved in return by the hero.

In reality, she'd endured two unsuccessful social seasons and had had her heart broken when the man she had come to care for had thrown her over for a woman who wasn't "new money" and had no limp. But even if Gwen was still known around town as Randolph's cast-off sweetheart, even if she ended up a spinster as her mother feared, even if she never gained back the agility in her foot, she would try not to complain. Surely there was something of value she could offer the world at large, limp or no limp. After all, she had her faith and a purpose in helping at the orphanage, as well as the relative freedom to come and go as she pleased, and for that she would remember to be grateful.

⌒๑๏᠔๑⌒

Gwen slipped into the house through a back entrance to avoid coming face to face with the butler. Stealth was difficult to achieve with her injured foot, but she managed to inch her way undetected to the stairs. If she could just change for dinner without being spotted first . . .

The murmur of voices coming from the parlor and not the dining room made her pause. Surely her mother wouldn't be entertaining visitors at this hour. Gwen didn't recall being told they were to have guests join them for dinner this evening, either.

As she hesitated beside the grand staircase, she heard footsteps nearing the parlor door. Too late, she started up the stairs.

"Gwenyth, there you are," her mother called from below. Her tone held none of the censure Gwen had expected. "Come say goodbye to the Rinecrofts."

7

Syble had been here? A flicker of disappointment at missing the chance to spend time with her friend cut through Gwen as she turned to face the small group. "I'm sorry I missed your visit. I was delayed on my way home from Heartwell House."

"Not to worry, dear." Mrs. Rinecroft turned and followed Gwen's mother toward the front door.

Gwen descended the stairs to join Syble. "I didn't know you were coming over today."

"Neither did I." Her best friend gave her a quick hug. As Syble eased back, she pressed a book into Gwen's gloved hand.

Glancing down, Gwen felt a thrill of anticipation as she studied the volume. "A new romance?" she whispered.

Syble's smile widened as she nodded. "Come along, Syble," Mrs. Rinecroft intoned. "We shall be late for dinner if we don't hurry."

"I can't wait for the trip to London," Syble murmured softly, her blue eyes sparkling with excitement.

Gwen threw her friend a puzzled look. "Don't you mean Newport?" Like the Bartons, the Rinecrofts were "new money," but they also made the pilgrimage to Rhode Island each summer.

"Oh, we'll be heading there too."

Her confusion grew, but there wasn't time to ask what Syble meant. The moment the butler shut the door behind the two women, Cornelia spun to face her daughter.

"I'm sorry I was not home sooner, Mother." Better to face the firing squad outright than wait and let it spoil dinner. "I had an unexpected . . . errand . . . come up."

To Gwen's astonishment, her mother waved away her apology. "We need to dress for dinner. I told Cook to delay the meal by thirty minutes, but that doesn't give us long to change."

"How was your visit with the Rinecrofts?" Gwen asked as she trailed her mother up the stairs.

"It was unexpected and yet most . . . enlightening."

Gwen lifted her eyebrows in bewilderment. "Oh?"

"Do you remember Clare Herschel?"

"Yes." Clare had debuted into society the same year as Gwen and Syble. "Isn't she in London this summer?"

Cornelia nodded. "She and her mother went for the season, but now Clare is engaged to an earl. She'll be Lady Linwood come October." Her smug expression almost made it seem as if she herself had orchestrated the match. "Mrs. Rinecroft and Syble came by to show me the announcement in the newspaper."

"How . . . wonderful . . . for Clare." Gwen liked the copper-haired heiress—Clare had always treated her kindly—and wished her well in marriage. But Gwen wouldn't want to marry an Englishman who would expect her to live away from New York. Away from her work at Heartwell House.

Stopping outside her bedroom door, Gwen caught a calculating gleam in her mother's brown eyes. Something more was afoot than a wedding announcement for Clare Herschel, but Gwen couldn't ascertain what it might be.

"Is that all Mrs. Rinecroft wished to discuss?"

"Oh no, that was merely the beginning of our discussion." Cornelia opened her own door and stepped inside. "I'll share the rest at dinner."

Uneasiness settled in the pit of Gwen's stomach as she entered her bedroom. Her maid was already waiting for her, which meant that changing out of her sticky, wrinkled gown into a fresh one took little time. Gwen didn't wish to prolong the suspense of what her mother wanted to share any longer than necessary. Still, her parents were already seated when she entered the dining room. Her father asked about her day as the servants placed dishes in front of the family.

"It went well," Gwen answered with hesitation.

Normally, she received a sniff of disapproval or a curt remark from her mother whenever Gwen talked about the orphanage. Tonight, however, Cornelia appeared to be lost in thought, a bemused smile on her lips. The sight of it worsened the churning inside Gwen.

Silence reigned for a few minutes as they ate, though Gwen hardly tasted the normally delicious fare. At last, her mother cleared her throat and dabbed at her lips with her napkin. "I have wonderful news, Gwen."

Gwen gave a mute nod before taking a sip from her glass, mentally bracing herself for whatever blow was coming. In the past, what her mother deemed as wonderful news had been far from it in Gwen's opinion.

"You and I are going to London."

The liquid in Gwen's throat collided with her startled gasp and she sputtered. "W-when? What for?"

"Don't stammer, Gwen." Cornelia shot her a frown. "We're going next spring, for the season, of course."

Prickles of both heat and frost broke out on Gwen's skin. She glanced at her father in a silent plea for help, for some protest at the outrageous plan. Gwen had no interest in experiencing another season, especially not one a whole ocean away from everything familiar to her, where her injury would invite ridicule and disdain all over again. In New York, the practice of treating her like a sideshow spectacle had faded with time and familiarity. Acceptance had never come, but at least here, society had reached the point of indifference. In London, she would have to start all over again. She wanted to beg her father to spare her that mortification. But he seemed unusually intent on finishing his dinner.

Disappointment cut sharply through her. Charles Barton would brook no argument in his daughter's favor.

"I've already had two seasons," Gwen managed to say calmly. Perhaps an appeal to logic would work this time, even if it hadn't before. "I hardly see the point of financing a third, particularly in another country."

Cornelia swatted away her words with an impatient hand. "No expense is too great if you can land an earl as Clare Herschel has done."

"Miss Herschel is marrying an earl?" her father asked.

"Yes, Charles. And our daughter can do the same. In fact, I wouldn't be surprised if she won the heart of a duke or a marquess." A wistful look settled onto her face. "There are yet titled Englishmen in London who don't mind a rich American wife."

Gwen set her napkin on the table. She couldn't stomach another bite. Not when panic churned inside her middle. "Mother, I don't need to marry an earl or a duke. I'm perfectly happy as I am."

"How can you possibly know what will make you happy?" Cornelia's gaze snapped with irritation. "As a titled lady, you won't be barred from entering the highest echelons of society. Nothing will be withheld from you."

"Except the full use of my foot."

Her father winced at Gwen's harsh tone, but her mother did not. "You know what you must do to compensate for your limp."

Yes, she did. Gwen had heard the firm reminders dozens—if not hundreds—of times. *Take small, measured steps. It will minimize your limp and keep you looking like a lady. Tell them you don't enjoy dancing, not that you can't dance. Never look as though you are in pain, even if you are.*

"I don't wish to go." Gwen cringed at voicing such a vulnerable statement out loud, but it was the truth. She didn't want to go to London or be foisted off on some Englishman with a title—provided one could even be found who would want her. More than likely, it would be another exercise in futility. Painful, boring, embarrassing futility, a world away from the orphanage, where she felt useful and valued. Her place and purpose were here.

Cornelia smiled, though it held more determination than warmth. "It will be wonderful. We'll stop in Paris to have new Worth gowns made, and Mrs. Rinecroft and Syble will be there too."

So that's what her friend had meant earlier about a trip to London. Though wealthy and pretty, Syble had also struggled to find a match in New York. There was the issue of an old family scandal, the details of which Syble didn't even know. She was also considered by many, especially men, to be far too outspoken in her opinions and independent in her thinking.

The knowledge that her best friend would be at her side brought Gwen a tiny seedling of relief. At least until her mother spoke again.

"Although, once we arrive in London, your friend will again be your greatest competitor." Cornelia picked up her fork once more. "But I'm confident you'll snag the better match."

The ache in her foot felt as if it had lodged itself inside her lungs. Gwen fought for a calming breath, her mind grasping at any excuse, any reason her mother's plans might be altered. None came.

How could her future change so drastically from one moment to the next? She knew the answer, though. At present, as an unmarried, financially dependent young lady, she was at the mercy of her mother's whims.

She hadn't felt this small or alone in a very long time. Not since Randolph had abruptly ended things between them.

Her fortune hadn't been enough for him to overlook her physical shortcomings. It seemed silly to believe it would be enough for the type of gentleman her mother had in mind. And even if someone wanted her fortune badly enough to make an offer, could she bring herself to marry such a man—one who valued wealth over everything else? Would she even find a man in England who exemplified the qualities she deemed more important than a title? Qualities such as love, respect, a shared faith, a pleasing sense of humor. Not to mention a man who saw her as more than her money or her limp when he looked at her. Could a man like that be waiting for her in England?

Yes, if my life were a fairy tale.

But she'd stopped believing in fairy tales sometime during her first season. There was no dashing prince waiting to claim her as his own—there was only her quiet, ordinary, useful life that she was destined to spend alone. She'd made peace with that. And if it took going to England and enduring several months of uselessness and humiliation to convince her mother of such a thing, then that was what Gwen would do. After all, what other option was open to her until she turned twenty-one?

"Very well." She pushed back her chair. "I will do as you ask."

A satisfied smile lifted Cornelia's mouth. "I'll write your sister straight away, Charles, to see if we may stay at her London residence. Remember, Gwen, she was also an American heiress who went to England to find a husband, though she only married a baronet." She intoned the last word as if Aunt Vivian had married a chimney sweep instead of a titled gentleman.

Gwen rose from her seat. "I'm going up to my room."

Without waiting for a reply, she slipped out of the dining

room and limped toward the staircase. Memories of her inspiring day and the new book waiting for her upstairs couldn't dispel her sorrow and regret.

Gwen plodded painfully up the stairs, gripping the banister with a tight hand. She would need every ounce of strength she could muster if she hoped to weather another disastrous season.

A niggling of an idea made her pause and brought momentary relief to the ache inside her. If she were London-bound, then perhaps she could seek out Dr. Smithfield. Even if Gwen wasn't successful in convincing him to uproot to America, the man might be willing to provide letters of introduction to suitable colleagues of his in the States. Perhaps he could even help her with correcting her own childhood injury. A surge of determination carried her the final yards to her bedroom.

The beginnings of a smile tugged at Gwen's lips as she grabbed her book and sank into her favorite armchair. She might not have the power to dictate her life right now as much as she wished, and yet that didn't mean she was helpless. Her mother might have plans for her, but Gwen wasn't without a few of her own.

Chapter 2

London, May 1908

Avery Winfield had little trouble following the Italian opera being acted out on the stage below. After all, Italian was one of three languages he spoke fluently. But he couldn't slip fully into the music or the story. Not with the tight feeling inside his gut, the one his grandmother had admonished him never to ignore. Tonight that feeling kept him on edge, his fingers drumming the arm of the chair inside his best friend's opera box. Emmett Markham, the earl of Linwood, had insisted Avery attend the evening's opera, even in Linwood's absence.

Shifting his weight, he stilled his fingers and attempted to relax. The soprano's solo rose in a crescendo, stirring an unnamed longing within Avery. In his opinion, the Italian operas were the most well-written, the most moving, the most—

The curtains behind him rustled. Someone was entering the box. The knot in Avery's stomach wound tighter. Was this why he'd felt uneasy? He sat unmoving, listening to the sound of the other person's breathing and the whispered tread of shoes against the plush carpet. Then Avery whirled around in his chair.

The stranger looked momentarily startled before a wide grin broke over his mottled face. "'Ello, gov'nor." His blackened teeth stood out in sharp contrast to the impeccable evening suit he wore. No doubt it belonged to whoever had sent him. Avery's attention quickly moved from the other man's clothes to his hand as the lights from the stage glittered off the knife he held.

Jumping to his feet, Avery kept the chairs positioned between them, his heart thumping faster. "What do you want?"

"Just a bit o' a chat."

If he could keep the assailant talking, perhaps he could lure the man into the hallway. Avery didn't want the occupants in the boxes on the opposite side of the theater witnessing whatever happened next.

"Who sent you?" he demanded, alarm chilling in his veins.

The man narrowed his gaze. "Now you don't think I's as daft as to tell you that, do you?"

"Maybe, maybe not."

Avery leapt toward the curtains, the man right behind him. The knife slashed downward, but Avery was expecting the attack. He ducked and jumped to the side, giving himself a split-second advantage. He seized it by gripping the man about the collar with one hand and clamping the other around the stranger's wrist. Holding tightly, he jerked his attacker through the opening in the curtains and into the empty hallway.

"Who sent you?" Avery repeated in a hiss. "Someone working for the Germans?"

"You'll never know," the man gasped. He squirmed, but Avery held fast.

"How much did he offer you to get rid of me?"

"More than enough."

Sudden applause sounded from the other side of the curtains, yanking Avery's attention back to his surroundings. It must be intermission, which meant any minute now the audience would come spilling out of their seats and boxes.

Too late, he realized he'd loosened his hold on the man's wrist. With a quick slash, the knife found purchase beneath Avery's jacket and through his waistcoat. Fire seared his side. The stranger jerked away from his weakening grip and grinned again.

"So long, gov'nor." He didn't spare a backward glance as he raced up the corridor.

Avery sucked in a breath as he touched his waist. His hand came back damp. He needed to hide until he could collect himself, bandage his wound, and determine how to get home without been seen.

He took a stumbling step back into the box, then stopped, swaying a bit on his feet. He was bleeding too heavily to pass it off as a nosebleed or a clumsy stumble in the dark, and the blood would most likely be discovered by the cleaning women after the performance. If they reported it to Linwood, what explanation could he give for bleeding all over his best friend's opera box? Dodging the question would only pique Linwood's curiosity. And Avery couldn't have that. Not even his best friend knew about Avery's profession.

The box next to Linwood's would be empty, since the Howells hadn't yet arrived in London for the season. The cleaning people would still be in for a shock, but they wouldn't be able to connect anything back to him. Avery lurched through the curtains of the other box, toppling a chair as he staggered along. The agony in his side had doubled in fierceness, lancing through him with ferocious intensity. He needed something to bandage his wound before he escaped the theater.

Think, Avery, he scolded. But his vision had begun to turn fuzzy, and his thoughts were a snarled mess.

He tried to sit on one of the chairs, but his knees would no longer support him. Instead, Avery crashed to the carpeted floor and rolled onto his back. One thought stood out above the rest, even as the darkness of the theater crept into his consciousness.

The attempt on his life could only mean one thing—his espionage work among the *ton* had been warranted. All the weeks and months he'd spent listening and learning who among London's upper class and his own acquaintances had any interest, knowledge, or connection to Germany hadn't been for naught. Avery was closer than he'd realized to identifying the traitor to England in their midst.

◦◦◦◦◦

She needed to escape. Gwen eyed the opera boxes at her right. If she slipped into a vacant one, even for a few minutes, during intermission, while everyone else sought refreshment . . .

The boyish-faced gentleman she'd met the week before— Mr. Nevil Fipwish, the eldest son of a baron—continued to stand at the end of the hallway, waiting for her. As Gwen watched, the man frowned in her direction as if he'd guessed her thoughts about escaping. Or had he somehow learned about her limp? Regardless of the reason behind his frown, she couldn't endure another moment in his tedious company.

"I'm afraid I've misplaced . . . something . . . back in the opera box." Her endurance? Her patience? Her sanity? All three had seemingly vanished after only twelve days in England. "I'll be along shortly, Mother."

Her mother turned, along with Gwen's aunt, Lady

Rodmill. Gwen's cousin Bert had been the first to exit the box and had already disappeared within the crowd.

Cornelia emitted an exasperated sigh. A lecture would surely be forthcoming later tonight about Gwen's efforts, or the lack thereof, in attracting a titled husband. "We'll wait here," she said, waving her gloved hand at Gwen.

"I don't wish to keep you. Please, go ahead."

"Very well. But don't dilly-dally." Her patronizing tone grated against Gwen's ears. "There are several gentlemen friends of Bert's here tonight whom your aunt wishes to introduce to you. Ones whom you have not yet met."

Gwen pressed her lips together, staying a retort. Surely she'd already met every unmarried, titled gentleman who resided in this country. But she would persevere—after all, arguing would accomplish nothing. Only it couldn't hurt to garner a few minutes of peace and quiet for herself, especially away from the tiresome gentleman attempting to move toward her against the tide of people.

The instant her mother's back was turned, Gwen hurried as well as she could in the direction they'd come. She bypassed her aunt and uncle's opera box, guessing that was likely where Mr. Fipwish would look for her first. Instead, she headed for the box two down from Aunt Vivian's, which Gwen had overheard was unoccupied tonight.

Slipping into the shadowed space, she concealed herself behind the curtains. Footfalls sounded on the other side. Gwen held her breath, ignoring the growing ache in her foot after practically running.

Would she be discovered? Most likely, with how hard she was breathing. She tried to squelch the noise but without success. The harried, pain-filled breaths wouldn't quiet, even when Gwen inhaled softly through her nose.

Which had to mean she wasn't alone in the opera box.

Her heart jumped into her throat at the thought. But her fear quickly gave way to concern when no one spoke or materialized in front of her. The other person sounded hurt—but what was wrong?

From the safety of the curtains, she peered into the box's interior. There were four empty chairs, though one of them had been overturned. She appeared to be alone, and yet she could still hear someone nearby. Gwen froze when an audible moan filled the space. She recognized the cry of pain—one she'd voiced herself countless times and had done her best to soothe in the children at the orphanage.

She emerged from the curtains. Only then did she notice a pair of masculine shoes sticking out from the corner of the box. A man was lying on the carpeted floor. Perhaps he'd taken ill or had stumbled.

Compassion nudged Gwen forward. The man released another groan. Anxious to help in some way, she knelt beside him, the skirt of her pale green velvet gown trailing behind her. Her eyes had adjusted to the dim light, but she could still make out very little of the gentleman's features. All she knew for certain was that he wore evening clothes and sported the chin of a young man, though she would guess he was older than herself, and he appeared to have brown or black hair. The other details of the man's face, save his closed eyes, remained obscured by the shadows.

"Are you ill, sir? May I be of some help?" She reached out and rested her hand lightly on his coat sleeve.

His eyelids flew open, and his fingers locked around her wrist with surprising strength. "Who are you? What do you want?"

"I—I don't mean any harm. I found you here."

"You're American," he stated matter-of-factly. More labored breaths filled the quiet box. "Are you squeamish about blood?"

20

Gwen shook her head. "No." Was the man injured rather than sick?

"Then I'd be obliged if you would help me remove my coat."

Her fingers felt corded muscles beneath his shirt as she pulled his right arm from its sleeve, then repeated the steps with his left. Each movement brought a sharp inhale from him. "Your coat is off."

"Can you detect any blood on it, on the left side?"

She squinted in the half-light, but she couldn't see anything marring the fabric. "I don't think so, no."

He grunted. "What about my waistcoat on that same side?"

Gwen leaned closer. A dark spot at his left side wasn't difficult to identify, even in the dimness of the box. "There is some blood there." She glanced toward his face as questions piled up inside her mind. "How badly are you injured? Will you tell me what happened?"

"Listen carefully," he said, ignoring her questions. His eyes had fallen shut once more, and his chest rose and fell rapidly, as if he'd been running instead of lying on his back. "I need the wound bandaged."

"I can see if there's a doctor here tonight." She started to rise, but he stopped her with another firm grip on her hand.

"You must tell no one you were here or that you helped me." His tone conveyed urgency. "Do you understand?"

His request made no sense, but Gwen didn't want to add to his distress by refusing. "I understand, and I think I can bind the wound for you myself." While Amie served as nurse at the orphanage, she'd asked Gwen to assist her now and again, particularly with the simpler matters of cuts and scrapes. If all the man required was a bandage to stop the bleeding, she could help.

"Good." He gave her hand a gentle squeeze, then released her. "See what you can find in the way of a bandage."

Gwen dismissed using the curtains. Their material would be too thick and heavy to tear. The velvet fabric of her gown would be useless too. However, the lightweight material of her petticoat would work.

"Give me a moment." Not that he had much choice.

Shifting away from him, she removed her gloves and located the hem of her petticoat. *Mother will be furious,* she thought as she began tearing the material. Perhaps Gwen, and the maid who assisted her at her aunt's home, could keep the ruined garment a secret.

"I have something to bind the wound." She returned to the stranger's side, the torn fabric in her hand. "I'm going to have to move you in order to get the bandage under you, though."

"Please proceed."

She blew her breath out slowly, then rolled the man onto his uninjured side as gingerly as possible. Despite her care, a pained grunt still fell from his mouth. He did manage to lift himself onto his right elbow, though, which allowed her to place the material underneath him.

After arranging the cloth, she guided the man onto his back again and gathered the end of the bandage around his waistcoat. She'd need to tie the bandage securely now, and from experience, she knew it would likely hurt.

Would it ease his discomfort if she padded the wound with more fabric first? The man's eyes were still closed, so Gwen didn't bother moving away from him this time as she tore away more material from her petticoat. She bunched the cloth together and placed it against the dark spot on his waistcoat.

"I'm going to tie the bandage now, sir," Gwen said, to

give him fair warning. After making sure the extra fabric would stay in place, she knotted the bandage as tightly as she could.

A low cry of agony filled her ears. Gwen swallowed back a matching cry of her own. Had she hurt him worse than what he'd already endured? "Sir? Can you hear me?"

She placed her hand against his chest and felt it rise. But the movement beneath her touch was more slight and shallow than she'd hoped. Should she go for help, despite his warning? No, Gwen dismissed the idea. She would obey his request.

A long minute passed with no other indication of life from him, beyond the slight lift and fall of his chest. Desperation warred with Gwen's resolve not to reveal his whereabouts. He needed to rouse, but how? She hated the idea of inflicting more pain on him by shaking his shoulders or tapping his face. There had to be some other way . . .

A scene from the romance novel she'd been reading the night before ran through her mind and gave her an idea. Placing a hand on either side of his jaw, Gwen bent close and kissed him. His masculine lips felt pleasant against her own, but she could scarcely appreciate that with how hard her heart knocked against her ribs at her boldness. She'd never kissed a man before, at least not on the mouth. Randolph had only ever pecked her cheek or her hand.

The stranger remained horribly still, filling Gwen with greater dread. Perhaps she ought to try shaking his shoulders after all. She lifted her chin, but to her surprise, the man gently cupped the back of her neck with his hand and guided her toward him again. Then he kissed her back.

Gwen told herself she ought to move away, and yet she sensed only innocence and gratitude in the man's touch, nothing untoward. Besides, kissing him filled her with a heady sense of freedom. Freedom from her fears that others would

23

discover her limitation, freedom from the pressure to find a husband in England, freedom from everything save the sweetness of his kiss.

Reality crept back in soon enough, reminding Gwen that this man was still bleeding. She eased back, though her pulse continued to trip as if she'd been the one running. "I—I'm sorry. I only meant to wake you." Heat burned her cheeks.

"For which I'm grateful, I assure you."

The deep rumble of his voice intensified her blush. She felt immense relief knowing he couldn't see her face any more clearly than she could see his.

"Is there anything else I can do?" She hurried to add, "For your wound?"

"No, thank you." His fingers wrapped around hers. "You need to go before intermission is over." He sucked in a sharp breath. "It will not bode well for either of us, but most especially for you, if we're discovered here alone."

"Will you be all right?" Gwen hated to leave him alone and bleeding, but he was right about not being seen together. "Can you tell me your name"—she pulled on her gloves—"so I might ask about your health?"

He gestured toward the curtains, acting as if she hadn't spoken. "You must go. Please."

She climbed to her feet. "Good night, then, sir." She didn't know if he was religious or not, but she couldn't help adding, "God be with you."

Giving his prone frame a final glance, she limped through the curtains and into the hallway. Several people were already heading back to their seats. Gwen returned to her chair inside her uncle's opera box. There was no point in meeting her mother and aunt for refreshments now. The performance would resume shortly.

Gwen pressed a hand over her heart, eager to calm her

pulse. She would have enough explaining to do when Cornelia returned. A breathless voice would only make matters worse.

Her fingers strayed to her lips, even as she tried to tell herself that their kisses meant nothing. They had only been a means to an end in rousing the stranger to wakefulness again. But her heart believed differently. She'd been astonished when the man kissed her back, though not upset or uncomfortable. If anything, his answering kiss had felt almost familiar. As if she were meant to kiss him, and only him, for the rest of her life.

But that wasn't possible, was it? Gwen didn't know his name or what he looked like. And even if she did, he would surely not be interested in a woman who couldn't walk without limping. She hadn't yet found the time to slip away to visit Dr. Smithfield and ask him about her foot and helping the orphanage.

Still, as Gwen waited for her family's return to the box, she couldn't dismiss her desire to learn the mystery man's identity. If only to know whom she'd helped. Because as long as she lived she would never forget that sweet and glorious kiss.

Chapter 3

With great effort and clenched teeth, Avery managed to keep himself upright as he moved from the cab to the front door of his London residence. No one could know he'd been stabbed earlier, though the fire in his side still burned with every breath.

The door swung open and his butler, Houndsley, stood at attention. "Back early, sir?"

"Yes." Avery decided against any explanation. "Which means I no longer require the carriage to be brought round to the opera house."

"Very good, sir."

A wave of dizziness washed over him, but Avery fought it off by tightening his jaw. *Just a little farther.* Once in the privacy of his room, he could finally see what damage the hired miscreant had done.

"His Grace called while you were out, sir."

Avery glanced over his shoulder. "My uncle is back in town already?"

Houndsley inclined his head. "Apparently, sir. He wishes to see you at your earliest convenience."

"I'm sure he does," Avery muttered, moving slowly toward the stairs.

Uncle Leo, no doubt, had come to check up on him. To see how his only nephew was getting along with his supposed duties of finding a wife and preparing to inherit. But Avery didn't want the title of the Duke of Moorleigh or the seat in the House of Lords. Just the estate house near Exeter where he'd grown up. And as far as a wife, well, that would only jeopardize his current employment.

By the time he reached the top of the stairs, he was completely winded. Avery waited until he was out of view from Houndsley's sharp gaze before he sagged against the wall to catch his breath. He likely needed a doctor, though he felt confident his valet, Gregory Mack, could stitch him up as effectively. Mack had served in the Second Boer War as a medic before returning to England and working his way up to the position of valet.

Inside his room, Avery collapsed into an armchair and carefully peeled off his coat. A familiar knock a few moments later alerted him to Mack's presence. "Come in," he called.

"You're back early," Mack said as he entered, his graying hair the only telltale sign of his age.

"Yes, and I'm going to require some hot water, a needle and thread, and your medical skills. In that order."

Mack's eyebrows rose to his hairline, but he nodded. "I'll have one of the maids put some water on to boil."

"Thank you," Avery said through gritted teeth.

Mack disappeared into the hallway. When he returned a few minutes later, he was carrying his medical bag. He shut the door firmly behind him, his expression grim. "What happened?"

Avery rested his head against the back of the chair. Most men wouldn't tolerate such direct questioning from a servant, even a valet, but Avery appreciated Mack's open candidness. He trusted the man explicitly too. Which was why Mack was the only one who knew that Avery was employed by Captain Vernon Kell of the Secret Service Bureau.

"Knife wound." He tapped a light finger against the bloodied fabric around his waist. "The assailant was a street thug, clearly given a set of evening clothes in order to sneak into the opera house. I prevented him from doing real harm, but he still exacted a piece from me."

"Then someone hoped you would be there tonight. Alone."

Though it wasn't a question, Avery still responded. "It would appear so. Now, help me get this waistcoat off so we can see what must be done."

Mack helped him onto his feet. The room began to tilt, forcing Avery to shut his eyes until the dizziness passed.

"Whose lovely garment supplied your bandage?" His valet's words were coated with as much amusement as curiosity.

Avery glanced down. His lips worked into a smile, in spite of the pain, when he realized the American girl had torn a length of material from her underskirt in order to bandage him. "That was the work of a rather remarkable American woman who happened into the box during intermission."

He didn't know why she'd entered that particular box, but Avery would be forever grateful that she had. The pain as she'd bandaged him had been acute and extreme, and yet it had faded the moment she kissed him. Such a superbly gentle kiss. One he hadn't wished would end, and so he'd kissed her back. And in doing so, Avery had momentarily forgotten his wound and the man who had clearly hoped to end his life.

"What has you smiling, sir?" Mack asked as he removed the bandage and then Avery's waistcoat.

Avery pressed his lips over a yelp of pain. "That is not a smile. It's a grimace. I think you tore off half my skin just now."

"If it's any consolation, your shirt should come off more easily now." Mack pushed aside Avery's stained shirt.

"Well? How bad is it?"

Mack scrutinized the wound. "It's deep, but it's nothing I can't stitch. You'll have a scar, though no permanent damage."

"Hallelujah for that," Avery murmured.

You ought to thank God you aren't gravely injured or dead. He considered the notion for a moment, then pushed it back to the corners of his mind. God was as distant as Avery's father had been before he died.

Feeling lightheaded once more, Avery sank into the chair to wait for the hot water. He was relieved when a maid knocked on the door a minute or two later, the water in tow. Once the girl was gone, his valet carefully cleaned Avery's wound in preparation for stitching it together. The process had Avery hissing with pain.

"I know your thoughts on drinking, sir," Mack said, setting out the needed supplies. "But you might want a bit of brandy."

Avery shook his head. Except for a small amount of wine with dinner, he had long ago sworn off drinking alcohol. The brandy in the house was something to offer his friends. His father had been the perfect gentleman, except when he was intoxicated, which was more often than not. Avery refused to follow in his footsteps.

With his hands braced against the chair's arms, he sucked in a deep breath and released it slowly. "All right, I'm ready. Do your worst, Mack."

"My worst?" The valet chuckled. "I'd think you'd want my best, sir."

Avery ignored the jest as he felt the needle slide into him. Stars danced before his vision, but he managed to remain conscious.

"What was an American girl doing in a deserted opera box?" He could guess the reason for Mack's question. It was his way of getting Avery's mind on something else in the absence of the brandy.

"I couldn't say. I didn't even learn her name."

Mack tsked. "What does she look like?"

Avery searched his memory, but he couldn't conjecture up anything beyond a vague recollection of the young lady's soft touch and her American accent. "It was too dark to see."

"Does she know who you are?"

"No." Avery flexed his fingers before fisting the chair's arms again. A glance at his side revealed that Mack was halfway through. "I didn't give her my name, for obvious reasons."

"That's a shame," Mack muttered.

Avery frowned. "A shame?"

The valet lifted his shoulders in a shrug. "Might have been a match orchestrated by an unseen hand. The way it was with Melinda and me." Mack's wife had passed shortly after his return from the war, but he claimed no two people had loved each other more.

"Hardly," Avery said with a bitter laugh. Although the memory of that kiss would likely remain with him always. "You know I can't marry, Mack. It would put too many people at risk." He gestured at his injury. "I only have to look at this to remember that."

"Aye. But if it's the right woman . . ."

"You're as bad as my uncle," Avery grumbled.

Mack grinned. "I'll take that as a compliment, being compared to a duke."

He couldn't help releasing a low chuckle. "It was not a compliment."

"Well, you'd better compliment my handiwork." His valet sat back. "All done."

Twisting to see, Avery studied the small, even stitches. "You are a horrible matchmaker, to be sure, but a brilliant medic."

Mack dipped his head in acknowledgement. "Thank you, sir." He rose to his feet. "What would you like me to do with your evening clothes?"

"Burn them." Avery toed his soiled shirt. "I can't have anyone knowing what happened tonight, not even the maids."

"What reason should I give for you sticking to your room?"

"How many days will I need to recover?"

"Two, at least."

Avery ran his hand over his now bristled jaw. "Tell them I have a head cold, but nothing that requires the doctor."

"Done."

After Mack helped him into nightclothes, Avery lay down on the bed, his mind full of questions. Had his assailant really been sent by one of the two men Avery now suspected of being a German spy?

Fear of such spies operating secretly in Britain had even ordinary citizens suspicious of anyone or anything connected to Germany. Hence the need for skilled men to investigate the possible truth behind such rumors. Avery's position among the upper class of society, his ability to speak German, and his prowess for observation had secured him a place as one such man.

His task was relatively simple, at least in theory: he must

discover if any of his fellow linguists from university had ties to Germany, then widen his search to members of the *ton.* However, the present fears and rumors often meant he and Kell's other agents had to follow up on a hunch or supposition rather than real proof. Still, an investigation of Avery's former colleagues had turned up two viable suspects for him.

Both men spoke fluent German; one was of German descent and the other had visited the country several times in the last few years. They'd both openly expressed an affinity for the country too. It wasn't the hard evidence Avery would have liked, but it was far better than asking waiters who claimed to be Swiss to provide a passport—something he'd read the public was being encouraged to do.

"Do you think one of your suspects hired your attacker?" Mack asked as he straightened up the room. Avery wasn't surprised his valet's thoughts were running in a similar vein as his. The older man's intelligent opinions had proven helpful in the past.

"I believe so." He never gave Mack names, as much to protect his valet as to avoid anyone else overhearing and warning the suspected individuals. While he could vouch for Mack's loyalty, Avery couldn't say the same for every member of his household staff.

Mack gathered the ruined clothes into a pile. "Is that all, sir?"

"Yes, Mack." Avery rubbed at the tight muscles in his neck, feeling exhausted in both body and mind. "Thank you."

Nodding again, Mack extinguished the light and left the room.

Avery drew the covers to his chest, the darkness soothing his fatigue. But he couldn't check his circling thoughts. What should his next move be? And who was the American girl who had come to his aid? He'd heard around town that there were

33

a number of American heiresses in London for the season this year. Could he figure out which one had helped him this evening without giving himself away?

His scoffing sniff sounded loud in the quiet room. He was a professional intelligence agent. Of course he could figure out the woman's identity. It wouldn't be easy, though. The intense pain he'd experienced earlier had dulled his normal prowess for observation. Even now, he couldn't recall the inflections in her voice or what color her dress had been. Still, study and deduction were second nature to him now. But did he want to find her? Finding her would mean interacting with her, and what if she recognized him in turn? If this girl learned who he was, she would likely want to know more about why he'd been injured.

Probably best to leave well enough alone, though part of him wished he were at liberty to thank her a second time. She'd risked her reputation and a possible attack herself by helping him.

His thoughts returned to their kiss. What would it be like to attend the opera with the woman of his heart at his side? To share more kisses such as that? He'd never had much of an inclination to marry—the institution hadn't proven to be a happy or ideal one for his parents—nor had a woman among the *ton* ever really captured his romantic interest. Instead Avery preferred bachelorhood. It certainly made his work in espionage easier.

And yet, in the wake of such an exquisite kiss, he couldn't help wishing things were different. That he could meet someone who possessed as much compassion, strength, and intelligence as the young lady from tonight had exemplified.

It would never work, though. His job was too important, to him and to Britain, to trade in favor of a wife and a family. He was meant to live and work alone.

Avery rolled onto his right side. His wound still throbbed, but the emptiness around his heart ached nearly as much. Ignoring it, he put the strange events of the night from his mind for now and shut his eyes, willing sleep to cloak the pain.

⁓ᴏᴏᴅᴅᴏ⁓

Gwen hung back at the conclusion of the opera. She was reluctant to leave without at least learning the name or seeing the face of the man she'd helped during intermission. Not after that wonderful kiss. Pretending to adjust her gloves, she guessed she had less than two minutes before her "dilly-dallying" would be noticed.

As her mother started down the hall, engrossed in conversation with Aunt Vivian and Bert, Gwen limped backward to the other opera box. Her pulse skipped erratically, out of rhythm with her measured steps.

Would the man be pleased to see her again or upset?

She pulled in a breath for courage, pushed aside the curtain, and stepped inside. This time, the box held no wounded occupants or overturned chairs. It stood void of anyone or anything unusual, save for a darker smear on the carpet. It was the only evidence that she hadn't dreamt their encounter.

Sharp disappointment pushed against Gwen's lungs as she exited the box. In her hurry to regain her party, she chose expediency over walking sedately.

"Gwenyth." Her mother's voice pierced her ears. "Slower steps."

Embarrassment washed over her, though Gwen kept her chin tilted upward as she altered her gait to disguise her limp and drew alongside her aunt. Her resolve to learn the identity of the injured stranger remained unchanged.

"Aunt Vivian?"

Her aunt turned, her dark eyes exuding warmth. The last time she'd seen Aunt Vivian, Gwen had felt slightly intimidated by the woman's regal presence and stunning beauty. However, since coming to London, she'd discovered her aunt had a kind heart too. "Yes, my dear?"

"Who occupies the opera box to the left of yours?"

If she found the question strange, Aunt Vivian didn't show it. "Lord and Lady Linwood."

"Ah. I'm acquainted with Lady Linwood. She debuted into society back in New York at the same time my friend Syble and I did."

If only Syble were here tonight. Her best friend would be thoroughly intrigued by the events in the opera box and likely just as determined as Gwen to solve the mystery of the man's identity. The voyage across the ocean and the stop in Paris had been almost enjoyable for Gwen with Syble at her side. But she'd seen very little of her friend since their arrival in London.

"I imagine then an invitation for a soirée or dinner will be forthcoming from Lady Linwood," Aunt Vivian said, interrupting Gwen's thoughts.

"I think we've already received one. Mother mentioned something earlier about dining at their home next Friday. It will be nice to see Lady Linwood again." Gwen was curious to know how Clare was getting along as the wife of an earl, living so far away from New York. Especially since this was the path Gwen's parents were determined she follow as well.

Now for her real question. "Whose box is next to Lord and Lady Linwood's, the one that was unoccupied tonight?" Gwen kept her tone conversational, even as her heart thrummed faster.

"That would be the Howells' box."

"Do they have a son, by chance?" The injured man might have come ahead of the family last minute. "Or a friend they allow to use their box?"

Aunt Vivian studied her, her expression full of unspoken curiosity. "I'm afraid they have only daughters and are very proprietary about their opera box. Family members are the only ones who use it."

Gwen managed a stiff nod of acknowledgement as regret lanced through her. The man she'd helped must have sought the empty box out of necessity, not because he had a connection to it or its regular occupants. His name—like his face—was to remain a mystery.

"Is everything all right, Gwen?"

Her aunt's gentle regard reminded Gwen of Dean and Amie. How she missed them and the children at Heartwell House. She was counting the days until she could return to them.

She blinked away her unwanted tears. "I'm well."

"We needn't linger long if you are tired." Her aunt dropped a quick glance toward the hem of Gwen's gown.

Gwen pasted on a weak smile and placed more weight on her good foot to curtail her limp. "I'll be fine."

"No matter who you are, the season can be exhausting." Aunt Vivian offered her an understanding smile. "It took me several weeks to acclimate too when I first came here."

Gwen was surprised to hear such an admission from her aunt. She couldn't imagine Vivian being anything but poised and confident. Was her aunt happy, though? Such a question would be impolite to ask, and yet Gwen hoped one of these days she might learn the answer.

Her aunt steered her gently toward a knot of young men, her son, Bert, among them. "Come. I want you to meet some of Bert's friends."

Gwen obliged, but she couldn't stop her gaze from sweeping the room as she moved alongside her aunt. Looking for whom, she couldn't say. Someone who appeared injured? A man whose face lit up with recognition at seeing her? But then, how would he recognize her? He likely hadn't seen her any more clearly or distinctly than she'd seen him.

"Miss Barton, may I present Lord Whitson?" Her aunt motioned to a young man with black hair and a square jawline.

"How do you do, Miss Barton?" Lord Whitson bowed, his dark eyes glinting with unmistakable mischief. "So you are the enchanting cousin to our Roddy here?"

Gwen chose to ignore the empty compliment. "I'm pleased to make your acquaintance, Lord Whitson."

"And I yours."

Aunt Vivian waved to another of the gentlemen, a sandy-haired young man with a serious expression. "Miss Barton, may I present Mr. Archibald Hanbury?"

Mr. Hanbury gave a curt bow. "Miss Barton."

"Mr. Hanbury."

"I am going to find your mother, Gwen." After touching her reassuringly on the arm, Aunt Vivian walked away, her head erect, her back straight.

Apprehension churned inside Gwen's stomach at being left to fend for herself with her cousin and his friends. How ironic that the most at ease she'd felt around any gentleman since coming to England had been while she'd helped bind up the wound of the one bleeding inside that opera box.

Lord Whitson appraised her silently before asking, "Did you enjoy the opera, Miss Barton?"

"I did." At least, she'd enjoyed what she could recall of it. She'd found it difficult to concentrate on the second half of the fictional drama being played out on the stage after her own dramatic experience.

"You didn't tell us your cousin was an American, or so lovely, Roddy," Lord Whitson said as he turned toward Bert. "Lots of *foreigners* in London these days."

Gwen threw a curious glance at her cousin. Lord Whitson's remark, and his pointed tone, struck her as odd, but she supposed it must be in reference to some private joke. Her cousin wasn't laughing, though. Tonight, Bert seemed more cross than she remembered.

"Yes, well, we were only reintroduced less than two weeks ago." He frowned, his attention on the crowd as if he too was looking for someone. "Prior to that, the last time Gwen and I saw each other was when my family traveled to America four years ago. Now if you'll excuse me, gentlemen. Gwen." With that he departed in the opposite direction his mother had taken.

"I'm afraid I have some business to attend to myself." Lord Whitson offered her another bow. "I do hope to see a great deal of you while you are in London, Miss Barton."

"Thank you, my lord," she said, unable to return a similar sentiment.

She didn't wish to see more of this man. Not after already experiencing his type of mindless flattery back in New York. As soon as young men discovered her limitation, their attention always waned. Was there no gentleman in either country who would love her as herself? She wanted to share a deep bond with her husband, to have the kind of relationship that Dean and Amie shared.

As Gwen struggled for something to say to fill the uncomfortable silence expanding between her and Mr. Hanbury, she caught sight of her vigilant admirer from earlier—Mr. Fipwish—heading directly toward her. She stiffened with dread. There was nowhere to disappear to now. She would have to endure another inane conversation about the man's large collection of decanters or his new mare.

"Is something amiss, Miss Barton?" Mr. Hanbury regarded her solemnly.

"I . . ." She swallowed, her eyes darting to the man moving like an ocean liner through the crowd. "There's this gentleman . . ."

Her lips closed over any further explanation. She couldn't bring herself to say aloud that she had no desire to talk to Mr. Fipwish. Or to any of them tonight. The only man she'd met in London who had succeeded in capturing her interest had disappeared as if he hadn't ever existed in the first place.

Mr. Hanbury followed her gaze. "Is that the gentleman you're referring to, Miss Barton? The one bearing down upon us?" A grim smile lifted one corner of his mouth.

Gwen couldn't prevent a light laugh. "I'm afraid so."

"Never fear. I shall deliver you safely to your aunt."

Throwing a dark look at Mr. Fipwish, Mr. Hanbury took Gwen's elbow in hand and led her through the press of people. There was enough of a crowd that no one would likely notice her limp. She cast a look over her shoulder at Mr. Fipwish. He appeared frustrated by her retreat, but he didn't attempt to follow them. Mr. Hanbury's silent message had been blessedly communicated.

"Thank you for your assistance, Mr. Hanbury," she said with sincerity as he stopped her near a group of jewel-bedecked matrons, her mother and Aunt Vivian among them.

He nodded. "Think nothing of it, Miss Barton. I shall bid you farewell."

She managed a sincere smile. "Farewell."

The next thirty minutes passed slowly. Gwen did her best

to engage in conversation, but her foot throbbed from standing and her head had begun to ache. By the time she climbed into her aunt's carriage for the drive home, her headache had become a full-blown pounding in her temples. She leaned her forehead against the window and did her best to tune out the conversation between her mother and Aunt Vivian. Cousin Bert hadn't rejoined them after leaving Gwen with his friends.

Perhaps she ought to have stayed home tonight or gone in search of Dr. Smithfield instead. But she quickly rejected the thought. If she hadn't attended the opera, she wouldn't have met the man in the box at intermission. And though it felt like a dream now, it wasn't an experience she would wish away.

Shutting her eyes, Gwen again recalled their kiss and the emotions it had motivated deep inside her. How could she possibly have felt so connected to a complete stranger? Even her initial affection for Randolph paled in comparison.

Was this expectant longing what her beloved romance novels meant about those first stirrings of love and adoration? Or was she simply feeling compassion for an injured stranger, and nothing else? She might believe the latter, except for those kisses. Somewhere in the midst of trying to revive the man and him kissing her back, something inside her had shifted.

Gwen had largely given up on the notion of marrying after her second season. But tonight's kiss had resurrected all of her girlhood yearnings for love and matrimony.

And yet she had a different perspective now than she'd had during her other two seasons. The broken heart Randolph had given her had taught her a painful but necessary lesson. She was *not* society's image of the consummate debutante or blushing bride. Her money was too new, her manner was too independent, and her physical impediment was too blatant.

Attempting to hide or disguise these facts would only lead to heartache. The only solution was to face them directly.

Gwen opened her eyes, renewed energy driving away the pain inside her foot and head. She had followed her mother's directives these last two seasons. And look where that had landed her.

This time she would do things differently. She would tackle society on her own terms—by being herself, just as she had tonight in the opera box. No more worrying about her limp being seen, no more playing the part of the demure young lady.

If she met another man, as she had tonight, with whom she felt safe enough to speak her mind, to be herself, then she would do so. She'd do everything in her power to find a gentleman with whom she could share a real love, a real marriage.

She would also make visiting Dr. Smithfield a priority. Hopefully he could offer help with more than just the orphanage; perhaps he could fix her foot too. Then whether Gwen found a love match and married or she didn't, she could still assist Heartwell House. She would provide them with a large part of her fortune, and if possible, with more physical labor once her foot's mobility had been restored. Either way, she wouldn't fail to meet the needs of the orphanage and her heart. From tonight onward, she would champion both.

Chapter 4

"His Grace, the Duke of Moorleigh, sir," Houndsley announced.

Avery tossed aside the book he'd been trying to read with little success and watched his uncle stride into the drawing room. While the distraction wasn't a pleasant one, it was a distraction nonetheless. After two days of convalescing, Avery felt bored and agitated.

"Your Grace, good to see you." Avery offered a moderately genuine smile.

Moorleigh sniffed. "You can drop the act, Winfield. Why haven't you come to see me as I requested?"

Avery waved a hand at the blanket across his lap. "My sincere apologies, but I've been a bit under the weather."

"Anything serious?" His uncle's gaze narrowed. He likely feared Avery would contract some sort of fatal illness and die without an heir, which would result in the title and estate going to some far distant relative upon the duke's death.

"I'm feeling much better today. Thank you."

Moorleigh frowned as he took the chair opposite Avery's. "I hope this illness doesn't prevent you from taking full advantage of this year's season." Avery resisted the urge to roll his eyes—he'd heard some form of this speech for the last seven years, ever since he'd turned twenty-one and had been, in his uncle's eyes, of age to "do his duty" to the family name. "You and I are not getting any younger, nephew. And I would like to see that the title and estate are properly cared for, at least for the next few generations."

"I'm certain you'll be around a great while longer, Moorleigh. Look at Grandmama." The woman was in her late seventies and still fit as a fiddle.

"Yes, but the men in our family haven't fared as well."

Neither had Avery's mother. She'd died shortly after Avery's fifth birthday. The day after the funeral his father had taken up drinking in excess.

Frowning, Avery glanced out the nearby window at the carriages and passersby moving outside the townhouse. He didn't want to think about his father or the man's premature demise four years ago. The memories inspired only shame and grief within Avery. Shame for being glad the man could no longer hound and criticize him and grief for what might have been had his father stayed away from drinking.

"My father chose a one-way ticket to an early grave," he said, unable to check the bitterness from his tone, "unlike yours."

The duke brought his right boot to rest against his left knee. "True, but he wasn't the only father who could be critical."

Avery glanced sharply at his uncle. Was the duke suggesting his own father had been similar in temperament to Avery's? He could remember so little about his grandfather, but perhaps Avery and his uncle had more in common than he'd previously thought. The idea surprised him. "Is there something you wished to discuss?" he asked, needing a change of subject.

"There is." Moorleigh cleared his throat. "I'm afraid it's not good news."

Bracing himself for the worst, Avery waited. He hoped there was nothing ailing his grandmother. It had been some time since he'd last visited Beechwood Manor to see her.

"The estate is not as profitable as it once was," his uncle said, his tone matter-of-fact. "My father spent a great deal more than he made during his lifetime, and your father's . . . expenditures . . . didn't help. We've been economizing for the past four years, but it may not be enough to save her." The pinched look in his eyes belied his casual manner.

Avery ran a hand over his face, hoping to hide his astonishment at his uncle's words. Why hadn't he been told about the estate's troubles sooner? Pushing aside his surprise, he settled on what he could control—new ideas for possible retrenchment. If they needed to sell his father's London residence—Avery's residence now—he'd do it. He could stay in a hotel while he continued ferreting out enemy spies among the *ton*.

"Being entailed, we cannot sell the land. However, Beechwood Manor is in great need of cash."

Avery released a frustrated breath. The amount of money he made working for the Secret Service Bureau wouldn't be enough to save the estate. It was barely enough to support himself, though he did like knowing he had his own money to spend as he saw fit, independent of his allowance from the Moorleigh coffers. "What would you have me do?"

"You could marry . . ." Moorleigh let the proposition hang in the air between them. Avery started to shake his head, but his uncle pressed on. "Aligning yourself with a woman of means would make a difference. It might be the *only* way to make a difference."

"And who, pray tell, would I marry?"

"There are a number of wealthy girls in town this year. Any one of them would do nicely."

An urge to stand and pace seized him, but Avery couldn't oblige it. His wound was still healing, and he couldn't afford the additional time it would take to recover should he aggravate it. "It's a wonder you never married yourself, Uncle, since you seem to think it the answer to *our* problems."

The duke's fingers stilled, and a sad expression settled in his light gray eyes. "There was a girl, many, many years ago." For a moment he looked much younger than fifty-two. Then the wistfulness passed and he straightened, his expression hardening. "However, my father found the match lacking in both fortune and connections."

"But you're confident I can secure both." Avery didn't state it as a question, but his uncle nodded anyway. He didn't want to consider marrying, especially for money. His employment gave him purpose, a way to prove his father had been wrong about him, that Avery wasn't a disappointment to those around him. Marriage would end all of that.

"I'm only asking you to consider the matter and to attend more social events this season." The duke's tone was surprisingly kind. "Don't follow in my footsteps. A wife can bring happiness, and at the very least, companionship. And there is no shame in finding a young lady of means who can benefit the estate as well."

Avery swallowed hard. His grandmother would be devastated to see the estate fall into disrepair. But he couldn't remain one of Kell's agents and take a wife. It would be too dangerous. "How much time do we have? Before things are . . . dire?"

"Six months, perhaps a little more."

Plenty of time for the two of them to work out a different,

more acceptable solution to the estate's financial woes. "I'll consider it and I promise to attend more events this season." Doing so would not only appease his uncle, but give him more chances to discover who among the *ton* was working for Germany.

Moorleigh released a sigh, but the exhale seemed to imply more than relief. There was something else weighing on the man's conscience.

"Was there anything else you wish to discuss?" Avery asked.

A knock at the door had them both turning in that direction before his uncle could answer. Houndsley appeared and announced, "Lord Linwood, here to see you, sir." Avery glanced at his uncle, lifting his brows in silent question. Did the duke wish for Avery to send his friend away so they could finish their conversation?

"We can discuss these matters again at another time," Moorleigh responded as he stood. "Good day, Winfield."

"Good day, Uncle."

The man exited the room. Less than a minute later, Linwood entered. "Winfield. Heard you'd taken ill."

"Nothing of consequence." Avery shook his friend's hand before Linwood took the seat the duke had vacated.

"How was the opera?"

Avery fought a grimace. "Most enlivening. Thank you again for the use of your box."

"Think nothing of it," Linwood said, shaking his head. "It's there whenever you'd like."

"I don't wish to impose. I'm sure you and your lovely wife have plans to use the box for yourselves."

His friend's normally bright demeanor dimmed. "I'm not sure how many operas Lady Linwood and I will be attending this season. And I'd hate to see the box remain empty."

There was something more to the man's simple statement, though Avery couldn't deduce what it was.

"How is Lady Linwood?" Avery had noticed some of the vibrancy fading from the young woman's large green eyes over the past few months.

"She is . . . well." Linwood straightened in his chair and smiled, but Avery didn't miss the hollowness in the gesture. "She is actually the reason for my visit. We are hosting a dinner at our home this Friday, and I come bearing an invitation."

Avery let out an audible groan. Just because he needed to attend more of the season's events didn't mean he wished to.

"I know, chap." Linwood chuckled. "But your presence will make it more tolerable, believe me." He bent forward, resting his elbows on his knees. "Besides, there's to be an American in attendance, a young woman of my wife's acquaintance. A raven-haired beauty, or so I'm told."

Stifling another groan—*would no one cease trying to marry him off?*—Avery managed to ask with mild politeness, "Who is she?"

Linwood's gaze gleamed with victory. "Her name is Gwenyth Barton. She's the niece of Lady Rodmill and the cousin of our old school chum Roddy."

"Roddy?" Avery echoed with surprise.

Bert Rodmill was more than just a fellow university student—he was one of the men Avery suspected of spying for Germany. And his cousin would be at the Linwoods' dinner party.

It would almost seem providential, if Avery believed in that sort of thing. He fought a grin as triumph swept through him. He would see what this Gwenyth Barton revealed about her cousin. Hopefully it would be enough information to more definitely conclude if Rodmill was actually a spy.

"Tell Lady Linwood that I accept the invitation."

Instead of smiling, his friend frowned and regarded Avery through a slightly narrowed gaze. "I've never known you to be so willing to attend a social engagement. And I've known you a long time."

Avery lifted his hands in mock surrender. "Can't a chap change?"

"Not you." Linwood scrutinized him again, then stood. "We're happy to have you. Though I will figure out the real reason for your easy acquiescence, Winfield. You'll see."

This time Avery let his grin break through. "Give it your best try, old friend. But you shall never guess."

⁓ෝ⁓

Gwen half expected to find the London residence of Lord and Lady Linwood to be uncomfortably lavish, given the heiress had married an earl. And while the furnishings and décor did speak of wealth, what Gwen saw on her way to the drawing room appeared more tasteful and welcoming than overly opulent.

"Miss Barton!" Lady Linwood held out both her gloved hands to Gwen. Her cream-colored dinner dress with sapphire accents highlighted the red-gold color of her hair and the green of her eyes.

Smiling, Gwen clasped the lady's hands in hers. "Lady Linwood. It's wonderful to see you again."

"I can't tell you how delighted I am to have you and your mother, fellow Americans, here with us tonight," Lady Linwood admitted in a mock whisper. "Especially one I consider to be a friend. And may I say, you look stunning in pink, Miss Barton."

The sincerity of her compliment and the warmth of her

49

gaze put Gwen immediately at ease. Clare Herschel might be an earl's wife now, but her kind regard for others hadn't diminished. Though Gwen sensed an undercurrent of sadness in the other young woman's smile that couldn't be completely masked. The realization tugged at her compassion. She hoped Clare had found—and would continue to find—happiness in her new life.

"Miss Barton, may I present my husband, Lord Linwood?" She motioned to the man standing beside her. He was nice-looking with dark blond hair and light blue eyes.

"It's a pleasure to meet you, Lord Linwood."

The earl bowed and offered Gwen a pleasant smile. "A friend of Lady Linwood's is a friend of mine, Miss Barton."

"Thank you, my lord."

He turned toward a gentleman standing slightly behind the couple. "Miss Barton, this is my oldest and most loyal friend, Mr. Avery Winfield."

While Lord Linwood was pleasing in appearance, Gwen found his friend to be far handsomer than any man she'd yet been introduced to. His brown hair and eyes were the color of coffee and perfectly complemented the strong cut of his jaw. And his charming smile at her prolonged silence elicited the sudden speeding of her pulse.

"I'm pleased to make your acquaintance, Mr. Winfield," she managed after a moment, though her cheeks warmed with embarrassment over her delayed reply.

Mr. Winfield bowed. "The pleasure is all mine, Miss Barton. I believe we have a mutual friend, in addition to Lady Linwood."

"Oh?" Gwen stepped toward him to allow the other guests to move through the receiving line.

"Your cousin Bert Rodmill attended university with me and Lord Linwood."

"Ah." She blushed again at voicing another one-word response.

If he noticed, Mr. Winfield thankfully didn't point it out. Instead he asked, "Are you and your cousin well acquainted?"

"Not really, no. Before this visit, the last time I saw Bert was four years ago when he and his parents visited us in America."

There, that was more than a single-word answer. But Mr. Winfield looked more disappointed than impressed. Did he think she ought to know more about her cousin than she did?

"Bert's a fine young man," she added belatedly.

Mr. Winfield gave a distracted nod as if he hadn't heard her. "How are you enjoying London, Miss Barton?"

"I don't know that I could say just yet. I've been here less than three weeks."

There was so much more she wanted to see and do while in London besides attend one dreary, monotonous social engagement after another. Like visiting Dr. Smithfield's office. She'd learned the address, but she hadn't yet formulated a plan for how or when to visit.

Mr. Winfield's answering chuckle took her by surprise. Did he find her honesty entertaining? Or did he think she was being intentionally coy? Since attending the opera the week before, Gwen had maintained her resolve to be herself—at least when out of earshot of her mother.

"Did I say something humorous, Mr. Winfield?"

He shook his head. "Not at all. But I assure you, Miss Barton, you may speak plainly to me about your opinions of our fair city."

"I *am* speaking plainly."

He leaned closer. "My guess is you find this place and its social pace rather tedious."

His candidness both confused and nettled her, though

she wouldn't trade it for the hollow pleasantries she'd received from other Englishmen. "I've seen a great many things and people I wouldn't call tedious." Though she was beginning to think Mr. Winfield wasn't one of them.

"You aren't here because you wish to be, though, are you?"

Gwen frowned. Perhaps he wasn't as handsome as she'd first believed. Certainly, his appeal was growing dimmer by the minute. It was almost as if he were trying to bait her, but she couldn't fathom why. "That may be true, but I don't see why that should matter to anyone." Least of all to this man she'd only just met.

"I meant no offense. I'm only surprised." He regarded her, his mouth twitching with a barely concealed smile. "You don't possess the same wide-eyed exuberance or veiled flirtation so many other socialites exhibit, especially the American ones."

Gwen wasn't sure if she ought to feel complimented or insulted by such an observation. His growing smile had her leaning toward the latter conclusion. But he wasn't the only one with a gift for scrutiny. Having spent a fair number of social functions along the periphery of the room, Gwen had developed a rather keen ability for observation herself.

"I don't think you wish to be here any more than I do," she countered in a soft voice.

He gave an impatient sniff. "How so?"

"I drew my conclusion by the way you were hanging back from Lord and Lady Linwood and the arched looks you've been throwing around the room." Gwen met his level gaze with one of her own. "You don't seem intent on impressing me either, Mr. Winfield, which leads me to believe you, thankfully, want nothing to do with my fortune."

He opened his mouth as if to speak, but Gwen wasn't

finished. "If this isn't where you wish to be either, I'm curious as to why you are here at all. Perhaps it's only as a favor to your good friend over there. However, if that's true, then I'd think you would choose to be more civil to the earl's guests and not interrogate them."

The look of astonishment that settled onto his face was more than satisfying. Gwen swallowed a laugh. The man might be attractive, but he was far too arrogant and intrusive for her liking.

"If you'll excuse me, Mr. Winfield."

She didn't bother trying to disguise her limp as she walked away from the insufferable man. Syble would be proud of her for speaking her mind instead of appearing to be the demure debutante she wasn't. When Gwen reached her mother's side, her heart was still beating too fast, though it was out of annoyance rather than attraction this time.

"Is something the matter, Gwen?" her mother asked a little too loudly. "You look flushed."

She shook her head and pushed out a calming breath. "Not at all, Mother." As long as she maintained a room's width of distance between her and Mr. Winfield for the rest of the evening, she'd be fine.

⁓⁕⁓

Avery didn't know whether to feel pleased or chagrinned at being seated beside Miss Barton for dinner. He'd hoped to glean information from her, not incur her ire. Perhaps he'd lost his charm in conversing with the ladies since becoming an agent for Captain Kell.

He cast a glance at his silent dinner companion and couldn't help thinking what an effective spy Miss Barton would make. Her gift for observation had been as shocking as it was impressive. Could those abilities run in the family? Was her cousin Rodmill using a similar talent for deduction by currently spying for Germany?

One thing he did know—Lord Linwood's assessment of Miss Barton's beauty had been correct. Avery found her quite attractive with her dark hair and expressive hazel eyes. Ones that had regarded him with genuine interest at first, then narrowed with anger before she'd walked away. He'd noticed a slight hitch to her step as she crossed the room, which made him wonder if she'd sprained her ankle recently or suffered from some injury in the past.

The possibility elicited a measure of compassion inside him. After all, he wouldn't be up and walking himself if Mack hadn't worked wonders with Avery's injury from the opera.

Briefly he considered whether she might be the American girl who'd helped him. But Avery threw out the notion almost at once. From what he could remember, his opera young lady, as he'd come to think of her, had been sweet and courteous— which made her far different from the other American girls he'd met during past seasons. Miss Barton struck him as much quieter than her compatriots from the States, but she was also far too observant and frank when she did speak her mind.

Although, Avery supposed he *had* goaded her after learning the disappointing news that she and her cousin weren't well acquainted with another. His grandmother would be just as appalled as Miss Barton about his ungentlemanly behavior, and rightly so. Even by American standards, he had been rude. He hated the idea of his grandmother thinking badly of him, which meant it was past time to rectify his earlier ill manners.

"Miss Barton?"

She turned to look at him, her olive-brown eyes no longer flashing with fire but veiled with wariness. "Yes?"

"I believe I owe you an apology." He cleared his throat. Had Mack tied his cravat too tightly this evening? "I was inexcusably rude earlier. I fear I've always been rather inquisitive, but that is no excuse for . . . how did you say it . . . interrogating my friend's guests?"

Her cheeks turned a lovely shade of pink. "I'm sorry as well, Mr. Winfield. I don't regret speaking my mind, but perhaps I could have been more . . . tactful."

"Actually, I found our exchange rather refreshing," he said, taking a sip of his wine.

She studied him with apparent disbelief before she must have sensed his sincerity. Then a fetching smile lifted her lips. "If we're speaking plainly, then I have to say I found it slightly refreshing too."

Avery laughed as he set his goblet back down. Miss Barton's smile deepened. "In that case, I am eager to hear what other less-than-tactful thoughts you have inside your head."

"Oh, no." Her eyes sparkled with amusement. "I won't be so easily pressed into speaking frankly again, Mr. Winfield. How about you speak plainly about yourself instead?"

"Touché," he murmured as he turned to study the other guests seated around the table. What could he share? His life of late hinged on his abilities of deception. "I don't care for soup."

Miss Barton eyed him curiously, though he could tell she was trying not to laugh. "Soup? Is this a lifelong dislike or a more recent one?"

"I've never cared for the stuff." Not after watching his mother dine on soup alone after she took ill. "Now it's your turn."

She glanced across the table. "I'd rather be reading or helping with my cousin's charity work back home than socializing."

The admission didn't surprise him. He'd noticed right away that she didn't appear to find enjoyment among the dinner guests and swirling conversations as some young ladies did, though she had masked her discomfort well. What astounded him was the absence of flirtatious coyness in her mannerisms. She wasn't trying to entice him with her honest answers; she was simply being herself. That knowledge was as inspiring as her frankness.

"Yet here you are," he said after a moment.

She smiled at him. "Here I am."

"How do you plan to make it through the season?" He truly wanted to know.

Miss Barton stabbed a morsel of food with her fork. "With a great deal of work and prayer."

"Prayer?" he echoed, more loudly than he intended. This was definitely not the answer he'd expected. He lowered his voice to ask, "Are you religious, Miss Barton?"

She gave him a puzzled look. "Yes."

"I wonder, then, which will drive you to the point of madness first," he said, half teasing her. "The shocking lack of reading time you'll have while in London or the absence of religion and faith you'll find among the *ton*."

Miss Barton frowned. "That sounds a bit extreme. I'm sure there are men and women among London's elite who are religious."

"Oh, they're religious, all right." He didn't bother to squelch his acerbic tone. "If you mean they attend church and occasionally give to the poor. But by and large, their intention is to safeguard their reputations, not their souls or the well-being of those less fortunate."

His father had been that way—appearing to be religious, while treating his own son harshly—and the hypocrisy of his actions still disturbed Avery. It was another reason he'd given up on his boyhood faith.

She lifted her chin slightly. "I imagine there must be

people among the *ton* who love and honor God. Who seek Him in prayer for guidance in their lives, and, having witnessed His love, wish to share that with others."

"That's a rather naïve point of view."

It was the wrong thing to say. He knew it the instant her gaze flashed with anger once more. "If that is naivety, then I'll accept that as a compliment, Mr. Winfield." She spit out his name as if it were a distasteful piece of mutton.

"Let me ask you this." He swiveled to face her, ignoring the warning in his head that told him to keep silent. "What do you value most in your future husband?" Before she could respond, he went on. "I believe I can guess. Love, faith, affection? Those are likely at the top of your list, are they not?"

Tension had stiffened her shoulders and thinned her mouth. "I know you're mocking me, but yes, those are qualities I wish for in a husband."

"Is a title not one of them?"

Instead of firing back a sharp retort as he'd expected, she threw a glance in the direction of her mother, her face turning slightly pale. "Not for me."

Avery could easily surmise what she wasn't saying. It was Mrs. Barton who hoped to tether her daughter to a titled gentleman. The woman certainly wouldn't be the first matron to do so. His own mother had been matched with his father in a similar scheme. And where had that left her, left their family?

He himself had fended off more than one scheming matron every season. There were plenty of mothers eager to marry their daughters off to the nephew of a childless duke, even if love and affection or even simple respect had no place in the arrangement.

"I'm not mocking you, Miss Barton." All the fight had left him. "I merely wish to offer some friendly advice." When she didn't protest, he continued. "Clinging to one's faith and to notions of romantic love is far more difficult than you might believe when you are living among London's upper class. It's like clinging to a buoy in the middle of the ocean during a storm."

"Then I'll take comfort in knowing the God I trust is Master of waves and sea." Her eyes glowed with flinty resolve. "I hope to marry someone I love, but if that isn't a possibility, then I'll remain as I am and trust that God has other plans for me and my life."

A flicker of memory darted through his mind—in it, he was a little boy sitting beside his mother, her arm cradling him to her side. *Remember to include God in your plans, Avery. He will make of them something far greater than you can accomplish on your own.* He shifted uncomfortably in his chair. He didn't want to recall his mother's faith. What good had it done her to hold to it?

Miss Barton didn't speak to him again, to Avery's relief, but her silence also left him feeling inexplicably frustrated. He was grateful when she and the other women finally withdrew from the dining room, leaving the men to their cigarettes and brandy, even if Avery didn't partake of either.

She'd proven to be no help in providing him with information about her cousin. Now that Avery knew that, he could go back to tracking down the enemy spy on his own and hopefully avoid interacting with Miss Barton for the rest of the season.

Chapter 5

Pressing her lips over a yawn, Gwen threw another glance at the clock on the mantle. Thirty minutes to go before their at-home day for callers would come to a blessed end. She thought longingly of the book she had set aside earlier. The memory prompted another, more unpleasant, recollection from the week before—when Avery Winfield had told her that she'd likely go mad from not being able to read due to all of the season's social engagements.

Fresh irritation rose inside her, pushing back against her boredom. Didn't he realize this wasn't her first season? She'd managed two others with time enough to read *and* help at Heartwell House as often as she could.

At least she'd had no concerns that Mr. Winfield would be among her visitors today. He'd seemed as frustrated with her at the end of the Linwoods' dinner as she had been with him.

She hadn't been surprised that Mr. Fipwish had called, though she hadn't been expecting visits from Bert's friends Lord Whitson and Mr. Hanbury. Her surprise at their appearance had soon given way to consternation.

Lord Whitson, the eldest son of a marquess, had talked

incessantly about himself whenever he wasn't showering Gwen with shallow compliments in an obvious attempt at impressing her and her mother. He'd apparently succeeded with the latter. In contrast, Mr. Hanbury, who would not inherit a title but was quite wealthy, had said very little. Gwen had been forced to carry most of the conversation for a quarter of an hour.

"Mrs. Rinecroft and Miss Rinecroft," the Rodmills' butler announced.

Gwen's fatigue and boredom faded at once. Her best friend was waiting in the foyer.

Her excitement did not extend to her mother, though. "Why are they calling now?" Cornelia frowned. "Come to crow about some titled match that Syble has made?"

"You know they aren't like that."

Cornelia sniffed. "Perhaps not. But if we allow them to call today, we will have to return the visit in the future."

"Please, Mother."

Sniffing once more, Cornelia looked at the clock. "Very well. But only because our at-home day is nearly at an end." She waved the butler out the door to grant the Rinecrofts admittance.

Eagerness had Gwen sitting up straighter. It was all she could do to suppress a grin when Syble and her mother entered the room.

"Hello, Mrs. Rinecroft," Gwen said politely as she stood. "Miss Rinecroft."

Her best friend smiled and crushed Gwen in a tight hug as if it had been months since they'd last seen each other. Over her friend's shoulder, she saw her mother's frown had returned.

"Mother was sure we'd only be allowed to leave a card," Syble whispered before releasing Gwen. "But here we are." She turned to face Gwen's mother. "Always a pleasure to see you, Mrs. Barton."

"Yes," Cornelia said with an imperious nod. "How do you do, Miss Rinecroft? Mrs. Rinecroft?"

As the two matrons greeted one another, Gwen took a limping step toward the door. "May I show Syble my room, Mother?"

Her lengthy sigh expressed her disapproval, but Cornelia finally motioned them toward the door. "I suppose there's no harm in it."

Syble winked at Gwen as they moved into the foyer. The moment Gwen was sure they were out of sight, she linked her arm with her friend's.

"I'm so grateful you're here, Syble."

"Me too," Syble said, slowing her footfalls up the stairs to accommodate Gwen's pace. "It feels like ages since I last saw you, and I have ever so much to tell you, Gwenie." She positively glowed in her light blue day dress and large feathered hat.

Once inside Gwen's room, Syble flouted convention by removing her hat from her blond hair. Then she sank into one of the armchairs. Gwen took a seat in the other.

"Don't you just love London?" Syble rested her gloved hands on the chair arms. "It's ever so much more fun than New York."

Thinking back to her conversation with the smug Mr. Winfield, Gwen gave a noncommittal murmur. "What have you loved the most?" she asked her friend.

"Oh, the theater, the dinners, and of course, all the handsome gentlemen." She raised her eyebrows, prompting a laugh from Gwen. "One in particular, actually."

Gwen listened as Syble spoke at length about a Mr. Elijah

Kirk, whom she'd met at the theater. He was the only son of a viscount, and the family had a country estate in Kent.

"He's ever so sweet," Syble gushed. "And unlike those bachelor bores back home, he seems to enjoy it when I'm blunt or prattle on about anything and everything."

"Speaking of bluntness, I finally spoke my mind to a gentleman last week." The recollection filled Gwen with new strength and prompted a smile. If only her best friend could have been there to witness her triumphant moment firsthand.

"And who was the beneficiary of your boldness?"

"A gentleman by the name of Avery Winfield."

Syble's blue eyes widened. "Avery Winfield?"

"Have you met him?"

Her friend bent forward, her incredulity palpable. "Of course I've met him. Not only is he incredibly handsome, but you know about his inheritance, right?"

"No."

An amazed laugh fell from her friend's lips. "Maybe that's a good thing. You might not have been so bold if you'd known he's the nephew and heir of the Duke of Moorleigh. Mr. Winfield will inherit the title and the estate from his uncle."

"Oh no." Gwen covered her face with her hands. Of all the men to choose to be herself around, she had to pick one who would one day be a duke.

"It's all right, Gwen." Syble touched her arm. "Perhaps he likes a forthright woman like Mr. Kirk does."

She lowered her hands to her lap. "Whether he does or doesn't, I'm not interested in him. I mean, I might have been at first, but he proved to be more pestering and patronizing than likeable."

"Interesting," Syble murmured, settling back against the cushions again. "The man hardly spoke more than a few words to me the night I met him, but nothing he said struck me as uncivil, and he certainly didn't pester me with his attentions." She loosely clasped her hands together. "Start at the beginning."

Gwen obliged, detailing her interactions with Mr. Winfield from the moment she'd arrived at the Linwoods' townhouse to their conversation during dinner. "I'll admit I allowed him to poke at me. But I don't regret what I said to him, especially not about my faith."

"I'm proud of you, Gwenie. And I don't blame you one bit for being annoyed with his arrogance. It sounds as if you handled things brilliantly."

She offered Syble an indulging smile. "You say that because I handled things a lot like *you* would have."

"Exactly." Her friend spread her arms wide. "Which is why I can knowingly say you handled them well."

They shared a laugh. "I've missed you, Syble."

"I've missed you too." Syble's expression drooped a little. "It isn't the same as it was back in New York, is it? I feel like we're supposed to be even greater rivals here. Just don't go falling in love with Mr. Kirk if you meet him, all right? He'll take one look at you and I'll be sunk."

It took Gwen a moment to realize Syble wasn't teasing. "Why would he like me?"

"Because you're kind and beautiful and quietly articulate." There was no jealousy in her friend's eyes, only vulnerability. "The men here seem to like when I blurt out what I'm thinking or want to discuss topics that are deemed too intellectual for a woman back home. But I'm afraid that, in the end, they'll prefer to marry someone quiet and discreet like you."

Reaching out, Gwen took hold of Syble's hand and gave it a firm squeeze. "We can only be who we are, Syble. And I hope there are men somewhere in this country who will love us because of that."

She lowered her hand to the chair arm and plucked at an errant thread. Her secret about the opera filled her thoughts and her throat, begging to be unburdened. It had been almost a week since that night. Surely she could tell Syble without betraying the man she'd helped.

"I met someone too."

"What?" Syble squealed as if they were fourteen again and not twenty. "Who? What's his name?"

Gwen released a sigh. "I don't know. I don't even know what he looks like."

"Then how can you know you like him?"

The memory of their kiss brought a smile to her mouth. "I know."

"Gwen! What aren't you telling me?"

She laughed. "All right, all right. I'll share the whole story. But you have to promise me that you won't breathe a word of it to anyone."

"I promise." Syble pretended to lock her lips with an imaginary key. "I won't tell a soul."

Satisfied, Gwen described her escape into the empty opera box and how she'd found an injured gentleman lying there. She told Syble how she'd bandaged him, then feared she had worsened his injuries in the process. Her cheeks flushed when she described their kiss.

"That is the most romantic story I've ever heard." Syble sighed dreamily. "Better than any of the books we've read. To think you helped him and had your first real kiss in the process. He's probably out there right now, wondering who you are too."

Gwen liked to believe so. "I want to figure out his identity, even if I'm not quite sure how." Or where she would find the time—with social events every evening, at-home days, and trying to figure out how to slip away to visit Dr. Smithfield's office. But she wanted to solve this mystery.

"Gwen?" Her mother's voice slipped through the partially opened door. "Mrs. Rinecroft is about to leave."

Climbing to her feet, Gwen threw Syble a firm look. "Please don't say anything—to anyone."

"I won't," Syble reassured her as she stood and put her hat back on. She scooped up Gwen's hand in hers as she added, "We'll figure out his identity together. I'll help you."

Gwen gave her friend a parting hug. "I'm so glad you came today, Syble."

"So am I."

Gwen trailed her mother and Syble down the stairs to the foyer. After leaving a card, the Rinecrofts departed. As the butler closed the door behind them, Cornelia turned to face Gwen. "I hope you weren't giving away any secrets to the enemy."

"No, Mother."

"Good. Then I think we can consider this at-home day a success. Especially given Lord Whitson's visit." She flashed a triumphant smile at Gwen.

Knowing she couldn't voice her true thoughts on the subject, Gwen held her tongue, allowing her mother to chatter on about the gentlemen who'd called as the two of them returned upstairs. The day had been successful, but not for the reason her mother believed.

Seeing Syble again had bolstered Gwen's spirits and her determination to be herself this season. It had also renewed her desire to learn the identity of her injured stranger.

"I'm going to lie down before dressing for dinner," Cornelia said, stopping outside her bedroom door.

Gwen tried to recall if they had plans for the evening, but

she couldn't remember which invitations her mother had accepted. "Do we have a dinner to attend tonight?"

"No, we're dining here, with your aunt and uncle, before we attend a dance."

"A dance?" Dread churned her empty stomach. Why had her mother agreed to such an event? "But I can't dance."

Cornelia pinched the bridge of her nose, her lips turning downward. "The hostess is a friend of your aunt's, Gwen. She is also the wife of a viscount and very influential among London society." She lowered her hand and gave Gwen a firm look. "So you will make your excuses about not dancing, but I still expect you to be charming."

She gave her mother a wordless nod, then moved toward her own room. The click of her mother's door closing sounded behind her. Casting a glance at the hall clock, Gwen guessed she had an hour, possibly two, before she'd need to dress for dinner. She could return to the book she'd been reading late into the night. Or . . .

Could she make it to the doctor's office and back in time? It might be days before she again had a few hours to herself.

With her heart beating double time, Gwen collected a hat from her room and headed downstairs once more. "I need the carriage brought around for an errand," she told the Rodmills' butler.

Would he question her? She wasn't doing anything wrong, though the clandestine way she had to go about it made it feel as if she were.

A flicker of surprise entered the butler's expression before he lowered his gaze to the floor and offered her a bow. "I'll see to it right away, Miss Barton." He exited the foyer.

Was he curious about Gwen's destination or surprised that her mother wasn't with her? Would he tell her aunt—or worse, her mother—about her mysterious departure? Gwen dreaded the thought of the ire that would descend upon her if he did. But regardless, she was finally going to see the famous doctor. She released her breath in a rush.

A heady sense of freedom and hope surrounded her as Gwen stepped outside to wait for the carriage. She couldn't help smiling when the vehicle appeared. At last she was doing something she wanted to do while in London.

⌒ᴓᴓᴓᴓᴏ⌒

From across the room at the club, Avery watched Bert Rodmill. The man appeared to be on edge as he polished off another glass of brandy. He kept checking his pocket watch and bouncing his leg. After another few minutes, Rodmill glanced around, then rose to his feet. It was Avery's cue to leave as well.

"I believe I'll head home," he said to Linwood as he stood.

His friend raised his eyebrows. "So early? What's the hurry, Winfield?"

"Feeling a bit peaked."

Which was true. Avery had stayed up later than usual the night before, reviewing all of the information he'd gleaned about his two suspects. But he hadn't come to any new conclusions. Not for the first time, he felt frustrated at the dead end he'd met with Rodmill's cousin, Miss Barton.

"You sound like an old man, chap," Linwood said with a laugh. "All you need is a nightcap and pipe to complete the picture."

"Ha. I'm no older than you." They were both twenty-eight. "Besides, I accepted an invitation to the Stouts' dance this evening, and I'd like to rest before I go."

Linwood eyed him with open suspicion. "You're attending another social event? Are you turning into a society man?"

"Hardly." Avery grimaced, prompting a smile from his friend. "But it is my hope that if I put in more of a show this season, my uncle will have less cause for complaint."

It was another truth. In addition, Avery hoped one or both of his suspects would be in attendance tonight. "Are you and Lady Linwood attending the dance?"

A shadow crossed his friend's face. "We were invited, but no, Clare and I won't be attending."

"Is something amiss?" If Linwood wished to unburden himself, then of course Avery would stay and listen. Besides, he already had a good idea where Rodmill was headed.

Linwood's smile didn't reach his eyes. "I'll be all right. You go on, old man."

"If you need anything, Linwood . . ."

He nodded, his expression uncharacteristically serious. "I know, Winfield. And I'm grateful for it."

Avery bid his friend goodbye, then exited the club before searching the busy street for Rodmill. Once his current assignment was over, he intended to get to the bottom of whatever was troubling Lord Linwood—at least, if his friend was willing to share it.

As he'd predicted, he discovered Rodmill walking a familiar route through London's various neighborhoods. Likely bound for the undistinguished townhouse Avery had followed the man to before.

Rodmill peered over his shoulder often, but Avery stayed far enough back to not be noticed. Members of the upper class, dressed in their finest, could be seen climbing into carriages and the occasional motorcar to attend a variety of social events.

At last, Rodmill stopped in front of the same townhouse. A servant opened the door, and the other man entered the house. Avery crossed to the opposite side of the street to wait. Rodmill's meetings typically lasted less than an hour.

His thoughts soon turned from his investigation to his concern for Lord and Lady Linwood. But that trail of thought went to the last time he'd seen them together at the dinner they'd hosted and that, annoyingly, led his mind to Miss Barton.

Nearly a week had passed since his disastrous conversation with the American girl. Avery had attended two other functions since then, but he hadn't seen Miss Barton at either. It was a fact he found as gratifying as he did disappointing. He'd wondered more than once how she was doing and if her philosophies on love and faith were holding up in the face of the season. He actually hoped they were.

He had met two more American heiresses since the Linwoods' dinner. But neither of them could be the girl who'd helped him. One of them, a Miss Syble Rinecroft, was pleasant enough, and yet she chattered too much to be his calm, serene young lady from the opera. The other, a Miss Snow, had a beautiful singing voice, which she prided herself on sharing. Her manners were a bit too showy, though, to be those of the woman from the opera box.

Had he only imagined the girl spoke with an American accent? *No.* Avery shook his head. He might have been in great pain that night, but he hadn't hallucinated his surprise when he'd heard her accent. Those three American girls might not be the one he sought. However, there were still other American heiresses he hadn't met yet.

The door to the townhouse suddenly opened, jerking Avery from his musings. Rodmill descended the steps to the street. Avery straightened away from the wrought-iron fence he'd been leaning against. Tonight the man looked uncharacteristically happy. Instead of his usual frown, Rodmill wore an actual smile.

Near the corner, the other man paused to pull out his

watch. A slip of paper fluttered from his pocket to the sidewalk, but Rodmill seemed to take no notice. Without looking down, he marched on.

Avery dashed in front of several carriages to reach the corner. He bent and picked up the paper. Could it finally be a clue as to why the man visited this part of town? Avery opened the note, and a surge of victory rolled through him when he saw the German words penned there.

"Now we're getting somewhere," he murmured to himself as he translated the message.

Komm heute Abend um 6:00 zu mir. "Come to me at 6:00 this evening."

He stuffed the note into his pocket. This was actual evidence that Bert Rodmill's meeting this evening had in fact been with the Germans. Could the man's happiness mean he'd at last delivered valuable information to those inside the townhouse? Could Rodmill be the one who'd commissioned that reprobate to try to kill Avery at the opera?

Avery had shared the incident with Captain Kell, along with his concern that his cover among the *ton* might have been blown. But the captain believed the threat was likely a lucky guess by the enemy spy's superiors—an attempt to do away with Avery in the event that he might well be a spy himself. With a very limited number of men to help him, Captain Kell had asked Avery to continue his work until they had the solid proof they needed to apprehend whoever was spying for and reporting to Germany.

He hurried past the corner and down the street until he had sight on Rodmill once more. As usual, the man's trail ended outside his parents' townhouse.

Not as exciting a final destination as Avery had hoped. But he still felt pleased with the note he'd discovered. It gave him an upper hand in this game of cat and mouse.

Before he turned to leave, he noticed a carriage pull to a stop in front of the Rodmills' home. Was Miss Barton inside? He paused to watch and felt something akin to pleasure when the young lady stepped down from the vehicle. Except she was the only one to disembark. The carriage moved on the moment she started slowly up the front steps. He could see, even from a distance, her guilty expression as she approached her cousin, who stood waiting for her.

How curious. Avery studied the pair. Rodmill looked annoyed as he spoke to Miss Barton, and Avery assumed the other man was scolding his cousin for her behavior. He had to admit he was surprised by her actions as well. Why would she travel unaccompanied around London? And where had she gone?

When the two of them entered the house a minute or so later, Avery started for his own home, his mind flooding with thoughts. Could Miss Barton be working with her cousin, and thereby, with the Germans too? Avery didn't want to believe it, especially given the disappointment expanding inside his chest. And yet he couldn't deny that the young lady possessed the skills of quiet observation and discreetness, which were so needful in a spy.

Perhaps she would be at the dance this evening. The possibility had him smiling to himself with anticipation. Because, whether Miss Barton accused him of interrogating her again or not, Avery planned to find out exactly where she had gone today and why.

Chapter 6

Everything swirled around Gwen as though she were caught inside a kaleidoscope for the senses—the lights glittering off the evening gowns, the buzz of conversation, the clashing scents of perfume. And it was more than the dancers moving around the Stouts' ornate ballroom. It was the eddy of emotions inside her too.

She'd felt so purposeful and independent heading to Dr. Smithfield's office. But her bravery had been vanquished by disappointment when the clerk had brushed her off after informing her that the doctor was away on a house call. That meant she would have to arrange another time to visit.

Then when she'd returned to her aunt and uncle's townhouse, she had been horrified to see Bert striding up the steps ahead of her, then pausing to wait for her. Gwen had exited the carriage as regally as she could, her head held high. To her relief, she hadn't been questioned about *where* she had gone. But Bert had plenty to say about the impropriety of riding in a carriage unaccompanied.

His irritation over her faux pas had mingled with her regret at missing the doctor and had stolen most of her appetite at dinner. Or perhaps that had been more due to the apprehension she felt over tonight's event, which was supposed to be *the dance* of the season. Anticipation of how awkward she would look and feel at sitting out added to the churning sensation in her stomach.

Gwen shifted on the cushioned chair, turning her gaze away from the whirling pageantry. It wasn't that she longed to dance, though she supposed it might be nice with an honorable man as her partner. She simply wished she had the option to decide for herself.

At that moment she caught sight of the dogged Mr. Fipwish heading her way. Gwen suppressed a frown. In good conscience, she couldn't ignore him, especially when he came to a stop in front of her.

"Mr. Fipwish."

He bowed to her. "Miss Barton. I was hoping you would be here this evening. May I say how enchanting you look? Like a decanter aglow in the firelight."

No, you may not.

The thought of saying such a thing out loud tweaked the corners of her lips, but Gwen hurried to hide the smile lest the man think it stemmed from his praise. "Thank you."

"Will you do me the honor of the next dance?"

All of her mother's advice, including another hissed reminder as they were helped from the carriage outside the Stouts' residence, reverberated through Gwen's head. She fisted one of her gloved hands as she attempted to silence the cacophony of thoughts. She'd committed to being herself, and that meant telling the truth—not making excuses. Hopefully doing so would send Mr. Fipwish fleeing for good.

"I'm afraid I cannot dance, Mr. Fipwish."

His eyebrows rose in a quizzical expression. "You mean to say you never had dancing lessons?" He seemed genuinely surprised. "I thought dancing lessons were part of every American heiress's education."

"Not for me." She sat up straighter. "I was injured as a child, and the result is a foot that can't bear much weight for long periods of time." A flicker of something entered his gaze. Gwen guessed it was a mixture of shock and dismay. "I limp when I walk, which makes dancing out of the question."

Gwen offered him a congenial smile, relieved to have the truth out in the open. After all, he wasn't likely to stick around in the present or the future after such a candid explanation.

And that made his answering smile all the more puzzling. The uneasiness returned to her middle as the man took the vacant seat beside hers.

"If you cannot dance," he declared, "then I shan't dance either, Miss Barton."

"That really isn't—"

He leaned close. "Never fear. I will gallantly take it upon myself to provide you with all of the conversation you could desire this evening."

She glanced around, desperately searching in vain for some reason to excuse herself. Her gaze met her mother's across the room. There was no mistaking Cornelia's pleased expression. Gwen felt trapped—she couldn't abandon her would-be suitor now that her mother had seen them sitting together. Why had being herself resulted in the very thing she'd hoped to avoid?

"How is that new mare of yours?" she managed to say from her tight throat.

If she could get him talking about himself, then she likely wouldn't have to talk at all. Instead she could think of how to ensure her plan to be herself didn't go awry again.

"She is a sight to behold. Have I told you how well she can jump?"

As Gwen had suspected, the man launched into an equestrian monologue. She tried to listen, but the longer Mr.

Fipwish talked, the more her attention and gaze strayed to the rest of those assembled. She noticed Mr. Hanbury standing to one side of the ballroom. The sight of another of her would-be suitors inspired an idea. Mr. Hanbury had kindly helped her out of an awkward situation before. Perhaps he'd do so again.

Gwen waited until he looked her way, then she offered him a genuine smile. He might be quiet, but he was nice-looking and not fond of talking only of himself. The man didn't seem overly fond of talking at all. Which Gwen now viewed as a great blessing. If he would only come over to speak with her, then maybe she could join him—to seek refreshments or step outside for some air—and blessedly leave Mr. Fipwish behind.

Mr. Hanbury acknowledged her with a dip of his head. However, instead of moving toward her as she'd hoped, he threw Mr. Fipwish a pointed look before disappearing among the press of people. Gwen bit back a disappointed sigh. Help would not come in the form of Mr. Hanbury tonight. She would need to come up with another strategy to shake the company of Mr. Fipwish.

At that moment, she noticed Mr. Winfield moving along the perimeter of the dance floor. Her heart gave a strange leap when he met her eye and smiled. Gwen didn't know whether to return the smile or frown instead. She was still mildly irritated at him for his bombastic comments at the Linwoods' dinner. And yet, when she realized he was coming her way, she felt more relief than annoyance. Debating with Avery Winfield sounded far more pleasant than listening to Mr. Fipwish belabor his fascination with decanters or his mare.

"Good evening, Mr. Winfield." She nodded to him when he stopped alongside her chair.

He inclined his head in return and bowed. "Miss Barton."

Turning to Mr. Fipwish, he acknowledged the other man. "Fipwish."

"Winfield," Mr. Fipwish replied with a frown.

Mr. Winfield turned his gaze toward the dancing. "Quite the ball, is it not?"

"Indeed." Mr. Fipwish glared in annoyance at Mr. Winfield.

If he noticed, Mr. Winfield chose to ignore the other gentleman's reaction. "I overheard Lord Dunstill talking about your mare, Fipwish." He leaned in as he added, "I'm afraid he still thinks he has a horse that can easily out-jump yours."

Mr. Fipwish aimed a glowering look across the room. "Is that so?" He stood and tugged his evening coat into place. "I'm afraid I must leave you, Miss Barton. The honor of my prize mare is at stake. If you'll both excuse me . . ."

"Of course," Gwen said, trying hard not to laugh. It was not an easy task with the way Mr. Winfield's brown eyes were twinkling with mischief.

"I shall seek you out later."

She held back her grimace by clasping her hands tightly together. "I'll understand if your other . . . conversation . . . requires a great deal of your time."

As Mr. Fipwish strode off, Mr. Winfield took his vacated seat. "Well played," he murmured to her, his mouth twitching with a barely hidden smile.

"You as well." She was surprised to find herself relaxing into her chair. "Was this Lord Dunstill actually talking about Mr. Fipwish's horse?"

"I did happen to overhear him." The merriment hadn't disappeared from his gaze. "However, even if I hadn't, I would have been safe in my claims. Lord Dunstill can't attend an event with Mr. Fipwish without disparaging the man's horses at some point during the evening."

Gwen studied him with a mixture of bewilderment and gratitude. "So you planned to approach Mr. Fipwish whether you overheard that conversation or not. Why?"

"Because I'm all too aware of how long-winded he can be. Especially when it comes to whatever new horse he's purchased." Mr. Winfield exchanged a smile with her, then turned to watch the dancing again. "I suppose you could say I was aiding a damsel in distress."

"Ha. I was hardly in distress." The laugh she'd suppressed earlier spilled from her lips. "All right, so I might have been experiencing a little distress."

He faced her once more. "I guessed as much. And as a reward for my benevolence, I should like to know why you aren't dancing this evening."

Had he been watching her longer than she was aware? Gwen found the prospect as unsettling as it was pleasing.

"I'll gladly tell you why I'm not dancing." She motioned to her left foot as she shifted it slightly beyond the hem of her ball gown. "As a child, I was in a carriage accident and injured my foot. In spite of the doctor's care, the foot didn't heal correctly."

Mr. Winfield nodded thoughtfully. "That's why you walk with a limp."

"Yes." She wasn't surprised that he'd noticed—not with how astute he'd been in his observations the other night. But she appreciated the lack of feigned sympathy from him. "It's also why I can't dance."

"And are thus at the mercy of Mr. Fipwish."

Gwen laughed lightly. "Exactly. But why aren't you dancing, Mr. Winfield?"

"Ahh." He leaned back in his chair. "Tonight, I find that I prefer enlightening conversation to dancing."

He found their conversation enlightening? Gwen wasn't

sure she could say the same. Except . . . he had seen her distress and responded to it. And after resolving her difficulty, he'd stayed and appeared genuinely interested in continuing to talk with her. Surprisingly, she found the idea of conversing with him less appalling than she might have earlier.

"What enlightening topic should we discuss, then?"

Mr. Winfield appeared to think her question over. "Are you finding the season's social events to your liking? And, remember, I expect you to speak plainly." He waved his gloved finger at her.

"That's what you deem enlightening?" she countered with another laugh. He offered a shrug, though his expression conveyed his amusement. "Fine. I've enjoyed the theater and the opera and some of the dinners. Although I did have a rather irritating companion when I dined at Lord and Lady Linwood's home last week."

Placing his fist against his chest, he shook his head as though deeply pained. "You wound me, Miss Barton."

"I'm sorry." Though she wasn't, not really. The man had been much too free with his views that night. "I couldn't resist."

"Nor could I," she thought she heard him murmur. "Have you seen much of London besides townhouse drawing rooms and the theater?"

It was her turn to shake her head. "Not as much as I'd like."

"What do you wish to see?"

Besides Dr. Smithfield's office, Gwen considered where else she wanted to visit. "I'd like to see Hyde Park and St. Paul's Cathedral. Oh, and an orphanage for crippled children if there's something like that here."

Mr. Winfield looked momentarily taken aback by her response. "Why would you wish to see an orphanage?"

"I work at the one my cousin founded back in New York, and I'm curious to see how they operate in London."

He cleared his throat. "Will your mother be accompanying you on your visits to such sights? Or perhaps one of your suitors?"

"I don't know," she answered honestly, glancing to the spot where she'd last seen her mother. Gwen felt relieved when she noted Cornelia was no longer there. Her mother didn't need to see her daughter conversing with the nephew of a duke. Cornelia would inevitably view it as something more than two people talking and would likely push Gwen toward Mr. Winfield.

He also appeared to be studying something across the room. "You won't attempt to go somewhere alone again, will you?"

"Again?" She threw him a sharp look. Some of the affability between them began to bleed away at the bizarre turn to their conversation. "How do you know I've gone anywhere alone?"

Mr. Winfield shifted slightly away from her as if uncomfortable. "I happened by your aunt and uncle's townhouse earlier today and saw you alight from their carriage—alone."

"No need to bother with offering 'friendly advice' in that regard, Mr. Winfield." Gwen clasped her hands tightly in her lap as frustration rose warm inside her. "My cousin Bert already did that. Apparently well-bred ladies don't travel in carriages alone here in London."

Was she mistaken in thinking the man looked relieved? "That is correct. I take it you didn't understand that before today?"

"No, I did not." It was her turn to inch away from him. Her welcome champion was fast becoming a bothersome offender.

His smile looked a bit forced as he asked, "Searching for a new hat or some other piece of costuming?"

"Hardly," Gwen muttered. She wasn't ready to tell anyone about her important errand, not even Syble. At least not yet. Not until she'd seen the doctor and learned if he'd be able to help her or not. Speaking of it to another person before then would only raise her hopes and expectations, which might very well be dashed. Besides, if word got back to her mother from her cousin or one of the servants, Gwen might not be allowed to make another visit to the doctor's office, especially by herself.

She glanced at Mr. Winfield as the tense silence stretched long between them. From the outside, he appeared to be the charming gentleman. And yet she sensed tightness in the line of his shoulders and an irritation his sociable words and expression couldn't hide.

"Do you live near my aunt and uncle, Mr. Winfield?"

He looked as if he'd been startled out of his thoughts. "No," he answered quickly. "My residence is in Belgrave Square."

"How interesting." Gwen cocked her head and eyed him shrewdly. She was beginning to learn the best way to manage her interactions with this man and all his contradictions was to turn the table on his questioning. "And yet you just so happened to come by the Rodmills' townhouse in Mayfair while I was climbing out of the carriage?"

The man stood up so abruptly he nearly trampled on the train of her dress. "If you'll excuse me, Miss Barton. I have another commitment to attend to. Thank you for indulging me in conversation."

"Oh . . . you're welcome." She hadn't exactly meant to drive him off, though she wished they could have kept their exchange as easy and friendly as it had been at first after he'd come to her aid. "Thank you for helping me earlier."

He bowed, the lines around his brown eyes softening. "My pleasure."

With that he strode away. Gwen lost sight of him after a few moments. He hadn't been as blatantly offensive tonight, and yet she couldn't riddle him out either. Who was the real Avery Winfield? The sharp-eyed gentleman of many questions or the gallant, appealing one? She found she actually wanted to know—and that was likely the most startling observation either of them had yet made.

⁓⁕⁕⁓

Avery sought refuge in the card room, though he didn't join any of the current games. Instead he found a comfortable seat in the corner to collect his thoughts and plan his next move.

His interaction with Miss Barton had gone dreadfully awry. Avery shook his head. That wasn't entirely true. He'd felt that same measure of compassion for her that he had at the Linwoods' dinner when he had noticed Fipwish blathering away to her. A desire to come to her aid had been his motive as much as finding out where she'd gone alone earlier.

He'd enjoyed their friendly banter. Perhaps a bit too much. He had nearly forgotten what he'd gone over to ask her in the first place.

Something about Miss Barton intrigued him. She'd matter-of-factly told him about her injured foot and its resulting consequences without an ounce of pity for herself. The young lady also possessed a quick wit along with unexpected fortitude. And she hoped to see an orphanage while in London. An orphanage! By the earnest, animated light in her hazel eyes he knew she wasn't overstating the truth of her commitment to children in need.

It was at that moment he began to question if he'd made an erroneous assumption about her. Surely she wasn't involved with her cousin and the Germans. And yet not only had she refused to mention where she had gone, she'd also reverted to questioning *him*. How had an American girl, with supposedly no spy connections, caught the inconsistency in his story about happening by the Rodmills' when he lived elsewhere in the city?

He tugged at his cravat in irritation, trying to determine where and how he'd mucked up his chance to glean more information from her. Was Miss Barton a dead end? He wanted to believe it. If so, then she wasn't acting in order to appear normal, as he often felt the need to. She was merely being herself.

Which is something I've never been able to be.

The idea of truly being himself felt as liberating as it did sobering. As a spy for Captain Kell, Avery *couldn't* be himself, even if he wanted to. But tonight, that thought didn't bring its usual relief. Having shared another fascinating exchange with Miss Barton, Avery suddenly wished he could be himself. At least with her. That's how he'd imagined he would be with his opera young lady if there were no impediments to their meeting again.

Avery gave the chair arms a resolute slap with his gloved hands and rose to his feet. He might have learned nothing particularly new about Miss Barton, save for why she limped and was required to sit out from dancing. However, the evening wasn't over yet. For now, he would put aside his hopes at catching a German spy and would turn his attention to his own mystery. The final American heiress he had yet to meet was here, and Avery had managed to place his name on her dance card.

A glance at the clock confirmed it was nearly time to claim his partner. Determined once more, he quit the card room for the ballroom. He looked for Miss Edith Dyer, but he couldn't find her. The music began again, signaling their dance had started. Where could the girl have gone? At last, Avery decided it would be best to ask the young lady's father if he knew where his daughter might be.

Avery approached the older man, who was conversing with several other gentlemen, and waited to be acknowledged. When the American turned to face him, Avery wasted no time in getting right to the point. "Mr. Dyer, I am Avery Winfield. I believe I was to have this dance with your daughter. Do you know where I might find her?"

"I'm sorry to say Edith has left, Mr. Winfield." The man gave a sad shake of his head. "Such a pity too. She was looking forward to the evening."

"Has she taken ill?"

Mr. Dyer shook his head again. "Not in a manner of speaking." He glanced around and took a step closer to Avery. "Some girl was accidentally knocked in the nose after one of the dances. Unfortunately, her nose started to bleed. And when Edith saw it, she fainted dead away." The father gave a helpless shrug as he grimaced. "My daughter really can't abide the sight of blood."

If this American girl couldn't handle seeing blood, then she couldn't be the one who'd bandaged Avery's wound in the opera box. He fought to hide the frustration the revelation brought him.

He'd met every American girl in London this season, and yet not one of them seemed to be his mystery young lady. "I imagine that was very distressful for her," Avery managed to say. "Please inform her that I hope she recovers quickly."

The man nodded. "I will. Thank you, Mr. Winfield."

Avery bowed, then headed in the opposite direction before realizing he wasn't sure where he was going. Dancing or talking held little interest to him now. He turned and made his way to the grand staircase, more than ready to make his exit.

Once inside his carriage, he sank back into the corner of the seat. He'd met with disappointment after disappointment rather than success tonight. Even the satisfaction he'd felt at finding Rodmill's incriminating note earlier had paled. The German spy among the *ton* and the girl from the opera were both still mysteries to him.

Which led Avery to wonder, as the carriage rolled toward home, if he should have followed his best friend's example and skipped the dance altogether. Of course he needed to attend the most popular social events—both for his espionage work and for his uncle. But tonight, the rest of the season stretched painfully long before him and made him wish, if just for a moment, that he'd chosen some other profession than the Secret Service.

Chapter 7

"You're plodding along like you're riding a nag, Winfield. At this rate, we won't be through exercising the horses until luncheon."

Avery frowned and urged his horse into a canter to match the pace of Linwood's mount. Thankfully it was still early enough that the crush of horses and riders hadn't yet begun to fill Hyde Park, though Avery had noticed two of Rodmill's friends, Lord Whitson and Mr. Hanbury, were here as well.

"Sorry," Avery muttered with a shake of his head.

Linwood turned to look at him. "Something on your mind?"

He had plenty on his mind—unfortunately, most of which he couldn't share with his best friend. After showing the note he'd recovered to Captain Kell, Avery had been instructed to put all of his focus into Rodmill. Avery had watched the townhouse Rodmill frequently visited and wasn't surprised to learn the occupants were German. However, other than Rodmill, they rarely received any visitors.

Avery didn't mind having a specific task to focus on, but he'd been much more careful regarding how he went about fulfilling it. Especially after Miss Barton's keen remark at the ball about Avery "happening" by the Rodmills' residence when he lived in a different neighborhood.

Miss Barton was the other subject of his thoughts of late. It had been five days since he'd last seen her, and yet, he had mulled over their conversation again and again since. Avery now believed, whatever her secret errand had been, that it wasn't anything which would compromise the safety of Britain. Still, that didn't ease his conscience over nettling her once more.

For reasons he couldn't fathom, given the two of them had only conversed twice, he wished for Miss Gwenyth Barton to enjoy talking with him as much he did with her. At the very least, he didn't want her thinking he was an ill-mannered cad.

"Winfield?"

His friend was waiting for some kind of answer to his question about what was on Avery's mind. He didn't want to throw out a glib response, so he countered with a question of his own. "How well does your wife know Miss Barton?"

"I couldn't actually say." Linwood shrugged. "They debuted into New York society together. And I believe Clare is grateful to have two other Americans and ones she considers more than acquaintances here in London this season. Why?"

It was Avery's turn to shrug—and ignore the gleam of curiosity in his best friend's gaze. "No reason. Did you know Miss Barton suffered an accident as a child? That's why she walks with a limp."

"I don't know that I noticed a limp at all."

Avery wasn't surprised. If noticing details weren't so imperative for his employment, he might not have been aware of Miss Barton's impediment either. As it was, there were a great many other details he'd noticed about her too. The way her eyes readily expressed her displeasure or delight. Her intelligent humor. Her obvious compassion for the downtrodden. Her genuine smile and the way it lifted those lovely, rose-colored lips . . .

He cleared his throat in an effort to rein in his thoughts.

"Does her limp bother you?" Linwood asked, eyeing him unabashedly.

Shaking his head, Avery urged his horse slightly ahead of his friend's. He hadn't meant the conversation to follow the convoluted thoughts inside his head. "Not at all."

"Then you approve of her."

He shifted uncomfortably in the saddle. "She is . . . an agreeable young lady."

"Aha." His friend gave him a smug smile. "I knew it. Clare had her doubts about matching the pair of you, but I didn't. I knew you'd like Miss Barton."

"She and I have shared less than a handful of interactions, Linwood. I hardly think that qualifies as anything noteworthy."

Linwood's expression of triumph didn't dwindle in the slightest. "For other chaps, yes. But not you. I've been your closest friend for years, Winfield. And you have never called a girl agreeable before, except for Clare, after I told you I wished to marry her."

"I find my grandmother agreeable too. So your wife and Miss Barton aren't the only ones who hold that distinction."

His friend laughed heartily. "Deny it all you like, but I stand by my claim. You and Miss Barton are a worthy match."

"I still don't wish to marry." He'd meant the admission to sound as decisive as it usually did. But this time the words brought a niggling of doubt and regret.

Linwood pulled his horse to a stop. "Clinging stubbornly to being a bachelor even now, are you? Your uncle won't go in for such a scheme."

Avery glanced away. "He hasn't married either."

"Right, but he has you to take over. Need I remind you that you'll lose the title and the estate to someone you've never even met if you choose to follow his same path?"

"I am well aware of that, Linwood. But that could still be the fate of things if I marry and am unable to have a son."

A furrow of pain creased his friend's brow, though Avery didn't understand its source. "Enough talk of matrimony," Linwood said, facing forward again. "This horse of mine has been pining for a race, even a short one. What do you say? Are you game?"

"Of course." Avery banished his introspective mood and smiled.

They selected a landmark up ahead as the finish line, then Linwood counted down from five. When he reached "one," he and Avery each spurred their horses into a gallop. The exhilaration of the morning air rushing past him and the speed of his horse deepened Avery's smile. It had been ages since he'd ridden at this pace. Probably not since his last visit to Beechwood Manor.

Despite considering himself a decent horseman, he still didn't cross the finish line first. Linwood was an exceptional rider, but Avery wasn't about to admit that fact in his moment of defeat. Once he and Linwood had stopped their mounts, he affected a sad expression. "I believe my horse is feeling a bit poorly."

"Oh, no you don't," Linwood said, grinning as he shook his head. "You used that same excuse last year when we raced at Beechwood."

"Perhaps I did. But a horse that's feeling off doesn't perform well."

Linwood dismounted and held his horse's reins. "Then I challenge you to another race. Only this time I'll ride your mount and you ride mine."

"All right," Avery conceded.

It wasn't likely to make a difference as far as securing a win. But Linwood's beast was a fine specimen of horse flesh, and Avery didn't mind riding the animal. Even if he lost—again.

The two of them traded horses, and Avery counted down. The speed was no less thrilling from atop his best friend's mount, and this time he was able to stay right alongside Linwood. Maybe there was something to his feigned claim after all.

The two horses were neck and neck, each vying for the winning position as they thundered down the road. Then up ahead and to the left, Avery noticed another rider bearing down on them, almost as if the man intended to join their race. Instead of directing his beast in line with the other two horses, though, he began to barrel straight toward Avery's best friend.

"Linwood, look out!" Avery hollered, jerking his horse hard to the right to give his friend room to do the same.

His friend glanced over his shoulder at the charging madman, then attempted to turn. But Linwood wasn't quick enough. The other man, his chin down, slammed into Avery's horse. The animal shrieked in pain and reared. Linwood managed to stay seated, but in the hubbub, the other rider rode off before Avery could get a proper look at his face.

He jerked his friend's horse to a stop. Then he dismounted, hurriedly threw the reins around a nearby post and rushed toward his own mount. "What happened?" Avery seized his horse's reins. "Are you hurt, Linwood?"

"No. A bit rattled, though." Linwood slid from the saddle. His face had turned pale. "What in the world was that chap thinking, plowing into me like that?"

Avery looked his horse over carefully. Even before he saw

the trickle of blood on the beast's left flank, he had a sinking suspicion he knew exactly what *that chap* had been thinking.

He and his best friend were of similar height and build. The assailant had assumed Avery would be riding his own horse, not his friend's. The knife that had nicked Avery's mount had likely been intended to nick him, a second time.

The thought set his heart to pounding hard and furious within his chest. Someone—*could it be Rodmill's superiors?*—still wanted him out of the way. But they were being rather discreet about it by threatening Avery in public places, where the dastardly deed would be less noticeable.

"What do you think hurt her?" Linwood gestured to the horse.

Avery schooled his expression to convey none of the dread or anger he felt. "Who knows? Perhaps there was a sharp edge somewhere on the other horse's tack. Thankfully it doesn't look deep. I'll have my stable master take a look. You probably prevented it from being much worse by getting out of the way."

"I was only following what you did." His friend ran a hand down his face, which was returning to normal color. "Thanks for the warning."

He gave Linwood a grim nod. "I believe I'll walk her back."

"I'll join you," Linwood said as he collected his horse from where Avery had left it. "I don't have much inclination to race or ride anymore today."

The walk back toward their respective townhouses was a somber one. Avery felt confident his horse would be fine. Though he couldn't help feeling he was to blame for the injury. After all, the other horseman had intended to hurt the beast's rider, not the animal itself. If Avery needed further proof regarding the foolishness of taking a wife, he had it right before him in the form of his injured horse. Worse still, it could have been Lord Linwood who'd been hurt if the man hadn't acted as quickly as he had in getting out of the madman's way.

Avery gritted his teeth against the awful possibility that his best friend might have been seriously injured, all because of Avery's involvement with tracking down supposed German spies. His feeling of victory at apprehending Rodmill's note had disappeared entirely. Now he felt only urgency and angered determination. It was time to track down this traitor once and for all—and find a trusted watchman to place in front of his own house from now on—before someone else he cared about was caught in the crossfire.

⁓⁕⁓

The trees surrounding the walled garden provided plenty of shade for afternoon tea outdoors. Gwen had expected her mother to decline the invitation from the Rinecrofts, but Cornelia had pursed her lips for only a moment before relenting. She hadn't even brooked a complaint when Syble had asked if the two friends could take their tea outside.

Was her mother scheming again? Or did Cornelia possibly feel as her daughter did—relieved to visit with an old friend rather than managing the usual whirlwind of conversing with near strangers?

Whatever the reason, Gwen was grateful for another rare moment with her best friend. The loveliness of the garden behind the Rinecrofts' rented townhouse added to her pleasure. Perhaps there was a way to turn a section of the courtyard at Heartwell House into a similar space so the children could sit among the leaves and flowers.

"Shall we begin?" Syble asked, brandishing a notebook and pencil.

Gwen took another sip of her tea. "Begin what?"

"Narrowing down the identity of your mystery man." Her friend opened to a blank page. "I promised to help you, remember?"

Setting down her cup, Gwen smiled. "I remember. But how is this going to help?" She motioned to the writing utensils.

"I was thinking now that we've been in London for four weeks and have met a significant number of society's young men, we could make a list of everyone you can recall seeing that night after the opera was over. That way we can narrow down who your young man isn't."

"That's a brilliant idea, Syble."

Her best friend grinned. "I know. Now who are some of the gentlemen you recall seeing that night?"

Gwen sat back in her chair, thinking. "Let's see. I met . . . Bert's friends Lord Whitson and Mr. Hanbury for the first time that night. Mr. Fipwish was there too."

"Ah." Syble wrote their names down. "Your three ardent suitors."

"Maybe to my mother but not to me."

"You don't find any of them agreeable?"

Studying the nearby flowering bush, Gwen shook her head. "So far, when the earl isn't offering me false flattery, he's boasting about what elite events he's to attend. Mr. Hanbury, on the other hand, says little, and Mr. Fipwish only wants to talk about decanters and his new mare." Her next words felt vulnerable to voice, even to Syble. "I want to find someone I love and admire to marry. Not settle for someone who's just agreeable and willing to overlook my shortcomings."

"Deep down, I think that's what most of us want," Syble admitted in a low voice as she glanced toward the house.

Her admission surprised Gwen. "Do you love Mr. Kirk?"

"I think I could learn to love him." Syble straightened in her seat and pointed her pencil at Gwen. "Speaking of Mr. Kirk, was he in attendance at the opera that night?"

Gwen tried to remember. She'd finally been introduced to Syble's suitor at the Stouts' dance. But could she recall seeing him at the opera?

"I don't think he was there." At the distressed look that crept onto her friend's face, Gwen hurried to add, "But didn't you tell me the other week that he doesn't enjoy attending the opera?"

Syble visibly brightened with relief. "Yes. I don't think he's attended the opera at all this season, so I'll write his name on our list too."

They continued adding names as they reviewed the different young men they'd both met. The prospect of whittling down whom her opera man couldn't be felt far less challenging as she watched their list grow in length.

"What about Mr. Winfield?" Syble looked up from her notebook. "Did you see him after the opera?"

Gwen frowned, as much at the reminder about Mr. Winfield as at the mental struggle to recall if she'd seen him from afar that night. The man was a mystery all right, a mystery of contrasts and contradictions. Or maybe that was just the feelings he'd evoked in her after every one of their conversations. Her frown deepened at the thought.

"No, he wasn't there."

Syble's expression revealed her excitement at Gwen's response. "Do you think he's your injured gentleman?"

"I doubt it," Gwen replied with a shake of her head.

She couldn't imagine the insufferable yet sometimes charming Avery Winfield as the stoic man from the opera box. Certainly his kiss wouldn't inspire the same sort of sweetness. *Or would it?* a traitorous thought whispered.

Only then did Gwen notice the way her best friend was watching her. "What?" She brushed at her mouth, wondering if she had crumbs from the tiny cake she'd eaten with her tea.

"You like him." Syble punctuated her statement with a nod. "I haven't seen you this agitated over a young man since Randolph."

Gwen lowered her hand to her lap. "And look how well that turned out."

"Randolph was a devious rogue, Gwen, pretending to be an admiring suitor."

"What if these other men are the same?" She waved a hand at Syble's list, though inside she was thinking only of Mr. Winfield. "They don't seem to mind my limp as the bachelors back home did, but I don't think they care about me as much as they do my fortune."

An uncharacteristically somber demeanor settled over Syble as she fiddled with her pencil. "I know what you mean. And yet we didn't expect any less, did we? Or we shouldn't have, I suppose. We're here to make good matches, and hopefully in the process find husbands who will come to care as much about us as they do our money."

Syble's speech lacked her usual animation. Instead, she sounded as if she hoped to convince herself of its validity as much as she did Gwen.

"Is that really what *you* want, Syble?"

Her friend offered a little shrug. "Does it matter? If we go against our parents' wishes and refuse to accept a match that meets with their approval, we'll be cut off financially and socially." She twisted her teacup around in its saucer. "I'm not afraid of having to find employment, but I am afraid of . . . ending up alone."

"Whatever you choose, you won't be alone, Syble." Sitting forward, Gwen reached out to squeeze her friend's hand. "You'll always have me and you have God."

Syble squeezed her hand in return. "You're right. And truth be told, I do want a love match. Just like you do, Gwenie." She eased back, a sad smile on her lips. "But I've decided I have to be realistic too. A love match may be too much for me to hope for in the beginning, but given time, years even, a marriage can become that."

How ironic that the usually impetuous Syble seemed almost content with the idea of working and waiting for a marriage to become one of mutual love. On the other hand, Gwen didn't want to wait. She wanted her marriage to be built on love from the start—if such a thing was even possible.

Mr. Winfield's words from the dinner party ran through her mind. *Clinging to one's faith and to notions of romantic love is far more difficult than you might believe when you are living among London's upper class.* They were certainly proving to be true, especially when Gwen felt no stirrings of romance or love in the company of any of her would-be suitors.

And yet, foolish as it might sound, she had felt that very thing when she'd kissed the wounded gentleman inside that opera box. Surely that meant Gwen could feel the same with someone else.

"Your mother is ready to depart, Miss Barton," a footman announced as he stepped into the garden.

Gwen rose to her feet and Syble did the same. "Thank you for your help, Syble." She gave her friend a parting hug. "I'm going to keep praying we both find love matches," she whispered before stepping back.

"I think I will too," Syble responded with a smile. "In the meantime, I'd like to get to know this Mr. Winfield better."

Gwen tried to shrug off the flicker of jealousy such a plan sparked inside her. It wasn't as if she had any claim on or understanding with Mr. Winfield. However, the image that rose into her head—of Mr. Winfield bantering with her best friend as he'd done with Gwen at the ball— threatened to sour her mood.

"I only meant to see if he was right for you, Gwen. Not because I'm interested in him myself."

Gwen took a shuffling step toward the house. "Of course. I didn't think you were interested in him."

"No, you didn't," Syble said, linking her arm through Gwen's. "But that look of dismay on your face just now certainly did."

There seemed no way to respond without incriminating herself, so Gwen settled for saying, "I appreciate your concern, Syble. But Mr. Winfield and I are not a match."

"Very well, but I still won't pursue him. I've already concluded Mr. Winfield isn't right for me."

"Oh?" Gwen hoped the bizarre relief she felt didn't leak into her voice or expression. "Why is that?"

Syble shrugged. "Because he isn't my Mr. Kirk."

They shared a laugh as they entered the house. But as Gwen followed her mother out the front door and into the waiting carriage, she couldn't help wondering what it would be like to have someone in her life she could call hers. Someone who felt she was his in return.

Memories of the events from the opera flitted through her mind again. Once she learned who the man was, could he be someone she could call her own?

She straightened on the seat, half-listening to her mother recount her opinions of the Rinecrofts' townhouse. With Syble's help, Gwen had made significant progress on figuring out who the occupant in the opera box wasn't. Now she just had to keep trying to figure out who he *was*. It was no small task, especially with so many possibilities among all of the young men in London. But Gwen hadn't survived a childhood accident and relearned to walk with an injured foot only to weaken at the sight of hard work.

She might not have a love match yet, but she did have determination—and faith. And hopefully both would serve her well as she continued to forge ahead through the season.

⚬ৡৡ ৡৡ⚬

"May I say you look dashing, sir?" Mack brushed Avery's evening coat. "You will certainly make an impression on the young ladies tonight."

If he hadn't felt a bit apprehensive about the ball this evening, Avery might have cracked a smile at his valet's remark. Or at least rolled his eyes. Instead he settled for a simple, "Thank you."

The older man knew Avery's real purpose for attending tonight's engagement—and it had nothing to do with impressing young ladies. He was more than ready to confront his target at last. Mack had successfully obtained word from the Rodmills' servants that the entire family would be in attendance at the ball tonight. Including Miss Barton.

Avery schooled his thoughts from the American young lady to the situation at hand. He couldn't allow himself to be derailed by memories of their past conversations. His horse had, thankfully, recovered from the incident in Hyde Park. But Avery couldn't be sure his attackers wouldn't strike again, though he'd hired two men of Mack's acquaintance to discreetly watch his home day and night. Still, he'd kept to himself for the past several days. Tonight's ball would be his first social event in a week.

Blowing out a slow breath, he tugged at his cuffs and eyed his reflection in the full-length mirror. "I believe I'm ready, Mack."

"Everything properly tucked inside your pockets?"

He opened his coat to double-check the spot where he'd concealed a small knife. Avery didn't want to try to apprehend a spy unarmed, even if his chances of needing a weapon were slim. He'd already arranged, through Captain Kell, for several policemen to meet him and Rodmill at eleven o'clock in the small park opposite the house where the ball would take place. All Avery had to do was procure proof of Rodmill's involvement with spying for Germany, then entice him to duck across the street with Avery. The police would handle the rest.

"Everything's secure," he replied, dropping his coat back into place.

Mack stuck out his hand, which Avery clasped firmly in his own. "Good luck, sir. I'll be praying for you."

"I'm grateful for it, Mack." He meant it too. While God didn't care much for Avery, He surely would listen to the appeals of an honest, upright man like Gregory Mack. Or Miss Gwenyth Barton.

Again, Avery attempted to push thoughts of her from his mind, but as usual, he wasn't successful. Would Miss Barton be devastated when she learned her cousin had betrayed his native country? A twinge of regret for her and her family shot through him. For his part, he was more than ready to see his hard work finally pay off. In his own small way, he was saving Britain from future disaster. Surely that meant he—and his life—amounted to something. Though if his father were still alive, Phillip Winfield would likely still find some flaw, some disappointment, in Avery and his mission.

"Have a *successful* evening, sir."

The smile Mack likely meant to conjure up lifted Avery's mouth. "I plan to."

Settling his hat on his head, he drew on his gloves as he headed into the corridor. A few minutes later, he was settled inside his carriage. He could have walked, given the drive took less time than it did to ready the vehicle, but Avery needed to look the part of the quintessential gentleman tonight and not draw any questions or suspicion.

The ballroom was already teeming with people when he arrived. It wasn't difficult to locate Miss Barton, seated to the side as she'd been at the last ball. However, this evening Mrs. Barton hovered near her daughter along with the arrogant Lord Whitson. Avery felt a flash of compassion for Miss Barton. Tonight he wouldn't be at liberty to save her from a tiresome, one-sided conversation as he had done before.

Finding Rodmill proved harder. The young man wasn't dancing, so Avery widened his search to include the billiards room and the card room. At last he located Rodmill in the smoke room.

Avery had no desire for a cigarette, so he feigned interest instead in talking at length with a friend of his uncle's who was puffing away on a cigar. When Rodmill finally stood and left the room, Avery followed a few moments later. This time the young man went to the ballroom, but he didn't dance. Instead, Rodmill stood along the periphery of the room, looking sullen and clearly ignoring the pointed looks from the young ladies not dancing and their mothers.

After checking his pocket watch, Avery knew he had less than thirty minutes before he was to meet the police in the park—with Rodmill in hand. He couldn't secure proof of spying here, though. Not among all these people. He needed to get the other man away from any listening ears. But how?

He discarded several ideas before settling on one that seemed to have the greatest potential to work. Avery would reveal just enough information from what he'd gathered about Rodmill to surprise the man and pique his interest enough to leave the party.

Decision made, he moved slowly toward Rodmill, whose back was to him. Avery stopped slightly behind him and to the side. "I know about the secret meetings," he whispered, loud enough for Rodmill alone to hear him. "If you wish to know more, meet me in the library. Now."

Rodmill's shoulders tensed. But before the other man could turn around, Avery strode off in the direction of the library. He could only hope—and perhaps pray a little—that his plan would work.

Chapter 8

With the train of her pink satin ball gown in one gloved hand, Gwen edged slowly away from where her mother and Lord Whitson sat, deep in conversation. They hadn't asked Gwen a question in several minutes and didn't seem aware of her presence anymore. Which suited her splendidly. Unlike at the Stouts' ball, she didn't want to simply sit and observe those around her. Tonight Gwen felt restless and in desperate need of a quiet corner after listening to the earl drone on for nearly a half an hour.

She reached the ballroom doors and allowed herself a small sigh of relief. Not that she couldn't still be overtaken. But a glance over her shoulder revealed she hadn't yet been missed. And that was a tiny miracle in itself.

Gwen smiled as the cooler air in the hallway greeted her, pushing away the stifling warmth of the crowded ballroom. She considered which way to go to find her moment's reprieve. From the open doors to her right, raucous laughter and a constant drone of conversation spilled outward. Gwen turned to the left and its promise of stillness. An open doorway farther down the hall to the left beckoned. She entered the room and immediately felt at home when she realized she'd discovered the house's library.

In the light of the single lamp, she studied the shelves filled from floor to ceiling with books. A fireplace with a large ancestral picture over the mantle reigned supreme on one side of the room, while a settee and armchairs gathered before the hearth. Other small seating arrangements were tucked into various corners.

Gwen walked to the nearest shelf. After removing her glove, she slid her fingers along the leather bindings. Some of the uneasiness she'd felt at her mother's exuberance toward Lord Whitson faded at the familiar feel of old books. She didn't see any novels until she perused the titles on the next shelf. Sir Walter Scott's *Ivanhoe* stood out. Gwen slipped the book from its perch and limped to one of the corner chairs nearest the window. The heavy curtains had been drawn back, which acted like a screen around the chair and made this spot difficult to see from the door. It was the perfect place to spend a few minutes alone reading.

She'd read this book before, but it seemed more than fitting to read some of it again, now that she was actually in England. Gwen became so immersed in the story that she didn't realize someone else had entered the library until she heard the door click shut.

Jerking her chin upward, she saw two men standing near the door, facing each other. They clearly hadn't noticed her, though. Should she say something?

A large part of her longed to simply stay where she was, safely hidden away. She had no desire to return to the ballroom. But on the other hand, she didn't like the idea of overhearing what was surely meant to be a private conversation. As she debated what to say, she recognized her cousin's voice.

"How long have you known?" Bert demanded.

The second gentleman shrugged and glanced toward the fireplace, allowing Gwen a view of his profile. She was startled to realize it was Mr. Winfield. "Long enough."

Withdrawing a piece of paper from his pocket, Mr. Winfield read aloud the words clearly penned there. But they weren't English. They sounded German.

"*Komm heute Abend um 6:00 zu mir.*"

"Wh-where did you get that?" The color drained from Bert's face.

Mr. Winfield causally pocketed the note. "You happened to drop it the other day. Although that wasn't the first time you've met your German friends."

"You don't understand." Bert ran his gloved hands through his hair, mussing up the black locks, as he began to pace the floor behind the settee. "Everything has to be kept secret."

"Of course." Mr. Winfield's tone dripped with sarcasm, but Bert didn't seem to notice.

Her cousin jammed his hands into his pockets, looking glummer than Gwen had ever seen him. "If my family finds out, they'll think I've turned traitor."

"Undoubtedly."

His gaze pleading, Bert ground to a halt in front of Mr. Winfield. "So what's a chap to do? I love her, Winfield. I have since we met on the Continent three years ago."

Gwen covered her mouth with her hand to stifle the gasp that nearly escaped. This had to be the reason Bert had been so morose lately. He didn't think his family would approve of the girl he loved.

"I don't care where she hails from," Bert continued with a defiant shrug. "Africa, Brazil, Germany? It makes no difference—"

"Wait." Now Mr. Winfield's face had turned a shade gray. "Who are you talking about, Rodmill?"

Bert frowned. "Miss Anna Müller. Who else?"

"Am I to understand . . ." Mr. Winfield fell back a step as

if the force of Bert's news had pushed him there. "Your secret meetings have been to see a young lady?" He wiped a gloved hand across his jaw.

"Yes," Bert ground out in obvious frustration. "With tensions so high between our two countries, we felt it best to keep our courtship a secret for now. Although, her parents know and have given us their blessing."

A recollection tickled at Gwen's memory. Was this what Lord Whitson had meant the night at the opera about there being "lots of foreigners in London these days"? Regretful compassion welled inside her for her cousin and this woman he loved but couldn't see openly.

"What do you know about her parents?" It was Mr. Winfield's turn to start pacing.

Bert shrugged again. "Nothing that would interest the nephew of a duke." There was disdain in his voice, though Gwen guessed it wasn't directed solely at Mr. Winfield but at the *ton* as a whole. "They haven't been accepted into society, even though they've lived in London for a year now."

"Do Miss Müller's parents wish to harm Britain because they've been ostracized?"

Her cousin glared at the other man. "That's a rather odd question, Winfield. What are you accusing them of doing?"

"Nothing at the moment." Mr. Winfield stopped his agitated steps. "Look, Rodmill. It's critical that I know where your allegiance and theirs lie. With Germany or with Britain?"

Bert crossed his arms. "What business is it of yours?"

"As with any loyal subject of His Majesty, it's my business to know if my neighbors are in league with Britain's adversaries." When he spoke again, Mr. Winfield sounded less resolute, almost weary. "It will go better for you and your young lady if you can assure others that you aren't involved with helping Germany to Britain's detriment."

"Are you speaking of . . . of spying?" Bert spit out the last word.

Mr. Winfield gave a curt nod and glanced toward the door. "Exactly."

"I'm no spy, Winfield, and neither are the Müllers." The fight seemed to drain from Bert as he added, "Anna and I are simply two people who fell in love at the wrong time. However, I still have hope that we'll prevail. That is, if our secret remains a secret for the time being."

He made it sound as if he were asking a question. Clearly, Mr. Winfield thought so too because he nodded once more. "I won't say a word to anyone." As if to prove his point, he pulled the note from his pocket again and handed it to Bert. "Probably best if you destroy this."

"I will." Bert accepted the note. "Thank you, Winfield."

"Your young lady isn't here tonight, then?"

Gwen's cousin shook his head as he pocketed the note. "I'll see her tomorrow, though." He moved toward the door. "I'd best return to the party. Have to keep up appearances, you know."

"I certainly do," Gwen thought she heard Mr. Winfield mutter. "I'll be along in another moment," he said with louder volume. "Go ahead."

The moment Bert disappeared out the door, Mr. Winfield braced his hands against the back of the settee. "How could you have been so wrong, Avery?" He hung his head and gave a scornful sniff. "Some spy you make, old boy."

Avery Winfield is a . . . a spy?

At the realization, Gwen jerked upright. But she'd forgotten about her book. It tumbled off her lap and smacked against the floor, as loudly as a shout in the silent room. Her presence in the library was no longer a secret.

Avery whirled around, his heart pounding with alarm at the unexpected noise. He wasn't sure which fact was most responsible for the cold sweat of shock breaking out along his brow—the reality he and Rodmill hadn't been alone earlier or that the intruder appeared to be none other than Miss Gwenyth Barton.

For one awful moment, he wondered again if she was a spy herself. Why else would she be here, listening in and hiding, if she wasn't working for the Germans? But the expression of startled bewilderment on her face appeared to be genuine. So there had to be some sensible explanation for her presence.

Although, how much had she overheard from her secret corner?

"Miss Barton." He offered her a mock bow, his jaw tightening with anger now that his shock had begun to dissipate. "I wasn't aware anyone else had sought this room for privacy." He stressed the final word of his statement.

"Mr. Winfield. I'm terribly sorry." She scrambled to stand, but her injured foot must have caught in the hem of her gown because she started to pitch forward.

Avery leapt toward her and managed to catch her by the elbow before she ended up on the floor alongside her book. Standing this close, he noticed the subtle fragrance of her perfume. It was floral in scent but light and pleasant, not showy or falsely sweet. Much like the woman herself.

"Thank you," she whispered.

He nodded but didn't feel the need to step away yet. It was vital he determine how much she'd heard. "Do you make it a habit of eavesdropping on others' conversations?"

"No, I don't." She yanked her arm free from his grasp. Only then did he realize she wasn't wearing a glove. That was the reason his own gloved fingers had touched warm skin. She snatched up her errant glove and pulled it onto her arm. "I was in need of some quiet, so I came here. I was reading," she said, motioning to the book, "and didn't realize anyone had entered until you and Bert began talking."

She might not have understood what they'd been discussing. Or that Avery had justifiably believed her cousin was a German spy. Now that he knew the man had done nothing more nefarious than fall in love with a girl his family might not approve of, Avery would turn his attention to his other primary suspect.

Unsure how to proceed with Miss Barton, he leaned down to pick up the book. "*Ivanhoe?*" he said, reading the title.

"I like novels." She commandeered the book back, her lips turned down.

"And that is an excellent one."

Her surprised look nearly made him smile, in spite of the unsuccessful evening. "You've read it?"

"Of course."

She moved slowly past him and replaced the book on a shelf. "If you'll excuse me, Mr. Winfield. I need to get back to the ball."

"One moment." He stepped between her and the door.

Miss Barton's eyes widened in fear. Then she narrowed them in determination. "I demand that you move away from that door."

"I'm not going to harm you, Miss Barton. I promise."

Her chin didn't lower a single notch, but the line of her shoulders relaxed slightly. "What do you want, Mr. Winfield?"

If his current situation weren't so concerning, he might

have chuckled at the directness of her question. Miss Barton might be a bit reserved in personality, but that didn't mean she would tolerate being bowled over. Hopefully that determination also extended to not giving in to her mother's choice in suitors. Not that that was any concern of his, of course.

"I need to know how much you overheard." If she wanted candor, he would give it to her. "More importantly, how much of it did you understand?"

This time she broke eye contact, her gaze flicking away from his. "I . . . um . . . heard everything." She clasped her gloved hands together. "I'm sorry for that. I certainly had no intention of eavesdropping on a conversation that was clearly meant to be private."

"What did you glean from our conversation, Miss Barton?"

She released a long breath and looked directly at him. "It sounds as if you were concerned my cousin had some secret tie to Germany."

"I was. Especially given that there were some not-so-secret ties."

Her eyebrows suddenly rose in what Avery could only deem as understanding. "You thought he was spying for them, didn't you?" She took a step toward him. "That's why you asked me how well I knew him. You thought he was a spy because you yourself are—" She pressed her lips together.

"Are what?" he retorted, matching the distance she'd narrowed. Had she heard his self-deprecating remark?

A measure of panic flitted over her pretty face and provided Avery with the answer he needed. Miss Barton knew he was a spy.

"I promise not to say a word to anyone, Mr. Winfield." She half rushed, half stumbled around him and gripped the door handle. "I won't, honest."

He didn't doubt that. And yet, he needed her to understand the gravity of what she'd inadvertently discovered about him. "It's not that simple."

"What do you mean?"

Avery rubbed his hand across his face, feeling as exhausted as he had felt after realizing Rodmill was secretly seeing a woman and not meeting with German sympathizers. "I work for the Secret Service Bureau, Miss Barton. As you can imagine, it is a profession often fraught with some degree of peril and danger."

"How much danger?"

To his relief, he could tell she was beginning to glimpse the burden he carried. A burden she would now need to shoulder as well, though he wouldn't give her the particulars about the two attempts at maiming him or ending his life.

"Enough to keep me on my guard at all times."

She released the door handle, her eyes growing large with apparent worry, but she didn't say anything. Avery sensed she was stoically waiting for him to continue.

"My life is at risk as a spy." There was no way to soften his next remark, so he simply stated it. "And I don't wish any harm to come to you should others learn that you know of my profession. They may then suspect you know much more than that."

He watched her visibly swallow. Other than that telltale sign of nervousness, there was no hysterics, no acting like she might faint. "What of my . . . my mother and family?"

"I believe they'll be fine, Miss Barton."

Now that she understood, he hoped to reassure her that all was not lost. Especially if she kept her promise. There was little reason to suppose she or her loved ones would become a target.

She gave a staunch nod—one his fellow Brits would

applaud. But Avery sensed she felt as much resignation as she did regret at having stumbled into the wrong place at the wrong time. Was there something he could do to make things up to her? To ease the weight of carrying his secret upon her shoulders?

"Since you've agreed to keep what you heard tonight confidential, may I ask if there is something I may do for you in return?" If she wished, he could certainly get Lord Whitson to leave her alone, at least for a few minutes.

Miss Barton studied him, then smiled. It wasn't a calculating smile. Rather it was one full of warmth, hope, and a bit of amusement. Seeing it, Avery no longer felt tired or burdened. He felt strangely buoyed up.

"There *is* something you can do to help me. Meet me tomorrow at my aunt's house at three o'clock for an errand."

"Will you be bringing along a maid to accompany us?"

Her impatient sigh elicited a chuckle from him. "No, Mr. Winfield. I'd rather not involve the servants. I would like to keep the particulars of this errand to myself."

"Very well," he conceded. "I will call for you at three o'clock tomorrow in an open carriage." While certainly not as discreet as having a servant with them, a ride in an open carriage ought to keep too many tongues from wagging.

As Miss Barton opened the door, Avery stepped backward in alarm. Both their reputations would be ruined if anyone saw them exiting the private confines of the library at the same time. "It will bode better for us both, but more especially for you, Miss Barton, if we aren't seen leaving this room together."

She furrowed her brow as if thinking carefully about what he'd just said. Then she partially shut the door. "All right. Should I leave first?"

"I believe that's wise. However, before you leave, will you tell me where we are going tomorrow?"

The single light enhanced the mischief shining in her hazel eyes. "You'll see."

"How exactly will I be of any help on this mystery errand?"

"You and Bert were both quite concerned about me travelling around town alone. This way I can accomplish what I need to without drawing more *unwanted* and *unwarranted* attention." She gave him a pointed look, and this time he couldn't help smiling in response. "I'm also hoping that having a gentleman with me will help the clerk take my request more seriously."

Avery had to admit he was more than a little curious about her errand, but he held back from asking her any further questions. He'd made enough inquiries for one night.

"Very well."

"Wait a minute." She tilted her head and regarded him with blatant curiosity. "All those pointed questions you've been asking me . . ." Miss Barton lowered her voice, though no one was likely to hear her through the marginal crack in the door. "Did you suspect me of the same thing you falsely accused Bert of doing?"

Avery didn't need to ask what she meant. Once again, she'd outsmarted him with her perceptiveness. It had been ages since he had last known the stinging heat of embarrassment—probably not since his father was still alive—but it crept up his neck now.

"I did," he admitted. "But I would consider it a compliment, Miss Barton, and not an affront. You are incredibly observant, and your unaccompanied carriage ride did raise my suspicions."

Her earnest laugh brought him a mixture of surprise and

pleasure. "I will definitely take that as a compliment, Mr. Winfield. However, as you will see tomorrow, my errand is nothing so dubious."

"I am intrigued."

"Tomorrow, then."

"Tomorrow."

He watched her slip out of the library. When another minute or two had passed, he exited the room as well. Upon entering the ballroom, he saw that she had returned to her seat. Lord Whitson no longer sat nearby, but Mrs. Barton did. The older woman appeared to be reprimanding her daughter in whispered tones. But Miss Barton didn't flinch or hang her head.

Avery felt a glimmer of pride for her. She was certainly made of stern stuff.

After leaving the ball and informing the bored policemen that there would be no arrest tonight, Avery returned home in his carriage. In spite of his mistake with Rodmill, he felt less disappointed than he would have otherwise been. He still had another man to investigate. As well as the errand with Miss Barton to attend to.

Not only did her mysterious errand intrigue him, but he found he was still very much intrigued by her. For the first time in a long while, Avery was actually looking forward to the morrow—and it had nothing to do with his spy work this time.

Chapter 9

The minute their at-home day ended the following after-noon, and the door had been shut behind Mr. Hanbury, their last caller, Gwen went upstairs to ready herself for her errand with Mr. Winfield. A strange sensation churned inside her as she pinned a blue straw hat with its spray of coordinating flowers on top of her coiffed hair. Why should she feel nervous, she wondered as she pulled on her gloves. If anything should inspire anxiety, it should be the conversation she'd overheard last night. And yet Gwen felt more flustered at the thought of spending time with Mr. Winfield today than she did about anything she'd learned during their encounter in the library.

With steps as hurried as she could make them, she returned downstairs to wait for Mr. Winfield's carriage. Her mother, who was writing letters in the drawing room, glanced up as Gwen crossed the foyer.

"Gwen! Where on earth are you going?"

She drew herself up straight. "I'm going on a drive."

"Alone?" Cornelia's tone was full of horror. Apparently she'd adopted the English views on such things as unmarried young ladies riding alone in carriages.

Gwen saw no use in pointing out how often she'd done just that in their carriage back home. Instead she shook her head and moved toward the door. "Mr. Winfield is accompanying me—in his open carriage."

"Winfield?" Cornelia called back loudly. "We met him at Lady Linwood's home, didn't we?" She didn't wait for Gwen to respond. "I learned last night that he's the nephew of a duke."

She could practically hear her mother's calculating thoughts from one room away. "Yes, he is. I'll be back in a while." Gwen managed a smile for the butler, who opened the door for her.

Her mother suddenly appeared in the drawing room doorway. "What a clever plan, Gwen."

"I'm sorry?"

"Giving your other suitors some competition by going for a drive with Mr. Winfield. It's a splendid maneuver."

Frowning, Gwen glanced at the butler. The man, of course, pretended not to be listening. But Gwen knew better. While Jenkins and a few of the other servants back home were loyal and discreet regarding her comings and goings, her aunt and uncle's staff had no reason to be the same.

"I'm not trying to give anyone competition, Mother."

"Nonsense." Cornelia waved her hand impatiently. "You have three men who seem besotted with you. However, this will serve as a small reminder to them that they aren't the only ones vying for your affections. You have other interested suitors."

Mr. Winfield was certainly not her suitor. He might be easy to talk with sometimes, and he was unarguably handsome, but she didn't fully trust him either. Not after the mercurial way he'd behaved around her. He thought little of her faith too. However, she saw no point in explaining all of

116

that to her mother. Not when there was a more pressing issue to be established.

"Lord Whitson, Mr. Fipwish, and Mr. Hanbury may enjoy my company, but the feeling isn't mutual." She added in a quieter tone, "It's still my decision if and whom I marry."

Her mother's eyebrows shot upward, then her gaze narrowed. "That may be true in part, Gwenyth." Cornelia's voice had taken on a warning edge. "But you mustn't forget your rightful place as the daughter of a Barton. Or that your father has the right to change his will at any time, regarding your inheritance. Especially if you refuse to marry someone who meets with our approval."

"I won't forget," she countered with quiet firmness. Movement through the open front door pulled her attention in that direction. Mr. Winfield's carriage and driver were here. "Goodbye, Mother. I'll be back in an hour or so."

Gwen didn't wait for a reply. Keeping her head lifted as she descended the front steps, she fought to release the sting of her mother's parting words. And the despair that accompanied the reminder that she still wasn't as in control of her life as she wished to believe. She could lose all of her inheritance, especially if—as her mother put it—Gwen refused to marry someone they deemed worthy. Of course her cousin Dean would likely agree to employ her at the orphanage, but her financial help would surely be of greater benefit to them and the children than her physical help.

Mr. Winfield had alighted from the carriage and stood waiting for her. "Good afternoon, Miss Barton."

She mustered up a smile. "Good afternoon." The driver handed her inside.

"Now then, where are we off to?" Mr. Winfield asked as he took the seat opposite hers.

Gwen gave the driver the address to Dr. Smithfield's

office. A few moments later, the carriage joined the other traffic along the street. She sensed Mr. Winfield's gaze on her as she glanced out her side of the vehicle.

"How are you today?"

"I'm well, thank you," she answered without looking at him.

His low chuckle had her turning to face him. "Miss Barton, given all we discussed last night and that I am now accompanying you on a rather mysterious errand, I would hope you could be as refreshingly honest with me today as you have been in the past."

"Refreshingly honest?" She couldn't help returning his laugh. "Is that what you're calling it now?"

He shrugged and gave her a lazy smile. "I believe that sounds far more polite than shockingly frank, don't you?"

"Agreed." Gwen relaxed against the cushioned seat as she pondered how to honestly respond to his inquiry about how she fared. "I feel a little weary after another at-home day."

Mr. Winfield dipped his head in a thoughtful nod. "More than five minutes with Lord Whitson or Mr. Fipwish often leaves a person feeling that way."

"We had other callers." Her cheeks heated with a blush as Gwen realized how arrogant that must sound. "What I mean is that Mr. Hanbury called on us today too, along with several new friends of my mother's."

"Mr. Hanbury is a suitor of yours?" The sudden interest in his voice didn't make sense to her.

She watched the other carriages moving along the street. "My mother would call him that."

"What sort of a chap is he?"

Gwen lifted her shoulders in a shrug. "I'm not really sure. He speaks very little, but there's been at least one time when he acted kindly towards me. Like the others, he doesn't seem bothered by my limp either." She hadn't exactly meant to share that last thought aloud.

"Why should it bother anyone?" he asked, causally leaning back into the corner of his seat.

After taking a moment to study his face, Gwen was relieved to find no flippancy there. "The bachelors back home weren't keen on the prospect of their would-be bride limping about the house." Her thoughts turned to Randolph and brought a prick of old pain. Before she knew what she was doing, she was sharing the story with Mr. Winfield.

"During my first season in New York, I was seriously courted for six weeks by one young man. But when he discovered I had a limp, he promptly engaged himself to another girl. She didn't have an impediment, physically or socially, since her family was a part of New York's most elite circle."

His brow had furrowed as she relayed her past, but Gwen didn't expect the question he asked. "How could this gentleman not have known you had a limp at any point during those six weeks?"

She blushed again. "Because at the time I was heeding my mother's counsel to disguise my limp." But she wasn't doing that ever again. "If I walk with small steps, I can hide it. And when asked to dance, I would feign some excuse."

"Yet you didn't do that the other night."

He spoke it as a statement, but she nodded anyway. "I'm not hiding it this season." She lowered her gaze to her gloves. "My mother was furious when she found that out the other week. But she's relented since then." At least as far as Gwen's injured foot was concerned. Securing marriage to a titled gentleman was still a different matter altogether, especially after Cornelia had realized as Gwen had that the bachelors in London didn't care a whit about her limp—only about her bank account.

From the corner of her eye, she watched Mr. Winfield reach across the space between the seats. He lightly touched her gloved hand before sitting back, but the connection still inspired the same stirring effect inside Gwen that she'd experienced last night when he had clasped her arm to prevent her from falling.

She could recall feeling this way only one other time in her life—after that wonderful kiss in the opera box. Could Mr. Winfield be the injured man she'd helped? His choice of words last night, about it not boding well for them to be seen leaving the library together, had sparked a memory from the opera. The man in the box had used a similar turn of phrase. And yet, Gwen couldn't completely reconcile that gentleman with the one seated before her.

If the stranger had been Mr. Winfield, he certainly wouldn't have kissed her back. He likely would have reprimanded her for her bold, unladylike behavior at reviving him.

"It takes a great deal of courage," Mr. Winfield said, bringing Gwen's thoughts back to the present, "to be who and what we really are."

The wise, almost caring, statement warmed her. "Thank you." For a man who could be rather pointed in his questioning, he was also proving to be a rather good listener too. "What about you, Mr. Winfield?"

"What about me?" His blasé tone belied the tightening of the lines on his forehead.

Making sure to lower her voice to a whisper, Gwen said, "I'd think your profession capitalizes on you being anything but who and what you really are."

The man appeared momentarily at a loss for words. "You are correct, Miss Barton," he murmured after a long moment.

Something unnamed passed between them when he fully

met her gaze. But it was gone the instant the carriage settled to a stop. They'd arrived at the office of Dr. Smithfield.

"This is it." Gwen gestured to the stone building before Avery climbed down and assisted her to the sidewalk.

He led the way up the steps. "Is this Dr. Smithfield an acquaintance of yours?"

"Not yet." Mr. Winfield opened the door for her. "You see," Gwen told him in hushed tones to avoid being overheard by the clerk seated at the nearby desk, "Dr. Smithfield specializes in the care of children who have suffered long-term illness or injury."

He followed her into the small foyer. "Your mother doesn't deem this errand worthy enough for her to accompany you, though?"

"Something like that. You have to understand something, Mr. Winfield. In America, no one finds it improper for an unmarried young lady to ride alone in a carriage. I'm accustomed to attending to this type of errand alone."

She didn't wait for his response and instead approached the clerk. "Good afternoon. I'm Gwen Barton. Is Dr. Smithfield in?"

"Ah, you again," the clerk said, lifting his head from the book he'd been reading. "You dropped in last week, didn't you?"

Gwen smiled, though she couldn't tell if the clerk was simply stating a fact or was displeased by her unaccompanied, impromptu visit the week before. "Yes. We'd like just a few minutes with the doctor, if he's around this afternoon." She waved a hand to encompass Mr. Winfield, who stood watching the exchange.

The young man sized him up, then stood and circled the desk. "The doctor's 'ere. But I don't know if 'e's even got a few minutes to spare for questions. I'll see."

Hopefully they wouldn't be turned away. "We appreciate it."

"Are you here to ask him about your foot?" Mr. Winfield asked her from behind.

"If there's time," she admitted. "I'd really like to know more about his work and how we can implement some of his practices at my cousin's orphanage back home."

"This orphanage is quite important to you."

"It is." Purpose and enthusiasm rose inside her, along with a feeling of homesickness for Heartwell House and its young occupants. "Most of the children there have been the victims of accidents like my own or of childhood illnesses. We want to find a doctor who better understands these cases to help us in our work."

Mr. Winfield regarded her silently again as he pocketed his hands. "You are unlike any other society miss I've met, Miss Barton." He added in a quieter voice, as though it were an afterthought, "Save one."

What did he mean? And who was this other society miss? There was no time to ask him, though, because the clerk had returned. "Dr. Smithfield will see you both now. You 'ave ten minutes."

"We'll take it," Gwen said, throwing a smile over her shoulder at Mr. Winfield as she fell in line behind the clerk.

◇◇◇◇

"It was my younger brother's childhood fight with illness that initially inspired my desire to become a doctor . . ."

Avery tried to pay attention to Dr. Smithfield, but his focus kept straying to Miss Barton. Perched on the edge of her chair, she listened to the doctor with open interest. A lock of her dark hair had fallen across her forehead, eliciting a bizarre wish in him to brush it aside and touch her smooth cheek. It was this same unexplainable yet pleasant longing that had compelled him to cover her hand with his own in the carriage earlier.

Clearing his throat, Avery twisted slightly in his chair to study the framed paintings and the clock displayed on the wall. But he couldn't stop recalling Miss Barton's vulnerable expression as she'd talked about her past and her decision to be herself. For a man such as him, trained to see past the pretense and hidden agenda of others, he continued to be surprised by Miss Barton's authenticity.

Of course there were others in his life who were also genuine—Mack, Linwood, his grandmother. But Avery had never met a young woman who was herself around him. He both applauded and feared the idea. If he spent more time in the company of Miss Barton, would she come to expect him to be himself too? And if he were himself, who would he be?

He shifted in his chair at the disconcerting question, unsure if it was the question itself or his inability to answer it that he found most uncomfortable. Avery glanced at Miss Barton again. He wasn't surprised she had a handful of suitors or that they weren't appalled by her limp. Certainly their interest wasn't just because of her beauty and her money, though. At least he hoped not. These other men would be fools if they couldn't see her strength, compassion, or clever sense of humor.

For reasons Avery could only chalk up to momentary insanity, he allowed himself to consider what it might be like to be one of Miss Barton's suitors. She would obviously have the means to help Beechwood Manor, though that wouldn't be his reason for courting her. Despite some of their more charged conversations, he liked being in her company. He could almost relax in her presence. Almost felt himself.

He mentally shook his head at the direction of his thoughts. Why was he even entertaining such an idea? He didn't wish to court or marry. Not if it meant giving up his position with Captain Kell. How many seasons had he already endured without the slightest inclination to align himself with a young lady? This year he'd already experienced that pull twice—after his encounter with the girl in the opera box and now with Miss Barton.

The young clerk popped his head into the room and coughed. "Your next appointment is 'ere, Dr. Smithfield."

"Yes, of course." The man rose to his feet. "Is there anything else you wish to know, Miss Barton?"

She stood as Avery did, casting a hesitant look toward the open door of the office. Through it, Avery could see a husband, wife, and their young daughter, her arm tied up in a bandage, waiting for the doctor in the entry hall.

"No . . . not today." Miss Barton took a step toward the door. "Thank you, Dr. Smithfield."

She moved across the room, her limping gait now familiar. Avery followed in her wake. Miss Barton paused long enough beside the girl to give her a sincere smile. Although the gesture wasn't directed at him, Avery still found himself smiling in return, as the child did.

"You didn't ask him about your foot," he said in a low voice as he opened the front door for her.

Hesitancy filled her gaze once more, along with a flash of what he suspected might be disappointment. "There wasn't time. I didn't even ask about his other colleagues who might do similar work in New York." She faced forward and slowly descended the stairs. "I suppose I'll have to figure out a way to come back."

"*We'll* figure out a way to come back." Avery gently

clasped her elbow to detain her at the bottom of the stone staircase.

He thought he heard her take a quick breath, and yet she didn't pull away. Rather she lifted her chin to peer at him from beneath the brim of her hat. Avery wondered why he'd never noticed until this moment that her eyes held glints of gold too, among the warm brown and cool green colors. If only he'd been able to see the eyes or the face of the girl from the opera box . . .

"Y-you want to come back with me?"

With a nod, Avery released her arm and took a much-needed step backward. "Of course. I wouldn't be much of a gentleman if I didn't extend my offer of help as long as it is required."

"Well, then, thank you."

He sensed the gratitude behind her words, but she hadn't smiled as she'd voiced them. If anything, her lips had tightened into a worried line. Had he somehow offended her? Avery sincerely hoped he hadn't. Accompanying her a few more times to see this doctor seemed a paltry price to pay for her agreement to remain silent about his espionage work. And yet perhaps there was something more he could do to show his appreciation.

A recollection from the Stouts' ball returned to Avery's mind. "Given this errand of yours took very little time, would you be interested in seeing St. Paul's Cathedral before I return you to your aunt's?"

"You mean we can go see it right now?" Her expression lit with excitement and hope.

Avery chuckled. "Yes, Miss Barton. We can visit the cathedral right now."

"That sounds wonderful."

She stepped closer to him. Almost as if she meant to

reward his suggestion with a kiss on the cheek or a friendly embrace, right here on the street, however improper it might be. But then she simply offered him a delightful smile and walked to where his driver held the carriage door open. After helping Miss Barton into the vehicle, Avery instructed his driver to take them to St. Paul's Cathedral.

As he reclaimed the seat opposite hers, he fought his own growing sense of disappointment. It didn't take Avery long to figure out its source. Improper as it might have been, he'd hoped, even wanted, that kiss on the cheek or a grateful embrace. That wasn't like him. He always kept himself strictly proper, never doing anything outside the bounds of propriety to avoid drawing attention to himself. And if he felt this off-kilter with Miss Barton now, maybe he ought to retract his offer for sightseeing and helping her again in the future.

But, no, unlike his father, Avery was a man of his word. He would take her to see the cathedral as he'd promised and he would return with her to Dr. Smithfield's office too. However, deep down, he was beginning to realize spying wasn't the only aspect of his life that had the potential to be dangerous. His time with Miss Barton this afternoon was a critical reminder that matters of the heart could be treacherous too.

⁂

Everything, from the wide stone steps leading up to the cathedral, to the black and white parquet floor, to the soaring dome, inspired awe. "It's magnificent," Gwen murmured as she attempted to take in every exquisite detail.

"It is, isn't it?" Mr. Winfield's tone seemed to suggest mild surprise.

Gwen turned her gaze on him. "When was the last time you were here?"

"Four, perhaps five years ago?" He shrugged. "Not much need for such visits in my line of work," he added, his smile droll.

She sent him a disappointed frown, then she began walking slowly again. "I would think in your line of work that faith of any kind would be important."

"Why?"

Putting one hand on her hat, Gwen tilted her head to study the arches and intricate ceiling. "Who has a greater need to ask God for help and protection than you, Mr. Winfield?"

Wordlessly, he furrowed his brow and tucked his hands into his pockets. Gwen felt a moment of triumph at rendering the man speechless—yet again. She left him to his own musings and returned her attention to the magnificence around her. It certainly inspired wonder, respect, and heavenly thoughts. Still, Gwen also felt close to God when kneeling beside her bed or reading the Bible in her room.

They wandered wordlessly about the cathedral for several more minutes before Mr. Winfield broke the silence between them. "There's something I can't wrap my head around."

"What is that?"

He gazed at something over her shoulder. "Why do you believe in a caring God, Miss Barton, after what happened to you as a child?"

She stopped and studied his expression. It was drawn and wearied. Clearly he wasn't mocking her. "You think God caused my accident?" she countered softly.

"No, not caused." Mr. Winfield shook his head. "But He certainly didn't prevent it, did He?" His next words were spoken in so hushed a tone, Gwen almost missed hearing them. "My mother had faith and she still ended up dead."

This wasn't the contrary dinner partner she'd met at Lord

and Lady Linwood's home. This was a man who was still hurting, all these years later.

Gwen couldn't keep herself from laying a gloved hand on his sleeve. "God could've prevented my accident, yes. But I don't believe He loves me any less because He didn't."

Lowering her arm, she stared at Mr. Winfield's tie, afraid she'd see derision in his eyes as she continued. "He loves me perfectly and because of that He wants me to grow, and change, and learn to love as He does. And sometimes, Mr. Winfield, the greatest catalyst to growth and change and loving more purely is to experience pain."

"Pain?" he repeated with a sniff. "How does that help anyone grow?"

The deep hurt she sensed behind his question made her wince, but she didn't regret speaking openly. "Though I didn't know it at the time, the pain of my accident made me more conscious of others' pain. It also led me to feel greater compassion."

"Then why do you still want Dr. Smithfield to correct your foot?"

Gwen snapped her gaze to his, no longer fearing what she might see there. "Because I'm hopeful if I can regain full mobility, I can help the orphanage in ways that I can't right now. It would also give me something else to offer them, other than funding, if I were to suddenly lose my inheritance."

Her last declaration slipped from her lips before Gwen could stop it. Immediately she felt exposed at having shared a portion of her earlier distress with this man she barely knew. Not wishing to say anymore on the matter, she limped toward a nearby alcove.

"Miss Barton, wait."

She kept moving as quickly as she dared across the polished surface, though Gwen knew it was silly to think she could outdistance him and his two fully functioning feet. Still, she would make a good attempt.

"Miss Barton." His voice came from right behind her. "Gwen!"

His hand on her elbow stopped her as much as the sound of her given name on his lips. "I—"

"Forgive me." There was no frustration or cynicism in his brown eyes now. "I know you didn't give me permission to call you by your Christian name."

She swallowed. Could he see how much his close proximity unnerved her? "Is that all you're asking forgiveness for?"

"Come again?"

He hadn't released her arm yet, though she didn't mind. Just as she hadn't minded when he had taken her elbow outside of Dr. Smithfield's office. As it had then, Gwen's breath hitched at his gentle touch.

"Are you only asking to be forgiven for calling me by my given name?" she clarified.

A slow smile lifted his mouth as he regarded her, and it sent her heart tumbling end over end. "No. Unfortunately, that is just one of my numerous offenses in the past five minutes."

"Agreed."

His smile deepened. "May I first make amends by asking if you would permit me to call you Gwen?"

She hadn't granted any of her suitors such a privilege, and they'd been calling on her for several weeks now. And yet Gwen didn't hesitate more than a second or two before she nodded. Her mother might not condone such an action. But in spite of their short acquaintance, it seemed only fitting to be on such terms with Mr. Winfield after all they'd shared and discussed.

"All right. You may call me Gwen. Am I allowed to call you Avery?"

Something warm filled his gaze. "I would like that very much."

"Me too," she whispered, unable to look away.

The charged moment ended when he let go of her arm. "I apologize for badgering you back there." He motioned to where they'd been standing earlier. "You were kind to answer my questions, and I repaid you by provoking you into defending your position. Please accept my sincere apologies."

"Thank you." She stepped backward on her good foot, hoping the extra space would restore her breathing to normal. "I meant every word, but I can't say I know the kind of pain you've experienced in your past."

He smiled again, but this time it held only sadness. "My mother used to talk about God as you did just now. So confident and hopeful." He ran his hand over his face. "I wanted to believe her. There may have even been a time when I did."

"And now?"

His hands slipped into his pockets again. "I haven't believed in much of anything for a very long time."

"That's not true." Looking around, Gwen ventured closer so that no one but him would hear her. "You believe in the protection of your country and its citizens."

He gave a thoughtful nod. "I suppose there is that."

"See? There's hope for you yet . . . Avery."

His gaze caught hers and held it again. "By any chance, were you in attendance the other week at the . . ." But he didn't finish his question, only shook his head. "It's of no matter. Is there more you wish to see?"

"No." Her foot was beginning to ache after so much

walking and standing. "Thank you again for bringing me here."

"My pleasure." At the quirk of her eyebrows, he chuckled. "I'm being honest, Gwen."

The same thrill she'd felt when he said her name the first time washed over her anew as she fell into step beside him.

"Would you like to drive past the Parliament buildings on our way back?"

She glanced at his face in surprise. "You don't mind?"

"Not at all."

As they moved in tandem toward the exit, his pace obviously slowed to match hers, Gwen realized he hadn't offered the latter request as a form of penance or tolerated assistance. Maybe Mr. Winfield—*Avery*—had enjoyed their time together as much as she had, religious debate and all. And maybe that meant that he, too, would feel the same measure of sadness later that she would when their time together came to an end.

Chapter 10

Standing opposite the mirror, Avery whistled to himself as he fiddled with his cravat. He didn't need gloves tonight, since he would be attending the theater and not a dance.

"I don't believe I've ever seen you quite this jolly before a social event, sir." Mack picked up Avery's coat from off the bed.

Avery chuckled. "I'm looking forward to attending the theater tonight. Lord and Lady Linwood will be there too." He hadn't seen Clare since the dinner at the Linwoods' home, and Avery hoped her presence this evening meant all was right once more with her and his best friend.

"I highly doubt it's the earl and his wife who've put that smile on your face."

Avery's smile increased as he turned away from the mirror so Mack could help him with his coat. "Then what, pray tell, is the reason for my good humor, Mack?"

"I'd say it's a young lady."

Arranging his face into a neutral expression, Avery chose not to comment as Mack brushed off his coat and readjusted his cravat.

"Your silence is very telling, sir," the man quipped.

"Perhaps you've learned the identity of the girl from the opera box?"

Avery shook his head. "I haven't." But he felt only mild regret over that fact. "I'm beginning to think I dreamt her American accent, Mack."

His valet stepped back and studied him. "You've met someone else, then." A slow grin spread across the man's lined face.

"Now why would you think that?" Avery deflected as he picked up his hat and placed it on his head.

Not surprisingly, Mack wasn't easily thrown off. "Who is she?"

Avery's mind called up an image of Miss Barton—*Gwen*—and the confident, passionate way she'd defended her faith to him two days ago in St. Paul's Cathedral. Or the compassion he'd glimpsed in her during their visit to the doctor. Almost against his will, he found himself smiling again.

"I knew it." Mack folded his arms, looking as smug as if he'd played matchmaker. "She must be quite a woman to batter down your defenses."

The words had the opposite effect than Mack likely intended. Avery sobered at the reminder of why he needed defenses in the first place. "She may have, Mack. But you and I both know that nothing can come of it. Not if I wish to keep serving king and country."

"If she cares for you, she'll support you." He collected Avery's day suit from off the armchair. "Just as my Melinda did."

Avery fought the vain hope Mack's words provoked and instead recalled how closely Lord Linwood had come to being seriously hurt. All because of his association with Avery. "If I come to care more for her, I can't ask her to take that risk."

"Perhaps." He waited as Mack stowed his clothes in the dressing room, then Avery moved toward the door. But his valet's next remark made him pause. "You're going to have to choose at some point, sir. Duty to family or to country. If you don't, the decision will be made for you and you might not like the result. Especially if it leaves your uncle and your grandmother disappointed."

Avery had begun to fear the same, though giving up his job with Captain Kell surely meant failure. How else was he to prove he had something worthwhile to offer the world?

Frowning, he lowered his gaze to his cuff links. They had once been his father's, but Avery had chosen to keep them, to wear them often, even. It was a physical reminder to himself that he would prove Phillip Winfield had been wrong about his only child and son. In spite of everything, Avery was worthy of notice and kindness.

Perhaps that was why he felt so drawn to Gwen. She'd seen sides of him that Avery typically hid from others, especially those of the upper class, and she hadn't rejected him for them either. Neither had she belittled or ignored his pain after glimpsing it the other day. Instead she had challenged him, while at the same time sharing her innate empathy.

"You're right, Mack." He lifted his head to look at the man he considered more than a valet. Mack was also his trusted friend. "I hope I'm not forced to choose too soon. There's still the business at hand to resolve."

The older man nodded thoughtfully. "What is your plan now?"

Avery had already confided in him that Rodmill had not turned out to be a spy. "I'm to focus on weeding out the other chap and seeing if I can find any other suspects."

That was the other reason for his anticipation about tonight. He knew Gwen would be in attendance at the theater, which likely meant her entourage of suitors would be as well. And one of them was Avery's next primary suspect.

"I have faith in you, sir."

Avery cleared his throat. "Thank you, Mack."

The man's parting statement lingered with Avery, long after he'd left the house and his carriage was rolling through the crowded streets toward the theater. Mack's unfailing confidence in him wasn't so different than Avery's grandmother's, especially after his mother had died. Or even Captain Kell's ongoing support. Even Gwen had reassured him the other day at the cathedral about his belief in the work he was doing for Britain.

At the reminders, he sat up straighter, fresh determination roiling through him. While he'd pursued the wrong trail with Rodmill, Avery still had one more viable suspect to investigate. He hadn't failed yet, and perhaps with some luck—and the faith of others—he wouldn't.

⟡

The performance was exceptional, in storyline, acting, sets, and costumes. However, by the time intermission rolled around, Avery was restless. He hadn't seen his suspect seated within any of the boxes across the theater, which meant the man either occupied a box out of Avery's line of sight or he wasn't in attendance at all. A visit to the refreshment room was the only way to know the answer.

"Did you enjoy the performance, Winfield?" Clare asked as he followed her and Linwood out of the box.

Avery nodded. "It's well done. What did you think of it?"

"I found parts of it rather sad." She glanced at her husband whose arm she held. "What about you, Emmett?"

Linwood shrugged. "I liked it so far. And I'm sure it will all come out jolly in the end, right?"

"Yes," Clare said with a smile, though it looked a bit forced and disappeared rather quickly. "I'm sure it will."

Avery couldn't help frowning over this brief but telling exchange between Lord and Lady Linwood. Clare clearly wished to discuss her thoughts on the play, and yet was reluctant to voice them unprompted. On the other hand, Linwood was eager to make her happy but couldn't see discussing the play would accomplish that, rather than reassuring his wife that everything would turn out. It was not Avery's place to interfere, though, no matter how much he cared for them. But he could at least acknowledge each point of view.

"I agree with both perspectives." The pair turned to look at him. "There were parts I found to be sad as well, my lady. And, Linwood, you're correct in that we can take hope that everything will turn out right in this particular story."

Their answering smiles eased the lingering tension in the air. "I do love that you hold to the happy ending, Emmett." Clare leaned into her husband's side.

"Thank you, my dear. But it wouldn't be a very satisfying happy ending if the way wasn't fraught with some difficulty or sadness." He covered her hand with his own. "I'm glad you came tonight, Clare."

It was Avery's cue to leave them to themselves. No longer frowning or worried, he held back as they stepped inside the refreshment room, then he entered alone. He searched the faces of the people milling about the room, eager for one in particular. It wasn't the face of his suspect, though. Instead he was unashamedly looking for Gwen.

He spotted her mother first, then a few moments later, he saw Gwen, sitting alongside another American girl. She and Miss Rinecroft were talking. Tonight Gwen wore a high-collared dress so deep blue in color it nearly matched her dark hair. The effect was nothing short of striking.

"Hello, Winfield," someone said from behind.

Avery startled. His embarrassment at being caught staring changed to surprise when he turned and found his uncle standing there. "I didn't know you were attending the theater tonight."

"Nor I you." A rare smile lifted the duke's mouth. "I'm glad to see you took our last conversation seriously." Avery's confusion must have shown on his face because his uncle added in a lower tone, "Participating in the season, nephew, so you can find yourself a bride."

"Ah, yes, that."

Moorleigh took a sip from the teacup he held. "Did you accompany a young lady?"

"No." Avery cleared his throat. "I came with Lord and Lady Linwood."

Nodding, his uncle studied the crowd. "Perhaps there's a particular young woman who's captured your fancy, though?"

"Not yet, I'm afraid," Avery answered, but he did throw another glance in Gwen's direction. Once again, he pondered what it would it be like to court her. To be the one to accompany her to the theater.

The duke frowned before sipping more of his tea. "I don't need to remind you of our deadline, Winfield." His cup hit the saucer with a loud tap. "The season will be over sooner than you realize, and I would like to know Beechwood Manor is secure before I . . ."

"Before you . . . ?"

Moorleigh straightened to full height, which put him eye to eye with Avery. "I'm only asking that you not squander this time in your life. Find a girl, preferably a rich one, and secure your happiness and the estate's future in the process." His expression softened. "That's all I'm asking."

His uncle made it sound so simple. As if all Avery had to

do was approach some heiress, tell her that he wished to marry her for her money, and set a wedding date. But it wasn't simple and the duke was asking far more than he realized, though Avery couldn't say so.

To marry would mean giving up his work with the Secret Service Bureau. It was a position he hadn't even sought out, but it had come to mean more to him than anything else. He would always be grateful that Captain Kell had approached him, after hearing of Avery's prowess with languages. Despite Avery's aversion to faith and God, the opportunity had still felt like a godsend. A way to finally be useful, to know he mattered in the grand scheme of things.

"Winfield?" his uncle prompted.

Avery gave a curt nod, the conflicting burden of his duties weighing heavily on his shoulders. "I understand."

"Good." The man offered him another smile. "I believe I'll say hello to Lord and Lady Linwood."

As the duke walked away, Avery remained where he stood, desperate to muster up his earlier determination. He still hadn't spied his suspect. Though that didn't mean he couldn't do so and speak with Gwen at the same time. Avery moved toward her, but his progress was interrupted again and again by the crowd of people.

He'd nearly reached her when a knot of women stopped him altogether. Avery politely cleared his throat, but the matrons didn't appear to hear him nor did they move. Finally he squeezed between them and the wall in an effort to inch his way toward Gwen.

"Do you think your injured stranger from the opera is here tonight?" he heard Miss Rinecroft ask.

Avery froze at her question. *Injured stranger . . . at the opera.* Could she possibly be talking about him? If so, how did Miss Rinecroft have any knowledge of that night? She certainly wasn't the young lady who'd helped him.

He shook his head, trying to focus his chaotic thoughts. Miss Rinecroft hadn't called the injured stranger hers. She'd used the word *your*. Did that mean . . . His gaze jumped to Gwen's face. Surely Avery had misunderstood her friend. But the rapidity of his heart and the immediate hope rising inside him told a different story.

"Shh, Syble." Gwen glanced around them. "We can't—"

Hanbury appeared beside them and handed Gwen a cup of tea. Avery kept very still, wondering if the other man had noticed him. But Hanbury only had eyes for Gwen. Or so the other man pretended. She thanked him for the tea, but he made no move to leave her side. Clearly Hanbury was hoping to monopolize Gwen's time during intermission.

Avery hesitated, his back remaining against the wall, contemplating if he ought to make his presence known to the trio or not. He did wish he could commandeer a moment alone with Gwen. Unfortunately, the signal for intermission's conclusion came before he'd come up with a plan. Hanbury waited for Gwen to stand, then walked beside her toward the door. Avery followed at a short distance.

When the pair was joined by Mrs. Barton and all three entered one of the theater boxes, Avery realized Hanbury had accompanied them here tonight. A jolt of irritation—or was it mild jealousy?—shot through him. But it also brought a sudden idea.

He could hardly concentrate on the second half of the performance, the happy resolve almost entirely lost on him. Instead he reviewed the details of his new plan and the events surrounding his injury at the opera. Was Gwen truly the woman who'd bandaged him, who'd kissed him? Somehow he would find out, though he wasn't sure what he'd do with such knowledge when he did discover it.

As the sound of the final applause died away, Avery was already on his feet and bidding the Linwoods goodnight. His earlier whistle returned to his lips as he waited outside for his carriage.

Despite the unpleasant conversation with his uncle, he sensed his good mood returning. His new plan, and overhearing Gwen's friend talking about that night at the opera, had the evening feeling more of a success than a failure. His one regret was not talking with Gwen. But if all went according to plan, he'd soon have more time to see and speak with her—all while learning a great deal more about his quarry too.

⌒⟨⟨⟨⟩⟩⟩⌒

In all of her time in London, Gwen couldn't recall feeling as fatigued as she did tonight. Her foot was growing numb as she limped along behind her mother up the front steps of the Rodmills' townhouse. After the theater, they'd come home to change before Mr. Hanbury had escorted them to a ball. Gwen had nearly fallen asleep twice as she sat inside the overly warm ballroom, trying her best to engage Mr. Hanbury in conversation when he wasn't dancing.

It was now well past midnight, and Gwen wanted only to sleep. But social duty still came first. Inside the foyer, she and her mother expressed their gratitude to Mr. Hanbury. Cornelia chatted a few minutes more about the lovely performance and how well Mr. Hanbury danced, while Gwen eyed the stairs with longing.

At last the door was shut behind her suitor, and Gwen hobbled across the foyer. "That man is most interested in you, Gwen," her mother said with self-satisfaction. "To be honest, I wasn't sure about him. But after learning tonight about his extensive land holdings in Scotland . . ." Cornelia reached the staircase before Gwen. "Well, my opinion of him has changed."

"Miss Barton," the butler said.

"Yes?" She turned slowly, though she still had to grip the balustrade to keep from swaying.

He extended an envelope toward her. "This came while you were out."

"Who's it from?" her mother asked from the landing.

Gwen accepted the note addressed to *Miss Barton* in an unfamiliar script. "Probably just from Syble." Though she doubted it. Syble had been in attendance at both the theater and the ball tonight, so she wouldn't have had time to send Gwen a note. Plus, it wasn't Syble's writing.

Thankfully, her answer mollified her mother, who continued up the stairs. Gwen followed more slowly, but she paused on the landing to open the envelope. Her gaze flew first to the signature. When she saw *Avery Winfield* penned there, her heart raced with anticipation.

She thought she'd caught a glimpse of him during intermission at the theater. After all, Lord and Lady Linwood had been in attendance. And Syble had pointed out Avery's uncle, the duke. But if Avery had been there with either the Linwoods or his uncle, he hadn't sought Gwen out. It was a possibility she'd found keenly disappointing. Yet he had sent her a note. A smile tugged at her lips, in spite of her fatigue, as she read the short message.

Miss Gwen Barton,

Would you allow me to accompany you a second time to Dr. Smithfield's office Monday afternoon at two o'clock? I believe that together we can politely press him for more time. There is also another matter I wish to discuss with you. We could visit another sight of interest as we talk. If this plan is

amenable to you, please send a note to my residence tomorrow morning.
Avery Winfield

He wished to help her again. Gwen's smile increased, though she hid it as she bid her mother goodnight and entered her own room. Tucking the note beneath her pillow, Gwen changed out of her ball gown with the help of a maid. Once she was ready for bed, she slipped beneath the covers and pulled the note out to read again.

What sort of matter did Avery wish to discuss with her? she wondered. She contemplated the question for a minute or two but couldn't think of a plausible answer.

Whatever the topic, she was happy to have another chance to speak with Dr. Smithfield and see more of London. However, it wasn't either of those opportunities that sent a flow of energy sweeping through her when she turned off the bedside lamp, her foot no longer bothering her. The vitality and happiness she felt in this moment had everything to do with seeing Avery again in three days.

Chapter 11

Gwen took extra care with her appearance Monday afternoon, though she chided herself for caring what Avery thought. It wasn't as if he were an actual suitor. If anything, she'd call him a friend. Much as she imagined she would feel toward the man from the opera box if she ever learned his identity, save that the kiss they'd shared had felt deeper than friendship. She was still determined to learn the identity of the injured stranger and had even added more names to her and Syble's list. But the more time passed, the more the experience at the opera felt like a dream. Something Gwen might have imagined or read about in one of her preferred romance novels.

For all she knew, her mystery man might have already left town. If only she could talk freely about him with her aunt. Lady Rodmill might be able to narrow down the possibilities of his identity better than Gwen and Syble had so far.

Gwen descended the stairs at two minutes to two o'clock for her outing with Avery. Thoughts of seeing him again produced an idea, one she wished she had thought of sooner. What if she asked Avery for help with learning the identity of the injured man? A smile of excitement lifted her mouth. As a spy, Avery would surely have contacts that none of the rest of them did. And Avery wasn't likely to be surprised or appalled by her actions to help a stranger either. Though perhaps she'd leave off any mention of the kiss.

The butler opened the door for her. As Gwen stepped outside, she saw Avery's open carriage standing at the curb. Her pulse quickened with eagerness as he climbed down from the vehicle and stood waiting for her.

"Miss Barton," he said, extending his hand to her. Reverting to her proper title was likely for the benefit of his driver, though Avery's full smile was anything but stiff or polite.

Gwen placed her gloved palm against his unencumbered one. The warmth of his bare skin breached the thin fabric of her glove and sent prickles of feeling up her arm. "Mr. Winfield." He helped her inside the carriage, and Gwen sat down.

Arranging her skirt, she was grateful for a moment to settle her emotions as Avery climbed into the carriage as well. She was acting as if this were a real outing with a real suitor. But it wasn't. This was Avery Winfield—as cynical as he could be charming, as kind as he could be annoying, and as unlikely to be interested in her as the king.

"I saw Lord and Lady Linwood at the theater last Friday," she said as the carriage got underway. "I noticed your uncle was there as well."

Avery nodded. "I attended with the Linwoods."

"Oh." Gwen's earlier disappointment returned. Avery *had* been there and hadn't bothered to find her. "Did you like the performance?"

"I did." He glanced around before leaning slightly forward. "What I would have enjoyed more was talking with you, Gwen. However, I was waylaid by a conversation with the duke and the crowd of people during intermission."

It was Gwen's turn to nod with acknowledgement, but she couldn't help smiling as well. He hadn't ignored her; he'd wanted to speak with her after all.

"Was that Mr. Hanbury I saw you with that evening?" he asked as he settled back against his seat.

His tone held a slight edge to it that wasn't lost on Gwen. Could it mean Avery was jealous of the other man? She doubted it. "He invited my mother and me to attend with him."

"With Hanbury, I'd imagine there was no need for someone to rescue you from his being long-winded about a horse or any topic of conversation, for that matter."

She laughed. "That's true. He doesn't say much, but he is polite and attentive."

A slight frown pulled at Avery's mouth, then quickly disappeared. "Will you ask the doctor about your foot today?"

"Yes, I'd like to." Although she would have to figure out a way to do so without Avery standing nearby. As much as she was coming to know him and be at ease in his company, Gwen didn't feel ready to have him present as she questioned the doctor about her childhood injury.

Their conversation returned to Friday's performance and what they had both liked and disliked. Before long, Avery's driver stopped the carriage in front of Dr. Smithfield's office. Gwen wasn't sure how they would be received, given she was showing up without an appointment for the third time. To her surprise, though, the clerk greeted them cheerfully.

"If you'll take a seat, the doctor'll be ready to see you in a moment." He motioned for them to wait on the two hardback chairs in the foyer.

Gwen and Avery sat. "Does he think we have an appointment?" she whispered.

"We do." His answering smile widened when she gaped

at him. "After receiving your note, I took the liberty of asking if the doctor had any available time today." He leaned close and added, "We've been granted half an hour."

He smelled pleasantly of soap. Gwen breathed in the clean, masculine scent before he sat back. She'd have nearly twice as much time to talk with the doctor today, and that was all because of Avery. He'd kindly arranged everything. But why? She shot him a surreptitious glance. Did he still feel indebted to her for her agreement to keep secret what she'd overheard in the library? Or was he simply being a friend?

"Thank you, Avery." She kept her voice low to avoid the clerk hearing. "I appreciate you coming with me again and setting up an appointment in advance."

"You are most welcome, Gwen."

"May I ask why you went to so much trouble on my account?"

Shrugging, he faced forward. "It seemed hardly fair that my help only amounted to a quarter of an hour last time."

"Yes, but you also took me to see St. Paul's Cathedral."

Avery glanced her way, though just for a moment. "That outing had nothing to do with our agreement." He focused on something on the opposite wall. "You said you hadn't seen it yet, and I figured it was high time you did."

A feeling of delighted excitement spilled through her at his words. She'd been right—Avery hadn't taken her to see the cathedral out of obligation. Did that mean he also considered her a friend? The possibility brought mounting hope as she followed him and the clerk into the doctor's office a few minutes later. Because, despite the rocky start between them, she wanted very much to know Avery better and count him as a real friend.

⁓⁓⁓

Our time must be nearly up. Avery peered at the wall clock. Sure enough, there was less than five minutes left to their appointment with Dr. Smithfield. Gwen had asked a great many questions and learned the names of two other doctors in America doing similar work with childhood injuries and illnesses, but she hadn't yet broached the subject of her foot.

Was she afraid to ask the doctor such a personal question? Avery wasn't sure he believed that—Gwen Barton wasn't timid. If anything, he considered her rather brave.

When the doctor bent over his desk to write down the name of his two colleagues, Avery caught Gwen's glance. He raised his eyebrows in question, hoping she'd understand his silent query. At first her brow furrowed in confusion until he trained a pointed look at her feet and tipped his head toward the doctor. Then recognition shone in her eyes, but she still shook her head.

The doctor's chuckle drew Avery's attention. "The two of you remind me of the wife and myself," Dr. Smithfield said with a smile. "When we were courting."

"Oh, we aren't . . ." A blush bathed Gwen's cheeks with color. A rather becoming color. She gave Avery what he guessed was a pleading look for help.

He didn't want to malign her reputation if the doctor learned they weren't actually courting, but he wouldn't lie about their relationship either. "Unfortunately, Miss Barton has a fair number of admirers," Avery said as he stood. "Of which I am only one. However, today's visit to your office has awarded me extra time with her. And for that, I thank you, Doctor."

Smiling, Dr. Smithfield stood as well. "I don't envy you having to choose, Miss Barton, which lad will win your hand in the end." Gwen blushed again as the doctor picked up the note he'd written and extended it toward her. "Here are the names of those two doctors I referenced."

She rose from her chair and accepted the slip of paper. "Thank you. I can't tell you how much I—we—appreciate your time today."

"Feel free to make another appointment if you remember anything I may have been remiss in explaining." The doctor circled his desk. "Your cousin's orphanage sounds quite novel in its vision. I hope you're able to secure the medical help you'd like in order to make it a long-term success."

Gwen rewarded the man's interest with a full smile. It wasn't the first time Avery had seen it, but it still had the power to charm him, almost making him wish he might be its recipient each and every day.

"I'm very proud of what Dean and Amie have accomplished. Given my own childhood experiences . . ." She lowered her gaze to the floor before lifting her chin in a clear show of courage, her gaze bright with determination. "I can understand why they're anxious to find a suitable doctor to assist them."

Dr. Smithfield nodded. "Did you have a bout with illness as a child?"

"Not illness." Gwen threw a glance at Avery.

He found himself impatiently watching her and the doctor. Would the man realize what Gwen was trying to explain? He didn't understand why she didn't come right out and share her past with Dr. Smithfield as she had with Avery. Perhaps her bravery knew some bounds. Or was it something else?

Avery studied her tight expression and realized with a

start that she wasn't uncomfortable discussing her foot with the doctor. It was having Avery standing there, listening in, that caused her hesitance. The conclusion sent instant regret through him. He didn't want Gwen to feel uncomfortable around him, over anything. Especially if she agreed to the plan he meant to present later. They would have to trust each other explicitly.

"I'll see if the carriage is ready." He knew it was, as surely as Gwen did. But it was the only excuse Avery could think of to give her a moment of privacy.

The relief and gratitude emanating from her proved he'd made the right decision. Of course she wouldn't wish to discuss her injury in great detail in the company of someone who wasn't her doctor, her affianced, or her family.

He didn't have to wait long. Several minutes later, Gwen descended the front steps. Avery handed her into the open carriage. He wanted to ask how the conversation with Dr. Smithfield had gone, but that seemed too presumptuous, too intimate.

"Ready to go?" he asked instead.

"Yes. Thank you for giving me a moment alone."

He dipped his head in acknowledgement of her gratitude. "I hope it went well."

"It did." Gwen smiled. "There wasn't time for him to examine my foot today, but I told him about my accident."

"Does he believe there's anything he can do?" He hoped she wouldn't fault him for the somewhat personal inquiry.

This time, she didn't look uncomfortable. If anything, Gwen appeared not only happy but lighter, as if some burden had been lifted. Avery felt a strange flash of envy.

"Possibly," she said, resting back against her seat. "He'll know for sure after he looks at it. I made an appointment for two weeks from today."

Avery offered a smile in return. "If you feel my presence might be helpful, I'd be happy to accompany you again."

"I appreciate the offer, Avery." She gave a soft laugh. "Your presence has definitely helped. The clerk seemed almost pleased to see you, which is a far cry better than the reception I got the first time I came alone."

The earnestness in her tone coupled with her use of his Christian name had his chest expanding with contentment of his own.

"Still . . ." Gwen stared down at her gloved hands, which she clasped together in her lap as if steeling herself against an awkward confession. "You didn't have to pretend to the doctor to be, as you put it, one of my admirers."

"I wasn't pretending." Avery hadn't necessarily meant to voice such a thought aloud, but the moment he did, the truth of it resonated through him. He *did* admire Gwen Barton, probably more than was wise.

Her gaze flew to his. "You weren't pretending?" The vulnerability of her expression revealed her uncertainty far more than the simple question did.

"Gwen," he said, resting his arms on his knees. "You are intelligent, compassionate, beautiful, and brave enough to banter with me." He succeeded in coaxing another smile from her, which chased the worried look from her face. "All admirable qualities."

Her cheeks grew a shade pinker before she looked away. "Where are we going now?"

"I thought a visit to Hyde Park might be enjoyable. We can find a bench and take in the view." That would afford them time and a bit of privacy to outline his plan. "If that's agreeable with you, of course."

She turned toward him again, no self-consciousness in her expression now. "I would love that. I haven't been to the park yet. Although, Lord Whitson invited me to ride with him there in two days."

An increasingly familiar prick of jealousy shot through Avery, but he wrestled it into submission. He had no right to such an emotion, not when he wasn't courting Gwen himself. Fortunately, he managed to keep such thoughts from showing in his expression as he kept up his end of the conversation. The closer they drew to the park, though, the more his jaw tightened with new tension. Would Gwen agree to his plan? Was it fair of him to ask her?

He helped her to the ground outside the park, then reluctantly released her hand. After instructing his driver to return in half an hour's time, he fell into step beside Gwen. He matched his footfalls to her measured ones. It was slower than his habitual stride, but he felt no impatience. The unrushed pace suited him well, especially when he was with her.

Ever popular, the park boasted a mixture of people. Nannies pushed perambulators, young boys watched the ducks swimming in the Serpentine, and other couples, young and old, strolled along the paths. Avery hoped to find an unoccupied bench quickly, so Gwen could rest her foot, and where they could discuss his plan. Not surprisingly, though, she raised the subject before he'd located a place to sit.

"Your note mentioned there is something you wanted to discuss with me." She regarded him with raised eyebrows, her curiosity evident.

Avery swallowed hard and forced a smile. This was it. "Yes, there is."

"Well?" Gwen asked with a laugh when he remained silent. "What is it?"

He cleared his throat. "It has to do with my . . . work." When she nodded, he glanced around, ensuring no one walked near enough to overhear him, before he continued. "In addition to your cousin, there is another gentleman I've suspected of working against Britain."

"Who?"

Up ahead, Avery finally spied an empty bench. He motioned to it and waited for Gwen to sit. Then he joined her, keeping a respectable distance between them. "It's someone else you know."

Her brows dipped downward. "Oh?"

"It's Mr. Hanbury, Gwen."

He watched her jaw drop and her eyes widen with astonishment. "Are you sure?"

"I am." He kept his voice low as he explained, "Hanbury is from Germany, but we don't know how deeply his attachment to his native country still runs. I've been tasked to no longer simply observe him but to learn everything I can about him."

She seemed to consider this. "That was the reason you asked me about him earlier."

"Precisely," Avery said with a nod.

"Are you warning me that I shouldn't be seen with him?"

He rested his elbow on the back of the bench and twisted to face her. "No, on the contrary, I'm hoping you'll help me in my investigation."

"Wait a minute." Gwen shook her head. "Are you asking me to . . ." She looked around before leaning toward him. "To spy for you, Avery?"

His certainty in the validity and strength of his plan unraveled a little in the wake of her incredulous tone. But there was no taking back what he'd half shared already. "Yes, that is what I'm asking, Gwen. However, you don't have to agree. I also don't feel you're in any danger if you continue to see Hanbury of your own volition."

He wanted to leave it at that. But he owed her more

reassurance, even if it pained Avery to admit it. "His interest in you appears to be genuine."

Turning away from him, Gwen stared straight ahead, her lovely face in profile. "I don't know what to say."

"You can think on it." Avery looked past her to where a young couple walked arm in arm. "There is one more thing." She made no protest, so he forged ahead. "If you do agree to help me, we would need to pretend to . . ." He shifted on the bench, far more uncomfortable with revealing this part of his plan than he was the other. "We would need to act as though we're courting, as if I'm one of your suitors. That would give us the time and wherewithal to share information with each other."

Silence lengthened between them, and with it, his self-doubt. "I know it's a great deal to ask. And in truth, you'd be doing me more than one favor—not just with my work but with my private life, as well." He offered a weak laugh, which she didn't reciprocate. "You see, my uncle is insistent I find a girl to court this season. My hope, therefore, is that a courtship, even a feigned one, will buy me more time away from his scrutiny to settle this matter with Hanbury."

Without looking at him, Gwen frowned, stirring his unease even further. Avery lowered his arm and shifted to face the same direction she did. "I wouldn't ask, Gwen, except that I believe you could be of invaluable help to this mission. Besides, I already suspected you of being a spy once before." One corner of her mouth tipped upward at the reminder, and the sight of it bolstered his courage. "If you do agree, which you most certainly do not have to, I would be eternally in your debt. Anything I might help with while you are here in London, anything at all, I will do it."

"Anything?" To his relief, she finally returned his gaze.

"If it's within my power, I'll gladly grant your request."

The breeze ruffled a strand of her hair from beneath her feathered hat. Reaching up, Gwen brushed it away, drawing his attention to her eyes. Interest and determination shone there. "If I agree, and I stress the *if,* Avery . . ."

"I understand," he said with a genuine laugh this time.

"I have two requests."

He cocked his head in a casual gesture to hide the grin that threatened to break through at her charming negotiation skills. "Name them."

"First, you agree to take me riding tomorrow." She shot him a look as if daring him to argue. "I haven't been on a horse in a very long time, and my mother insisted I accept the earl's invitation. However, I don't want my first attempt in years to be with Lord Whitson."

"Done." He smacked the back of the bench with his hand for emphasis, pleased she wished to go riding with him at all. "What about the other request?"

Once more, she wouldn't meet his eye. "Second, I'd like your help with finding someone. Or I guess I should say identifying someone."

"Who?" he asked, intrigued.

Gwen blew out her breath and kept her eyes averted from him, appearing to be watching a nearby child as he played with his dog. "I met a young man, a few weeks ago, at the opera."

Avery fought to keep his expression impassive, but his heart began to pound with anticipation. "Is there a reason you couldn't identify the man?" He prided himself on sounding matter-of-fact, even impartial.

"It was hard to see his face," she admitted, throwing him a sheepish look. "I found him lying injured on the floor of one of the opera boxes during intermission. Apparently he'd been hurt. He didn't tell me why." She straightened on the bench. "I helped bandage his wound."

And then she'd kissed him. The memory of her soft lips nudging him back to consciousness inside the opera box filled Avery's thoughts. Along with the sweet recollection of tugging her close and kissing her in return. Of course the young lady, who'd exemplified such strength and compassion, could only be Gwen. Now that he knew her better, he couldn't imagine it being anyone else.

A yearning to touch her, to ascertain her realness as he had that night, prompted him to stretch his arm along the back of the bench. "Is there a reason you wish to learn his identity?" His fingers were a hairsbreadth away from brushing her shoulder.

"I want to see if he's all right," Gwen said firmly as she faced him. Her eyes sparkled with a hopeful tenderness. "I suppose I'd also like to make his acquaintance." She laughed lightly as she lifted her shoulders in a shrug. "With a proper introduction this time."

Was this latter wish because she wanted to form a connection with the man from the opera box? Maybe she even hoped he might become a suitor? The truth rose into Avery's throat, beseeching him for release. He could grant this request of hers right here, right now, by confessing his identity to her. But a troubling thought held him in check and had him curling his fingers into a fist without touching her.

He'd been half-consumed with pain that night, yes, though not so far gone that he hadn't been fully aware of kissing Gwen. And he shouldn't have done that. While their kisses had awakened something in him—and he now suspected they may well have had the same effect on Gwen—it wasn't something he was free to pursue.

She seemed to squirm a bit at his silence as he'd done moments before. "I thought since you're a . . . I mean, with your profession . . . that you could help me figure out the man's identity."

The expectancy emanating from her twisted his heart. How could he say *no*? Especially if she agreed to collaborate with him in spying on Hanbury.

Perhaps Avery could wait to tell her the truth regarding the opera until after he'd resolved the German spy issue. But a familiar restlessness inside his gut told him the timing of such a confession wouldn't matter. Whether he told her now or later, he still wouldn't be free to court her for real. To see if those shared kisses and their deepening friendship might lead to something more.

He wanted to help Gwen and have her help him in return, and yet he feared the consequences of both. "Are you saying you'll assist me then?" he asked, hedging.

Pressing her lips together, Gwen finally dipped her chin in a decisive nod. "Yes. Will you help me too? I know it's a lot to ask."

"On the contrary"—he allowed himself to cover her hand briefly with his own—"it seems very little when compared with how you'll be helping me."

She peered down at where his fingers lay atop her gloved ones. "So you don't mind going riding with me tomorrow?"

"It would be a pleasure." The truth of his own words hit him. Avery released his hold on her hand and stood, needing space to breathe, to think.

Gwen climbed to her feet as well. "What of the other matter I asked about?" They began to walk back the way they'd come.

"I will look into it," he reassured her. But he averted his gaze the instant he voiced it, afraid she'd read the truth, and the longing, in his eyes.

Chapter 12

"Relax your grip on the reins," Avery instructed.

Gwen did so, though it took a great deal of effort not to continue to cling in fear. It had been so long since she'd last ridden. From atop her uncle's horse, she thought the ground beneath her looked frightfully far away. Gwen shifted on the side saddle, wishing her injured foot fit more securely in the stirrup. She hated teetering like this on such a narrow platform.

"You're doing well."

She appreciated Avery's encouragement and patience, but she wondered if he secretly thought differently. "Are you sure you aren't just saying that because you agreed to help me?"

"Not at all," he said, smiling as he easily swung astride his horse. "I will even compliment you on how fetching you look in your riding habit."

Gwen laughed, if only to hide her blush. She'd borrowed the tailored jacket and long skirt from her aunt. "Now I know you're just flattering me." He nudged his horse forward, and after a moment's hesitation, she did the same. "You don't have to pretend to be my suitor out of earshot of others."

"Who says I'm pretending?" The low quality of his voice and the teasing light in his brown eyes made her feel as breathless as climbing onto her horse had. "We'll take this first stretch as slowly as you'd like." He nodded at the wide dirt thoroughfare ahead of them, which was thankfully not yet crowded with other equestrian riders.

"Thank you."

They fell into companionable silence. Gwen studied him from the corner of her eye. He looked very dashing in his riding clothes. No one who saw him in this moment would suspect such a gentleman, the nephew of a duke, of being a spy. What had motivated him to take up such a dangerous profession?

"Why do you do what you do? It isn't as if you have to in order to support yourself, right?"

Avery twisted to look at her. "You mean . . ."

She nodded without speaking, but his gaze lit with understanding anyway. They'd experienced this same sort of cryptic communication during their last visit to Dr. Smithfield. A fact that had her smiling. It felt akin to real friendship, another secret only the two of them shared.

"I don't have to do this, no." His brow furrowed as if he were thinking how best to explain. "I like the purpose it affords me, though, and the chance to apply all that I learned during my time at university. I studied very hard there, despite my father's protests that knowledge of academia was of no use to a gentleman."

Gwen could relate in a way. Her brother had been allowed to go to college, but her parents saw no benefit in their daughter doing the same. "What did you study?"

"Languages and history, mostly. I can speak fluent Italian, French, and German. Over the last year, I've been slowly learning Russian too."

A recollection tugged at her memory. "Didn't Bert study the same thing?"

"He did, along with me and Hanbury."

"What does your father think of your profession?"

"He doesn't know." Avery's posture went rigid. "He died four years ago."

"I'm sorry."

He offered her a tight smile. "I appreciate the sentiment. However, we were never close, especially after my mother's death."

Empathy welled inside her. She might not be close to either of her parents, but they'd always been around—providing for her and wanting, she supposed, what was best for her. "How old were you when you lost her?"

This time his shoulders sagged as though the weight of past memories was too much for them to bear. "Just a lad. I only have a few recollections of her being well and not sipping soup in bed. Unfortunately, she was never very strong in constitution."

"Is that why you don't like soup?" she asked, suddenly remembering that detail from one of their first conversations. Their initial meeting felt as if it had taken place months instead of weeks ago.

The rawness and surprise in his expression nearly had her reaching out to touch his sleeve. "Yes, I think my dislike for it began in those anxious days of boyhood, watching my mother grow weaker and weaker."

Her heart sped up at the vulnerability behind his confession. This was the real Avery Winfield, or at least an important side to him. One she felt honored to have seen.

"Rather silly, isn't it?" he said, interrupting Gwen's thoughts and clearly trying to deflect his embarrassment at sharing something so personal. "To hate soup?"

Shaking her head, Gwen guided her horse a little closer to his. "It isn't silly. After my accident, I refused to ride in a carriage for weeks." She smiled self-consciously at him. "And one of the girls at the orphanage who burned her hand and arm told me she still gets nervous going anywhere near a hearth. I think wariness of situations or things or foods that spark painful memories is very normal."

"You are very wise for one your age, Gwen Barton."

If only her mother thought so. Then perhaps Cornelia would trust Gwen to make her own decisions when it came to love and marriage. "Wisdom is sometimes more about experience than age."

"Too true." His relaxed chuckle added to the camaraderie between them. "Perhaps that's why my uncle would like me to have a bit more of both—experience and age—before I inherit the title."

His teasing remark reminded her of something he'd mentioned the day before. About the duke wanting Avery to court a girl this season. "Is he hoping you'll be married before you inherit?"

"He is," Avery said, the merriment draining from his demeanor.

His flat response surprised and puzzled her. "You don't want that?"

"I'm not sure that I will ever marry, this year or in the future." He threw her a look, almost as if he was asking her to understand, but it only confused Gwen more. "If I continue in my current . . . profession . . . I believe remaining a bachelor is the wisest course."

Something akin to disappointment stung Gwen and increased the thudding of her heart. Yet why should she care about Avery's matrimonial opinions and aspirations or the lack thereof? "Are you saying a wife couldn't handle your profession?"

"No," he countered quickly, then he shook his head. "Well, possibly. Yes, I suppose so. My greater concern is that what I do can be dangerous at times, and I wouldn't want to worry or endanger a wife."

Irritation overcame her at his response. Gwen had to fight to keep it in check in order to reply. "While that may be true, isn't that a choice a future spouse should be allowed to make for herself?"

"I don't want to put anyone in jeopardy, Gwen."

"And yet you assured me that if I helped you, I wouldn't be in jeopardy."

The hard line of his jaw appeared to ease slightly. "I believe that's still true. However, it would be different with a spouse, where there is meant to be a sharing of hearts and lives. How could I ask someone to put all of that at risk by aligning with me?"

His words, though spoken in low tones, crashed over her with the force of a torrential wave, leaving the sands of regret behind it. But at least now she understood him.

Avery wouldn't be courting her or any other woman for real—not now and likely never. It wasn't simply because he was a spy, though. This brave, kind man with a devotion to serving his country feared something far greater than possibly endangering a spouse and family.

He feared endangering his heart.

"Shall we try cantering?" Avery suggested. He watched her carefully, but Gwen couldn't tell if he was attempting to read her reaction about cantering or about what he'd just revealed of himself.

Gwen forced a smile. "I'd like to try."

Avery guided his horse from a trot to a canter, and Gwen

did the same. The breeze strengthened, tugging in vain at her hat, as she and her mount picked up speed. The thrill of it evaporated too soon, though, as her thoughts turned back to Avery's confession.

The revelation that he had no intention of courting or marrying settled like heavy stones inside Gwen. But she wasn't sure why she felt so disappointed. Avery had made no promises to her, nor had he confessed a hope that their faux courtship might turn into something real. Yet that was exactly what she herself had been hoping for, wasn't it? She liked Avery very much and had felt a growing connection and attraction to him the more time they spent together. Did that mean a piece of her, however small, had wanted something more, something deeper between them?

Gwen resisted the urge to hang her head at her own foolishness. Avery's genuine compliments or his occasional touch and tender look might have inspired emotions similar to those she'd felt after kissing the man at the opera. However, that didn't mean Avery's feelings matched her own. They had helped each other as friends, and would continue to do so, but that was clearly all that would ever come from her relationship with him. Any expectations for more were hers alone.

For one brief moment, she let herself experience the pain and grief at her unmet longings. Then she released her proverbial grip on them and let them go with a long exhale of breath. She'd agreed to help Avery and accept his help in return—and that was what she would focus on. Not on hopeless imaginings.

As if to solidify her decision to remain focused, Gwen lifted her head and saw Mr. Hanbury riding toward them. A prick of panic shot through her. How was she supposed to act around the other gentleman now that she knew he might be a spy?

"Avery?" He didn't seem to hear her, so she spoke more loudly. "Avery!"

He glanced at her, his startled expression suggesting he'd also been immersed in his own thoughts. "What is it?"

"Mr. Hanbury is coming this way." Gwen pulled back on the reins to stop her horse, causing the mount—agitated from carrying an unfamiliar rider—to dance to the side. The unexpected movement disrupted her balance and she began to slip. She leaned the opposite way, desperate to keep her seat, when Avery reached out and assisted her with a firm hand on her elbow.

Immediately ripples of feeling skittered up her arm. The delightful sensation belied her fresh resolve and tempted her to relish his touch once more. But Gwen knew better now. Making more of this attraction, this relationship, than the friendship it was would only lead to heartache.

She nudged her horse a few inches to the right, breaking Avery's grip on her arm. "Th-thank you," she said.

"Is everything all right?"

Tipping her head in a nod, she tried to indicate the other man's approach without being too obvious. "Mr. Hanbury is here." Avery followed her gaze. "What do I say?"

"You should greet him as you typically would."

Of course, she thought with a wry shake her head. She needed to act as if nothing had changed with her suitor, as if she didn't suspect him of possibly spying for Germany. "Right."

"You can do this, Gwen."

His confidence bolstered her own as Mr. Hanbury drew to a stop alongside her. "Good morning, Mr. Hanbury." She managed to infuse her voice with a measure of casual cheer. "It's a nice day for riding, isn't it?"

"It is that, Miss Barton." He tipped his hat to her, then looked toward Avery, his eyes narrowing slightly. "Winfield."

"Hanbury," Avery returned in nearly the same tone of annoyance.

Gwen pressed her lips over a laugh. If this type of greeting was typical fashion for the two men, there had to be more to the underlying tension between them than Avery's suspicions.

"Enjoy your ride, Miss Barton."

She and Mr. Hanbury exchanged polite nods. "Thank you. You too."

Without acknowledging Avery again, Mr. Hanbury rode off. "Do you want to tell me what that was all about?" she asked as she and Avery guided their horses forward again.

"I don't understand," he said with a frown.

"Was that strained greeting how you normally address Mr. Hanbury?"

His frown increased. "I'd hardly say that was strained."

Gwen let her laugh escape this time. "Whatever you call it, I think you made it fairly obvious you suspect him of something."

It was another minute before Avery spoke again. "Very well. I'll admit I don't feel overly delighted in talking with that man. After all, he may be working for the people who tried to have me—"

He left off talking as he glanced her way. "Tried to have you what?" Gwen prompted.

"All I'm trying to say is that he may feel troubled by our brief interaction for the exact same reasons I do."

"Because of what you suspect his profession to be?"

"Exactly."

Gwen still sensed there was something more to the men's uncomfortable exchange. Almost an air of competition between them, as though they'd been sizing each other up. Was that what spies did? She didn't know, and clearly Avery didn't wish to discuss it any more.

It seemed they needed a change of topic. "What sort of information or questions would you like me to ask him?"

"Anything about his family," he answered, the tight line of his shoulders relaxing. "Or his pursuits and interests."

"He owns quite a bit of land in Scotland."

"I've heard the same. Does he talk much about it? Has he told you what purpose so much land serves in what I've heard is rather isolated country?"

She thought back over her largely one-sided conversations with Mr. Hanbury. "I think he told me he likes the solitude there. The property is on a loch, which joins the sea."

"Gwen, that's perfect. That's precisely the sort of information we need." His warm smile was another threat to the hastily formed boundaries around her heart. "A loch near the sea would allow access and communication by boat."

"I'll see what else I can learn."

Avery met her eyes. "I can't tell you how much I appreciate your help."

"You're welcome," she said, blushing at his sincere gratitude. "Thank you for riding with me today. I feel much better now about my ride with Lord Whitson."

He offered her a brief smile, then faced forward again. "You'll likely impress the earl." The words were teasing, but the way Avery voiced them wasn't. "I'm impressed with how well you ride, even with your foot." His glance strayed her way again. "You are rather remarkable, Gwen."

The compliment set her pulse tripping and nearly had her believing it hinted at deeper feelings. But whether he meant more than friendship by expressing such praise no longer mattered. He wasn't going to risk his heart, and that meant neither would Gwen.

"I'm grateful for the compliment, but you haven't seen me gallop yet."

His smile widened into a grin. "No, I haven't. Is that something you're game—"

Without waiting for him to finish, Gwen urged her horse faster. She glanced back over her shoulder to see Avery scrambling to follow. Another laugh escaped her lips. Only this time it was as full of pleasure as it was pain.

No matter how fast she rode, she couldn't outride her growing awareness of Avery. She'd conquered her reluctance about riding today. But she wasn't as confident that she could as quickly and effectively conquer her heart where Avery was concerned.

⁓⟡⟡⟡⁓

After seeing Gwen home at the conclusion of their ride, Avery returned to his own townhouse. He needed to head to the club in hopes of gathering more information for Captain Kell. But at present, he felt too agitated to listen to what typically amounted to rather tedious conversations with only hints of vital details now and again.

Not like his conversation with Gwen as they'd ridden. Conversing with her was never tedious. If anything, it had been downright dangerous to his peace of mind this morning. Avery had nearly slipped and told her about his injury at the opera. And that was after disclosing other vulnerable pieces about his childhood and why he couldn't marry. Then she'd gone and correctly identified an unusual tension between him and Hanbury. At least on Avery's part.

Try as he might, Avery hadn't been able to fully control the spike of jealousy he'd felt when the other man had ridden up. Hanbury wasn't just a possible spy; he was also Gwen's suitor.

Avery ran his hand over his jaw in frustration and glanced around. He'd wandered unthinkingly into the study—his father's study. When was the last time he'd ventured in here? He couldn't recall. Normally he avoided this room, though he had replaced some of the furniture and paintings after his father's death.

His gaze moved to the old cabinet, which still stood beneath the window. An empty decanter sat on top. It had never been empty when Avery's father had been alive.

Crossing the room, he picked up the cut-glass bottle. He uncorked it, releasing the stale but unmistakable scent of brandy. At once Avery was a young boy again, though not in this house. In his mind's eye, he was back at Beechwood, on summer holiday, waiting nervously in the doorway to ask his father a question. Avery could see the man's bloodshot eyes as if his father actually stood before him now. He could smell the alcohol on Phillip Winfield's breath.

"Don't stand there like a dormouse," his father had scoffed as he'd approached Avery. "Speak up, boy. What do you want?"

Young Avery had hazarded a single step forward, then another. "Would you like to go fishing in the pond with me, Father? As you promised?"

"As if I have time to go fishing." His arm shot out and he clumsily waved at the desk behind him. "I have more important things to do."

Something hot balled up inside Avery's chest. "You mean like drinking?" His voice shook with as much bravado as fear. "That's all you do anymore."

"What did you say?" Phillip grabbed him by the collar,

though his drunken grip only succeeded in moving Avery an inch or two from his rooted spot.

The tears in his eyes blurred his view of his father's angry face, but Avery couldn't seem to stop the words that poured from his mouth. "You don't care about anything or anyone!"

"On the contrary . . ." Avery watched Phillip visibly swallow. "I care too much." There was blatant anguish in his expression before it hardened once more. "Get out," he snarled, pushing Avery toward the door. "Leave me be. I have things to do."

After that, Avery had sought solitude beneath the large oak that had stood for more than three centuries beside the pond. His uncle had found him there. Moorleigh had come up from London on a visit. He took Avery fishing that day.

Why had that memory come to mind? Avery re-capped the decanter. Gwen was right—memories, pleasant or painful, were tucked away into so many of the objects and smells and situations of one's life.

I care too much.

Phillip's agonized sentiment repeated itself through Avery's mind as he gazed, unseeing, out the window. What had his father meant by that? Everything in the man's life, at least after his wife had taken ill, suggested he felt the opposite. The drinking had begun then and became excessive after Avery's mother's death.

How could his father care too much and still push away those who loved him? Who wanted to spend time with him? It made no sense to him. Unless . . . had his loss made him afraid of his own emotions?

Avery jerked upright. Could his father's behavior, which Avery had viewed for so long as proof that the man didn't care, actually be evidence Phillip cared too deeply? With caring deeply came the risk of losing and then hurting deeply too.

Isn't that the real reason I haven't seriously considered marriage?

The silent question shocked him enough that Avery stumbled to the desk and sank into the chair, emotion pushing painfully against his ribs. While his profession could mean possibly endangering a spouse and family, it also made for a convenient excuse not to marry. And if he were truly honest with himself, it wasn't just being a spy that made him uneasy about marriage and a family.

Propping his elbows on the desk, he dropped his head into his hands. This revelation changed nothing. If he was afraid of the pain and hurt that love could bring, then he had good reason for his fears.

What if he married, then died soon afterward as his mother had, leaving a grieving spouse and children of his own behind? Or worse, what if he lost his wife as his father had? Avery knew how badly one's heart could be broken by grief and loss—how it could change a person. What if, despite his best efforts, he became a husband and father exactly as Phillip Winfield had been? A shudder ran through him, and he pressed his palms against his smarting eyes.

No, he would never risk consigning a woman and children to what he himself had experienced in his relationship with his father. That was the real reason he couldn't—wouldn't—marry.

Avery stood and exited the room. Fresh determination swept through him and helped to quell the storm of other emotions. It was time to head to the club. He would continue to keep his focus on what he knew, on what he was good at doing. If that meant ignoring Gwen's gentle knocks on the door of his heart, then so be it.

"The soiree was a rather exclusive affair," Lord Whitson boasted as he patted the neck of his black mare. "I myself hadn't counted on an invitation, but of course I was humbly honored to accept it when it did come."

Gwen murmured agreement, then hid a yawn behind her gloved hand. Only politeness, Christian kindness, and acquiescence to her mother's not-so subtle demands kept her from turning her horse around and riding in the opposite direction. But she'd committed to this outing with Lord Whitson, and she would see it through.

Unlike with Avery, the conversation between her and the earl never ran smoothly. Though one could say, the earl's conversation with *himself* ran quite smoothly. Certainly he never seemed at a loss for words. When he wasn't talking about which *exclusive* events he'd recently attended, Lord Whitson talked about what food he'd recently eaten, whom he'd seen, and what he planned to buy in the near future. But it never seemed to cross his mind that conversations were meant to be shared experiences. The man rarely asked questions of Gwen or seemed interested at all in her thoughts and opinions—not like Avery did. It was another trait in a growing mental list about Avery, one Gwen knew she shouldn't be keeping track of anymore.

"What did you think of the concert last night?" she asked in an attempt to change the subject to something they could both converse on. "I thought it was very moving."

Lord Whitson sniffed. "Moving? I owned a bird once who could sing better than that prima donna."

Annoyance swelled inside Gwen at his rudeness, and she gripped the reins tighter than she should, causing the horse to toss its head. Avery's patient counsel from the day before entered her mind, and she forced her gloved fingers to relax. Surely there was something she could talk about with the earl that wasn't centered solely on him and his apparent indifference to her own preferences.

An idea had Gwen lifting her head with instant hope and relief. She might still be able to salvage this outing and fulfill her task from Avery at the same time. "Tell me, Lord Whitson. How long have you and my cousin and Mr. Hanbury been friends?"

"Since university," he answered with a shrug. "Although Roddy and I first met back when we were boys at Eaton."

"Mr. Hanbury didn't attend Eaton with you?"

The earl shook his head. "He lived in Germany until he was sixteen."

"Did his family come to England with him?"

"Only his mother and sister. His father died the year before they moved to Britain, but the man's brother was already living here."

Did Mr. Hanbury still have family members living in Germany? If not, did he feel enough affection for his mother country that he'd turn on England?

"Do his mother and sister live in London too?" Gwen couldn't recall Mr. Hanbury mentioning any relatives living nearby. Then again, the man typically mentioned very little about himself—or about any subject, for that matter.

"They usually come to London for the season, though they didn't this time. The rest of the year they reside at Hanbury's estate in Scotland." Lord Whitson nudged his mount closer to Gwen's. "Why the sudden fascination with Hanbury, Miss Barton? Aren't you interested in getting to know me better as well?"

Gwen didn't know whether to roll her eyes or physically

cringe at the man's conceitedness. "I'd like to hear about your family too, Lord Whitson." She had to push the words from her mouth.

"My father is a marquess and my mother is from an old royal line in Europe . . ."

The man arrogantly droned on and on. Gwen found her thoughts wandering before settling on what Lord Whitson had revealed about his friend. There certainly seemed to be great potential for continued ties with Germany for Mr. Hanbury. Were his mother and sister aware of his duplicitous activities? Or could they be involved as well?

Gwen couldn't wait to relay to Avery all that she'd learned. She would see him soon, when he came to call upon her and her mother that afternoon during their at-home day, which Cornelia had pushed back by an hour to accommodate Gwen's morning ride with Lord Whitson. But there would be no time to talk privately with Avery. His visit was solely to help establish his pseudo role as Gwen's suitor.

The idea of sitting in the parlor, listening to her mother's poorly disguised prying into Avery's inheritance and his intentions, sounded painfully awkward. Still, the thought of seeing him so soon brought a traitorous leap to her pulse. Even though it shouldn't. The doorway that led to more than friendship with Avery was shut and boarded up, if it had ever been open to begin with. If only Gwen could convince herself to believe that.

She needed to stay her current course of assisting Avery with his spying, seeing the doctor again about her foot, and learning the identity of the man from the opera. Hopefully Avery would have information on the latter soon.

The memory of that kiss prompted a smile from Gwen. It was difficult to be despondent whenever she remembered how she'd felt that night. Surely the stranger from the opera box, whoever he might be, would be the ideal suitor, one far more committed and willing to see and love her than any of the others, including Avery.

A surge of purpose had Gwen sitting up straighter in the side saddle and urging her horse faster. Lord Whitson broke off speaking for a moment in order to keep his mount in line with hers, but once that was accomplished, he began another monologue on the subject of his family's various country estates.

This time Gwen didn't feel so irritated. She'd discovered more information about Mr. Hanbury, and she hadn't even questioned him herself yet. If she failed to marry this season or to think of some way to better help the orphanage, then maybe she could make a career out of spying instead.

Chapter 13

Avery drummed his fingers on the side of the open carriage, waiting for Gwen to exit the Rodmills' townhouse for their scheduled outing. Over the past nine days he'd visited twice with her and her mother during their at-home day. He'd also secured as many invitations as he could to the social engagements Gwen was already planning to attend.

Mrs. Barton had easily accepted Avery as a viable match for her daughter, after receiving what appeared to be satisfactory answers to her plentiful, and at times slightly ill-mannered, questions regarding his family, their estate, and his uncle's history of health. In securing his role as an interested suitor, Avery believed he and Gwen had been successful. But each public interaction with her had left him feeling more disappointed than triumphant. It wasn't until last night, though, that he'd finally ascertained why.

He missed talking freely and openly with Gwen. Not that she didn't participate in conversation with him during his calls or their shared social engagements. But there had been moments when he couldn't determine what she was thinking or why certain questions from her mother made Gwen visibly flinch. He couldn't ask her, though, not while Mrs. Barton or others were seated nearby, listening to every word.

That had to be the reason for his eagerness at seeing her again today—a chance to converse with her without anyone else around. And there was nothing wrong with looking forward to speaking privately with a friend. Besides, he also couldn't wait to share with Gwen where they were headed today. He'd concocted the idea earlier in the week, then sent a note to Gwen instructing her to wear her most durable visiting dress and stating the time he would call on her with his open carriage.

At that moment, the front door opened and Gwen stepped outside. The instant her eyes met his, a familiar sensation of contentment and anticipation prompted an almost boyish smile from him. She slowly descended the stone steps as Avery climbed out of the carriage. Even without a hat and dressed in a simpler gown than he was accustomed to seeing her wear, she still looked as elegant and graceful as always.

"I'm going to dispense with the pleasantries," she said, her gaze sparkling. "Instead I want to know where we're going this afternoon."

He pretended to consider her request. "We might first wish to discuss what information you've gleaned." Gwen had mentioned in her answer to his note that she had a list of things to share in regards to her assigned task. The news had been nearly as welcome as her agreement to join him today.

"I can tell you in a minute. *After* I know where we're going."

With a chuckle, Avery helped her into the carriage, doing his best to ignore how much it affected him every time he touched her hand. Or how profoundly he'd been moved by their shared kiss inside the opera box.

He set aside such thoughts before his expression gave

anything away. "I believe it would be much more fun to have you guess."

"You are impossible." She shook her head with what appeared to be as much amusement as annoyance. He took his seat across from her, and the carriage rolled forward. "Fine," she said, throwing him an arched look. "May I at least have a hint?"

Avery nodded. "Certainly. Our outing has a great deal to do with something you feel strongly about."

Her brow furrowed. "My . . . faith?"

"No."

"Talking with Dr. Smithfield again?"

"Another good guess, but no." He was enjoying this, especially the play of emotions crossing her lovely face.

"My family?"

He shook his head.

"Avery!" Her tone implied scolding, but she was laughing too. "Just tell me."

"Very well." He leaned forward, not wanting to miss any part of her reaction. "I've arranged for us to tour . . . an orphanage."

Gwen's hazel eyes widened in surprise for a moment, then her gaze softened as she smiled fully. Not the polite smile he'd seen many times in public or the one she gave her other suitors. This smile implied more than courtesy. It offered him warmth and gratitude and tenderness. And it made him wish to inspire such a smile every day for the rest of his life.

"An orphanage? Avery, that's wonderful."

He shrugged, feeling self-conscious. When was the last time he'd chosen to do something similar for someone else? Something arranged purely for the pleasure it brought him to see their enjoyment? He couldn't recall.

Avery liked to think he was a good friend to Linwood and

that he treated his staff kindly. But he wasn't sure he'd truly given someone the gift of his time like this since his last visit to Beechwood, when he'd played whist with his grandmother for an entire day. Were there others in his life to whom he could give the gift of his time in doing something they loved like he was doing with Gwen today? Perhaps even with his uncle. The idea was certainly worth pondering more deeply.

"Did you hear what I said, Avery, about riding with Lord Whitson the other week?"

He would ponder his musings later. "My apologies, Gwen. What about your ride with the earl?"

"I was able to get him to answer some questions about Mr. Hanbury." She spoke in a low voice but also one that seemed to resound with happiness at her success.

"That's brilliant." Even he hadn't thought to broach the subject of Hanbury with the earl, though he knew the two men were longtime friends. "What did he say?"

Gwen shared what information she'd learned about Hanbury and his family. Most of it wasn't news to Avery, though it did serve to verify some of the facts. However, Gwen wasn't finished. She'd also seen Hanbury earlier in the week at a reception Avery hadn't been able to coax an invite to and had managed to glean additional details from the man himself.

"Mr. Hanbury may be a linguist like you, but at one point, he had a plan to join the German navy."

"He did?" How was it Avery had never heard this bit about Hanbury before?

It was Gwen's turn to look pleased at his surprise. "His grandfather was a ship builder, and Mr. Hanbury has always had a fascination for boats. If his father hadn't died, he would have joined the Imperial German Navy. As it was, he didn't want to leave his mother and sister behind for such long stretches after his father passed, so he changed his plans."

"Gwen, you are a wonder," he said with an admiring shake of his head. "This is exactly why I needed your help."

A blush drew attention to her cream-colored cheeks. "I have to admit it was rather fun. I hope the information will be useful too." Before he could reply, she changed the subject. "Tell me about this orphanage we're touring. How did you hear about it?"

"The proprietor is the son of one of my grandmother's dearest friends." Avery clasped his hands together and leaned forward. As much as the orphanage had a respected reputation, it was far away from the posh neighborhoods of the *ton*. He needed to prepare Gwen for what they might encounter during their visit. "The orphanage is located in a rather poor section of the city. Not the slums per se, though it isn't much of a stone's throw away from them either. If you'd rather we turn back and find something else to occupy our afternoon, I'll understand."

Gwen regarded him with a look that conveyed both resolve and a measure of sadness. "Do you really think the caliber of the neighborhood would deter me from wanting to see this place and its children?"

He felt an instant stab of chagrin. How could he have doubted Gwen's strength, even for a moment? She'd proven herself more genuine, more caring, and more courageous than any other woman he'd ever met. Of course she wouldn't faint or waver from her goal at the first sign of poverty.

"I should've known differently. I'm sorry, Gwen."

The disappointment in her expression faded. "Heartwell House may be in a respectable, middle-class neighborhood back in New York, but I'm not unfamiliar with the destitution that is rampant in the city either." She glanced out the side of the open carriage, seeing something Avery couldn't. "I've gone with my cousin and his wife to visit some of those poverty-stricken tenements. Most of the children living at their orphanage have known no other way of life prior to their arrival at Heartwell House."

Her words prompted more questions from him about her cousin's orphanage and about the man himself. Avery was as interested in her answers as he was at watching her as she talked. Her passion for caring for others, particularly children, shone in every word, inflection, and gesture. Before he knew it, his driver had parked the carriage beside a narrow street.

Turning on his seat, the salt-and-pepper-haired driver addressed Avery. "Afraid this is as close as I can get her, sir."

Standing, Avery exited the carriage. "It's quite all right. We'll climb out here." He turned to Gwen and helped her down. "I was thinking after this, we could view the Thames up close if you'd like."

"I would love that," she said with a smile.

He instructed his driver when and where to meet them in two hours' time. Then Avery glanced up at the buildings around them. "I believe it's this way." He motioned to the narrow street before them.

The daylight shrank behind them as they walked farther away from the main street. Simultaneously, the smell of spoiled food and rubbish expanded until it nearly choked Avery. People, mostly children, eyed them with as much suspicion as curiosity from rickety staircases and worn doorways. Gwen kept a slow, measured step alongside him, not once shrinking or looking appalled. Instead she walked with her head up, her sorrow-filled eyes studying the scenes around them.

The rise and fall of children's voices prefaced their arrival at the orphanage's front door. Avery knocked and they were admitted by a young lady in servant's livery. The proprietor, Mr. Shellings, greeted Avery warmly. Avery then introduced Gwen to the older man.

"I was delighted to receive your note, Winfield. Is there anything in particular that you wished to see?"

Avery smiled. "I'm actually here as an observer, Mr. Shellings." He motioned to Gwen. "Miss Barton, on the other hand, has done a great deal of work at her cousin's orphanage in New York, and it is her for whom I wanted to set up this tour."

"Is that right?" Mr. Shellings nodded with approval at Gwen. "What can you tell me about your own work, Miss Barton?"

Gwen briefly explained the history behind her cousin's orphanage and her desire to continue helping there. By the time she was finished, it was evident to Avery that she'd completely won over Mr. Shellings with her honest compassion.

"Shall we?" The older man led the way down the hall. Avery and Gwen followed behind him. They passed the stairwell, where two girls and a boy stared at them through the banisters. Gwen offered them a small wave and a smile. They returned the gestures shyly before racing upstairs.

The tour took them all over the building, through the classrooms and dormitories as well as outside to the small courtyard and vegetable patch. Along the way, the three of them were joined by a small entourage of children. Mr. Shellings gave them a scolding look, but he didn't dismiss them, even when he and Gwen remained conversing outside.

A tug on Avery's coat prompted him to look down. A young boy with blue-green eyes watched him with solemn eagerness. "Hello."

"Hello," Avery answered with a smile. "What's your name?"

"Edmund, sir."

"Pleased to meet you, Edmund. I'm Avery." He gave the lad's hand a hearty shake.

He didn't know any children personally and was never sure how to act around them, but he sensed a comrade in this boy with the curious expression and scuffed shoes. Avery had worn out a fair number of shoes himself as a child from all of his ramblings about the estate.

"Are you an inspector?" the boy asked, looking Avery over. "Come to see how the place is run?"

Avery crouched down beside him. "Actually, I'm with the lady over there." He tipped his head in Gwen's direction. "She helps orphans in America and wants to know how she can do more."

"She looks nice and very pretty."

"I quite agree, Edmund," Avery said, his gaze on Gwen. She was still talking with Mr. Shellings, but she was also deftly braiding the hair of a little girl leaning against her skirt.

"Is she your wife?"

Avery returned his attention to the boy. "Afraid not, lad."

Edmund's face scrunched with thought. "Do you have a mum and a dad then?"

"No, not anymore."

"Me neither. Suppose that makes us both orphans." His sorrowful look and truth-filled statement gently pulled at Avery's compassion. "I have me a sister, though. Do you have a sister?"

Avery straightened. "No, I don't have a sister or a brother."

"So you haven't got a mum or a dad, or a sister or a brother, or a wife, even?" Edmund sounded incredulous.

When Avery nodded, the boy continued. "Who takes care of you?"

He was tempted to laugh until he realized the lad's inquiry was in earnest. "I suppose I take care of myself, though I do have a grandmother and an uncle and some good friends."

"And God. You have him too, sir."

Did he? Avery shifted his weight from shoe to shoe as a sense of consternation washed through him. His mother would likely be saddened by his doubts if she were still here. Then again, might Avery have held to his faith with greater conviction and courage if she hadn't died? He supposed he would never know.

Looking at Edmund again, he couldn't help asking a question of his own. "Who taught you about God, Edmund?"

"Me sister, sir, and Mrs. Shellings and the vicar at the church we orphans go to."

"Do you truly believe them? That God knows and cares for you?"

The boy gave an enthusiastic nod.

"How do you know?" A part of him felt silly at having a religious discussion with a boy who couldn't be more than nine or ten. And yet Avery truly wanted to understand how a lad in such circumstances could still cling to faith. Just as he'd been interested in learning how Gwen's faith had remained strong after her accident.

Edmund lifted his thin shoulders in a shrug. "I know 'cause I asked Him."

"You asked . . . God?"

The lad gave him a look as if Avery were daft. "One night when I said me prayers, I just asked. Like me sister told me to. 'God, do you care about little ol' Edmund Morley or not?'"

"And did He answer?" Again Avery felt a wash of embarrassment, but he had no desire to end their riveting conversation now.

"Not that night." Edmund glanced down at the dirt. "But on that next Sunday, when we were all singin', I felt something . . ." He tapped his narrow chest. "Right here. Like after I drink some of Cook's hot cider, and it warms me up, head to toe. Me sister said that was God's answer. His way of sayin' He knows me."

The hopeful glance he threw Avery revealed the boy's desire for a bit more reassurance that his sister had been correct. But could Avery offer such a thing, especially when his own faith and relationship with God had grown rather dusty with neglect?

"I can't say I've had the same experience, chap. But I would trust your sister . . . and what you felt." Avery rested his hand on the boy's shoulder as a forgotten memory returned to his mind. "My grandmother once told me that God's love fills us with warmth and peace and confidence. Is that how you felt that day, Edmund?"

"I did, sir." His reverential tone was nearly as touching as his trust in telling Avery his story.

"Then I believe you got your answer from God."

The lad's relieved grin inspired the same from Avery. Or was the real source of his smile the feeling inside him of being buoyed up, of feeling lighter? It wasn't so different from what he experienced each time he was with Gwen. Almost as if her friendship had been heaven-sent. Though he wasn't sure how that could be. He'd been ignoring God for years. Wasn't He doing the same with Avery?

As if in direct opposition to his troubled thoughts, Avery felt two small arms wrap around his waist. "Thank you for that, sir. I'll trust me sister and me answer." Edmund lowered his arms as he stepped back. "But you've got to, too, sir."

"What do you mean?" Avery asked with a confused chuckle.

"You got to trust your gran, and then get your own answer." With that, Edmund gave Avery a parting wave and ran to join two other boys who looked to be his same age.

The lad's wisdom stayed with Avery as he slipped his hands into his pockets and went to join Gwen and Mr. Shellings. How many people in his life had patiently lived and shared their faith with him? His mother, grandmother, Gwen, even Mack. And now young Edmund today. Could it be that God hadn't forgotten or ignored him? That He wasn't disappointed in Avery as his father had constantly been?

The possibility enlarged the lightness within his chest, along with a sense of gratitude. He might have come up with today's outing, but Avery was beginning to suspect Someone else may have had a hand in his plans too. And this time he didn't mind at all.

Chapter 14

Even after thanking Mr. Shellings several more times for the tour and his counsel, Gwen was reluctant to leave the orphanage. It wasn't just how impressed she'd been by the facilities, either. The handful of children she'd met had reminded her of those back home at Heartwell House, and she didn't want to say goodbye.

"We can come again," Avery reassured her as they ventured back into the chaos beyond the orphanage walls.

Gwen nodded with grateful relief. "I'd like that." She cast a final glance at the orphanage before facing forward again. "Did you enjoy the tour?"

For reasons she didn't want to identify yet, she hoped Avery had enjoyed himself as much as she had. Especially after seeing him talking with one of the boys with such ease and comfort that it seemed as though the two of them had known each other for years. It was in that moment Gwen realized with a heartfelt pang that Avery Winfield would make a wonderful father someday. If only he were willing to risk his heart.

"I enjoyed it very much." His smile held nothing but sincerity.

"What were you and that boy Edmund talking about?" Hopefully her question wouldn't reveal she'd been paying as much attention to him as she had to listening to Mr. Shellings.

Avery shrugged and glanced away. "Nothing much."

"Who's not being forthright now?" she teased.

He chuckled, but he still looked slightly embarrassed. "All right. If you must know, we were having a rousing discussion on . . . religion."

It was Gwen's turn to laugh. Only Avery didn't join her. "Oh. You actually did talk about religion?"

"We did." The chagrin in his expression changed to thoughtfulness. "Edmund is rather wise for his age. Sort of like someone else I know." He threw her a meaningful glance, his brown eyes gleaming with amusement. "He answered all of my questions with aplomb, and I promise you I was not interrogating him. The boy started the questioning."

"I wasn't thinking that." His arched look inspired another light laugh from her. "Honestly. You both looked as if you were enjoying your conversation."

When they reached the main street, Gwen allowed herself to draw in a full breath. The air wasn't crisp and clean here either, but at least it wasn't as suffocating as it had been closer to the orphanage.

"Will you tell me what you and Edmund said?" She genuinely wanted to know, especially after seeing the intense contemplation on Avery's face as he'd spoken with the boy.

He regarded with a kind expression. "I will someday soon, Gwen. I promise. Right now, though, I want to show you the boat traffic on the Thames."

She felt only a flicker of disappointment. After all, Avery had promised to tell her soon—and she trusted him to keep his word.

"To the boats, then," she said, giving him a smile.

Truthfully, she didn't care what she and Avery talked about or where they walked. She simply enjoyed being with him—and not just to report what she'd discovered about Mr. Hanbury, though she'd been bursting to share that information for days. More than that, she'd greatly missed time alone with him and the way he encouraged her to be herself.

"Edmund does remind me of myself as a boy."

Gwen raised her eyebrows. "Really? In what way?"

Avery shared a few stories from his boyish adventures on his family's estate as he led the way toward the nearest bank of the famous river. It wasn't Gwen's first glimpse of the Thames, but it certainly felt different viewing it up close, at her own pace and not from inside a carriage. Vessels large and small moved along the water's surface or sat moored along the various docks. Workers transferred cargo from ship to shore or loaded the boats with freight bound for other ports. The sounds and smells were nearly as overpowering to Gwen's senses as those by the buildings and alleyways near the orphanage.

"It reminds me a little of home."

Avery glanced at her. "Do you miss New York?"

"I miss my father and I miss being at Heartwell House."

"And yet . . ."

Gwen wasn't surprised he'd heard her hesitation. "There's a lot about London that I've come to enjoy too. More than I thought possible." Especially her time with him.

"I'm glad you're here, Gwen."

The intensity in his gaze was as welcome as it was confusing. "Because I'm such a good"—she lowered her voice—"spy?"

"That isn't what I meant," he said, his voice devoid of any teasing.

How she longed to ask what he *did* mean. But doing so would only drudge up hopes and expectations that would not be met. Instead she had to keep things light between them. It was the only way she could be with Avery and not get caught up in the emotions he stirred inside her.

"Let's take a look at that large ship there." She gestured a short distance down the waterfront.

To her relief, he didn't argue or try to press his point further. He simply fell into step beside her, matching her pace with his own. Unlike many others, Avery never showed any sign of impatience at her limping walk. It was something else Gwen appreciated about him. Something else that made it difficult not to feel more than friendship for him.

They were nearly to the ship when Avery abruptly stopped and looked back the way they'd come. "Do you recognize that carriage?"

"Which carriage?" Her gaze had been on the boats and the river—at least when it wasn't surreptitiously on Avery.

He frowned. "It turned the corner, but I thought it looked like Lord Whitson's." He lifted his shoulders in a shrug and motioned for Gwen to continue. "Likely my mistake. I can't think of any reason the earl would be driving around down here."

The ship was even more impressive up close than it had been down the wharf. "Have you ever travelled beyond England?"

Avery shook his head. "I haven't, no."

"Is there anywhere you'd like to go?"

His expression turned reflective. "To the Continent, perhaps. Maybe even New York."

"Oh, really?" At his emphatic nod, she laughed. "If you ever do, I'd love to show you around the city."

The merriment faded from his handsome features. "If you marry a titled English gentleman, as your mother wishes, you won't be in New York to show me around."

"You're right," Gwen conceded, the admission bitter on her tongue.

She looked away, unable to face whatever she might see in his eyes at that moment. Across the street, she caught sight of a familiar lean figure, strolling in the direction she and Avery had just come. "Avery, look. Isn't that Mr. Hanbury?"

"Will you look at that?" He grinned. "I imagine there's reason for his interest in the river traffic, and it doesn't stem from nostalgia." Avery grasped her elbow and stepped into the street. "Let's follow him."

A thrill shot through Gwen, though it may have been as much at Avery's touch as doing something as spy-like as trailing a suspect. "You think he's gathering information?"

"I do." Avery led her to the opposite side of the street before releasing her arm. "We'll stay far enough behind that he shouldn't notice us but close enough to observe his movements."

Gwen gave a quick nod and kept her gaze trained on Mr. Hanbury's back. The man stopped after a minute or two, forcing her and Avery to stop too. Gwen's heartbeat ricocheted inside her chest. Had Mr. Hanbury seen or heard them behind him? But no, he didn't turn around, and he seemed more interested in the nearby vessels than anything or anyone else. Could he truly be making mental notes to aid Germany? She didn't want to believe it of the quiet man, and yet he had a great many reasons to help his native country.

When Mr. Hanbury began walking again, she and Avery did the same. The pattern of starting and stopping repeated itself several more times. Each time, Gwen feigned interest in the sights around her, though she'd already seen this stretch of river. No one would likely guess she and Avery were keenly interested in the comings and goings of a certain gentleman ahead of them.

She wasn't sure how much time had passed before Mr. Hanbury turned up a side street. "Hurry," Avery said quietly. "We don't want to lose him."

Gwen did her best to pick up her feet, but her limp still hampered her speed. "Why don't you go ahead and see if you can spot him at the corner? I'll be right behind you."

"Are you sure?" He hesitated until she waved him forward.

"Go. I'm coming."

Avery rushed up the street and soon disappeared around the corner. Gwen limped after him as quickly as she dared. Her foot had already started to ache even before she'd tried to hurry. She paused to rest beside a building that formed one wall of a narrow alleyway. Spy work was certainly not for the faint of heart—or foot. A wry smile lifted Gwen's lips as she pushed away from the building and started walking again. Hopefully her pace hadn't prevented Avery from catching up with Mr. Hanbury.

As she prepared to turn the corner, a person sprinted around it and bowled into her. Gwen reached out to steady herself. "I'm so sorry, Gwen." Avery's arms gripped hers and prevented her from crashing into someone or something else.

"What's wrong?"

His face held none of its earlier confidence. "I lost Mr. Hanbury."

"Oh no. Is there a way—"

Grabbing her hand, Avery tugged her forward before she could finish her sentence. "That's not the problem, at least not right now."

"What is the problem then?" Each smack of her shoe against the street sent pain up her left leg as she struggled to keep up with him.

He threw a frantic look over his shoulder without

slowing his pace. "I believe our ruse is up. Mr. Hanbury must have seen me—or us. I don't know. But we're the ones being followed now."

"What?" Her pulse raced wildly with panic. "By who?"

"A pair of miscreants with knives."

Her fear expanded as she stumbled. "Avery, I can't walk that fast." She glanced back the way they'd come, but she didn't know whose faces she needed to fear seeing. "You'll never outrun them with me at your side. If you go on ahead, perhaps they'll leave me—"

"I won't leave you here alone, Gwen."

The firmness in his tone and the determined set of his jaw brought her a glimmer of relief. She wouldn't be forced to deal with whatever was coming on her own. "Then what do we do?"

"We'll try and elude them another way."

He squeezed her hand, then led her into the same alleyway she'd rested alongside earlier. However, a wall of bricks blocked their escape in that direction. Gwen let go of Avery and rattled one of the door handles. "It's locked!"

"So is this one," Avery said, his expression more grim than she'd ever seen it.

He eyed the street behind her, but Gwen didn't need to turn around. Any moment now, the men with knives would find them standing here, helpless and trapped.

Gwen sent a short but earnest prayer heavenward before Avery grasped her shoulders. "I have an idea." He drew her closer to the wall, her back still to the street behind them. "Do you trust me?"

"Yes," she whispered without hesitation.

Dipping his head in a somber nod, Avery held her gaze as he settled his hands on either side of her waist. Then he brushed her lips with his own. Surprise and pleasure tumbled through Gwen. Though featherlike, the kiss still had the power to commandeer her pulse and cause it to trip with something entirely different from the alarm of moments ago.

How long had she imagined kissing Avery? For some time now.

The breathless feeling inside her grew and blossomed as Avery kissed her again, with gentle fervor this time. Fear fled Gwen's thoughts. She wound her hands around Avery's neck and let herself fall into the shared kiss. It felt new and exhilarating, yet at the same time, comforting and natural. Underpinning everything was a strong sense of familiarity too—as if this weren't the first time they had kissed.

When Avery inched back, his masculine mouth still a hairsbreadth away, Gwen wasn't sure if five minutes or five hours had passed. "Gwen," he said softly as if her name were the most precious utterance he could voice.

"Yes?" Would her heart ever beat at a steady rhythm after today, after such a kiss?

He pressed his forehead to hers. "I . . ."

At a shout from the street, Avery lifted his head and peered past her. "I believe they're gone."

"Gone?" The word slipped out before her thoughts caught back up with her. The moment they did, she blushed with embarrassment. He was talking about their pursuers, the ones with knives and ill intent.

Avery smiled and stroked her cheek. "Yes, we success-fully eluded them. We should be safe now."

The pleasure she'd felt at his touch, at their kiss, splintered as reality crashed upon her. Avery had kissed her as a means to hiding them from their assailants. Not because he'd been longing to kiss her.

It was a brilliant plan, really. No one would suspect the couple locked in an affectionate embrace inside the alleyway to be a man and woman fleeing for their lives. And yet Gwen couldn't be the only one who'd felt the wonder, the rightness, the familiarity of their kiss. Not since the night of the opera had she experienced such a strong connection to another person . . .

No. Gwen fell back a step, unable to meet Avery's gaze now.

He couldn't be the injured man from the box. She'd asked Avery to help her learn the identity of that man and he had said nothing. He would have told her if it was him, wouldn't he? But the more Gwen considered it, the more it made perfect sense that he and her mystery gentleman were the same person.

What kind of man sustained a knife wound while attending the opera? A spy intent on finding other spies. She also hadn't met Avery after that performance, but she had met Mr. Hanbury. Gwen pressed her back against the rough wall of the alley, her hand massaging her temples. Confusion eroded her strength and the loveliness of their kiss. Their second kiss.

"Gwen, are you all right?"

She managed a wordless nod, unable to answer out loud.

"We aren't in danger of them finding us anymore." When she didn't react to his obvious attempt at comfort, he added, "I can see if they're gone, if that would help."

He believed she still feared their assailants, and Gwen didn't bother to correct him. Besides, now that the frightening ordeal was over, she felt shaky with the frenzied energy of their escape.

Avery strode past her to peer out the alley's opening. After a moment, he turned toward her. "I don't see them. We can go meet the carriage now."

Nodding, Gwen pushed away from the wall. She folded

her arms against a shiver as she walked slowly toward Avery. "I—I'm coming," she said through her chattering teeth.

"You're cold." He approached her and, wrapping her in his arms, held her tightly against him. Warmth seeped pleasantly into her, and Gwen welcomed it. Whatever his true feelings for her, Avery had broken no promise regarding a future together. He'd been honest with her about his feelings toward courtship and marriage. He'd also likely saved their lives today. For all of those things, she could be grateful.

"Th-thank you."

His chin rested lightly against her hair. "You have nothing to thank me for." His tone was full of censure, but she sensed it was at himself. "I'm sorry, Gwen."

"For kissing me?" she couldn't help asking. She shifted so she could see his face, though she hated the thought of seeing the regret in his brown eyes.

"What? No." Avery frowned. "I wasn't apologizing for that."

She glanced away in confusion. "You mean you don't regret kissing me?"

"Seeing as it kept you safe, I don't regret it for a moment." He waited for her to look at him again, and when she did, a gentle smile lifted his fine mouth. "Truth be told, I've wanted to kiss you ever since . . . Well, for a while now."

His admission soothed her disappointment, and yet it couldn't mollify it completely. Gwen wanted more from him than friendship and stolen kisses. She wanted a commitment she knew he'd never give. But even if she couldn't have that, she at least wanted him to tell her himself that he was the man she'd helped in the opera box.

For a moment, she considered asking him outright if it had been him, but there must be a reason Avery hadn't yet shared the truth with her. And for now, she would respect his wish for anonymity.

"Then what are you apologizing for?"

Avery rubbed her sleeves with his hands. "For dragging you along to follow Hanbury and nearly being accosted by armed ruffians. And for assuring you that you wouldn't be in danger by helping me."

"I agreed to help you spy and to follow Mr. Hanbury, Avery."

"Be that as it may, I don't think you should go anywhere with him alone. Not even with your mother accompanying the two of you."

Gwen was more than willing to concede to that plan. She didn't wish to be alone with Mr. Hanbury either. "I won't. Do you still need me to gather information on him?"

His hands stilled on her forearms, his expression somber. "No. There's still a chance that Hanbury saw you with me, and you questioning him might make him respond . . . unpredictably. But even if he didn't see you, I think it's best if you don't make any inquiries of him or anyone else for the next week."

"All right." She nodded. "I suppose we don't need to meet to exchange information, then. At least for a while."

Avery looked surprised. "We could still meet as friends, couldn't we?"

Before she could answer, he released her and ran his hand through his hair. Somewhere in the shuffle earlier, he'd lost his hat. "I know I kissed you, Gwen, and I meant it when I said I don't regret doing so. My only regret is that there wasn't time to ask for your permission." Agitation saturated his entire demeanor as he paced beside the opening of the alleyway. "In light of that, I understand if you no longer wish to be friends."

"We're still friends, Avery," Gwen said, stopping his distressed movements with a hand to his arm.

She only wished she could feel the same relief that lit his handsome face. "Thank you. Shall we go?" He held out his hand to her.

"Yes." She locked her fingers with his. Proper or not, she needed the tangible reminder that she was well and safe, and she guessed Avery did too.

As she followed him back toward the direction of the orphanage, she struggled to keep her threatening tears at bay. She and Avery might still be friends, but everything else had changed for Gwen. Her hopes and dreams of a love match with the man from the opera would remain just that—a dream. Even though she was now certain of his identity, he would remain as unreachable and mysterious as he'd been that night. A man who had captured the feelings of her heart but who would never be free to return them.

Chapter 15

B y the time the carriage settled to a stop in front of the Rodmills' townhouse, Gwen was more than ready for the afternoon to be over. The visit to the orphanage seemed a lifetime ago, rather than merely a few hours in the past. A headache throbbed behind her eyes, and the ache in her foot felt as if it had lodged itself inside her throat too.

"Thank you for the chance to see the orphanage." She managed a semblance of a smile.

Avery's expression remained as troubled with bewilderment and sorrow as it had been since they'd located his carriage for the return trip home. "I'm glad you enjoyed it." He glanced down. "I'm sorry again for dragging you into the other . . . situation."

"You didn't know what was going to happen, Avery."

She started for the front steps, but his next question made her stop. "Will I see you this next week?"

Earlier today, Gwen would have responded with a resounding *yes*. But now? Her initial surprise at realizing he was the injured man from the opera had begun to give way to anger at his silence. Whatever his reasons, he should have still told her the truth the moment she'd asked for his help.

The other source of frustration wasn't so much about Avery as it was herself. Their kiss had revived Gwen's deeper feelings for him, and she wasn't sure how much longer she could bear spending time with him like this, all the while knowing they could never be more than friends.

"I don't know," she finally answered. "Our social schedule is very full."

He nodded slowly, his gaze unreadable. "May I send you a note, then?"

"That would be fine."

His own attempt at a smile appeared as unconvincing as hers likely had. "Good day, Miss Barton."

"Good day."

The easy camaraderie and connection she'd come to cherish with him had vanished, leaving this stiff formality in its wake. The realization tore at her already bruised heart. She hurried up the stairs, stumbling a bit in her rush to get inside. This time Avery wasn't beside her to help. Gwen grabbed for the railing to keep herself from falling, but not before striking her knee against one of the steps. Pain radiated up her leg and brought a fresh rush of moisture to her eyes. She bit the inside of her cheek to keep the tears from escaping as she fled into the townhouse.

Ducking her chin to avoid the servants' curious looks, Gwen limped toward the grand staircase. Movement through the open door of the drawing room caught her attention and she stopped. Aunt Vivian stood within the circle of her husband's arms as the two shared a lingering kiss.

Gwen knew she ought to slip away before they noticed they had an audience. But she couldn't make her feet move anymore. Instead, she watched the tender exchange between her aunt and uncle with pained fascination and longing. Had they initially felt this way for one another when they'd married? Or had this affection grown out of mutual rapport? She hadn't spent a great deal of time around Uncle Albert, beyond dinners and a few social engagements. And yet the man exemplified quiet patience, and a tender glint shown in his eyes whenever he looked at his wife.

That's what I want. It's what I've always wanted.

In spite of her love for the orphanage and her belief that working there would bring complete fulfillment, deep down Gwen still longed to marry. Not for money or a title or social station, but for love. She wanted to share her thoughts, her faith, her life with someone. Wanted to treasure a husband and children and be treasured in return. Was that path closed to her now? Did God wish for her to find contentment with her work at Heartwell House and nothing else?

"Oh, Gwen, you've returned from your outing."

She glanced up to find her aunt and uncle watching her. Her cheeks flooded with heat at being caught standing there. "Y-yes."

"Are you all right, my dear?" Aunt Vivian moved to the doorway.

Gwen considered giving an excuse, but her emotions were likely to betray her no matter what she said. Better to stick with the truth. "No, not really."

"I'll leave you two to talk," Uncle Albert said, pressing a kiss to his wife's cheek. He strode into the foyer and paused beside Gwen. "It's been a pleasure to have you here with us this season."

The warm sincerity of his tone resurrected the threat of Gwen's tears. "Thank you for having us." She meant the words. She'd been reluctant to come to England, but now she couldn't imagine having not come at all. Having never met Avery, even if she still felt angry with him.

"Come sit with me." Her aunt motioned for Gwen to join her in the drawing room.

Her hidden burdens felt twice as heavy as Gwen shuffled into the room and sank onto one end of the settee. Aunt Vivian took a seat on the other end, her expression full of concerned compassion.

"I hope you know you can confide in me, my dear. I will simply listen if that is what you wish."

Gwen nodded, words and emotions clogging her throat. Where to begin? And what could she share without sharing too much?

"Am I right to assume your distress has something to do with your different suitors?"

"Yes." Though it had more to do with one suitor in particular, and he wasn't even officially that.

Aunt Vivian gave her a knowing look. "It can be rather confusing trying to understand one's feelings and preferences." When Gwen remained silent, she asked, "What do you think of your two most persistent suitors?"

Her aunt meant the earl and Mr. Hanbury. Mr. Fipwish had dropped out of the running for Gwen's hand—he hadn't visited or approached her in more than a week. But what could she say about the others, especially since they were friends of the Rodmills? She didn't care for Lord Whitson, and Mr. Hanbury was likely spying for Germany and may have sent assailants after her and Avery earlier.

"Of the two, I find Mr. Hanbury's manners more appealing."

To her surprise, her aunt laughed. "A very diplomatic answer, and one I agree with. They may be Bert's friends, Gwen, but that doesn't mean I'm keen on either of them marrying my favorite brother's daughter."

"That's a great relief," she admitted with half a smile.

Aunt Vivian returned the gesture. "What about Mr. Winfield? What do you think of him?"

"I . . ." Gwen glanced away. "I consider him a good friend."

"He is a good man."

Gwen couldn't prevent her next question from spilling out. "What do you know about him, Aunt Vivian?"

"He's to inherit his uncle's title and the family estate near Exeter."

These were things Gwen already knew. "What of his character?"

"I think you know the answer to that question far better than I do." Her aunt tempered the chiding words by reaching out and resting her hand on top of Gwen's. "I will say, though, that I know him to be an honorable man and one who seems to be quite taken with my niece."

Could that be true—was Avery taken with her? "I'm not sure what you mean."

"I've observed moments between you and Mr. Winfield that remind me of myself and Albert when we first met." Aunt Vivian sat back, her countenance nostalgic. "Like oil and water at times."

"You and Uncle Albert?" Gwen couldn't imagine such a thing.

Her aunt's pleasant laughter rang through the room again. "You didn't inherit your strength from your mother's side only, Gwen."

"You think my mother is strong?" she countered in surprise.

Aunt Vivian's expression changed to one of quiet consideration. "Mothers of daughters have to be strong." She studied her clasped hands that now rested on her lap. "I would have loved to have a daughter, but there are days I'm grateful we only had a son. I don't have to worry as much about Bert because he can make his own way in this world, whatever he chooses. But a daughter . . ." She lifted her chin to reveal dark eyes glimmering with tears. "A daughter is so often at the mercy of others. All that scheming and prodding for a good match is often done out of great love and equally as great a fear."

Regretful understanding flooded through Gwen. Her aunt's words shone a different light on Gwen's mother's motives and actions of the past few years.

"Are you happy, Aunt Vivian?"

Her aunt's soft smile was as much an answer as her reply. "I am. Like anyone's life, mine hasn't been without challenges and disappointments. At one time, I felt certain my life's work would be helping secure women's suffrage."

"Really?" Gwen couldn't quite picture her demure aunt giving impassioned speeches, or chaining herself to a fencepost, or sitting inside a jail cell, all in hopes of winning a woman's right to vote. Then again, why not? Who better to assist in such a worthy cause than a former American heiress who was the respected wife of an English baronet? "Do you still feel that strongly about women's suffrage?"

"I'm still quite active in helping with the movement here, but I understand now that God had other things in mind for me." Aunt Vivian regarded her kindly. "May I share something else, Gwen?"

"Please."

"I've watched you when you've returned from spending time with Mr. Winfield." Her aunt leaned toward her, giving earnestness to her observation. "Apart from today, you are much happier with him than with anyone else."

It was true. But the knowledge didn't bring the relief Aunt Vivian likely thought it would. Her aunt didn't know about Avery's reluctance to risk his heart, his certainty that he could never marry. "What do I do, Aunt Vivian?" All of the emotions Gwen had felt earlier rushed over her anew, creating a tidal wave she felt powerless to swim through.

Her aunt surprised her by pulling Gwen into a hug. "You follow your heart, my dear," she whispered. "Then you trust God and yourself in following the answer it gives you."

Following the answer . . .

As her aunt released her, Gwen rose to her feet. She knew her own heart—she was falling for Avery. Unfortunately, that was as much a dead end as the alley had been earlier. That didn't mean she couldn't move forward, though, with the one answer she already had. To do all in her power to help the orphanage.

In all of the excitement of an outing alone with Avery, she'd nearly forgotten her scheduled appointment with Dr. Smithfield. "Would you be willing to accompany me on an errand tomorrow? I have an appointment with a doctor here in London."

Aunt Vivian stood as well. "Of course." The curiosity in her gaze was unmistakable, though she was too ladylike to satisfy it with questions. Gwen trusted her aunt with her secret, though.

"Remember what I told you about Dean's orphanage in New York?"

"Oh yes."

Gwen quickly explained the nature of Dr. Smithfield's work. "While initially my visits focused on getting recommendations for doctors in America who might help the orphanage, I'm also hoping he can fix my foot, so I can have greater mobility than I've had since the accident."

"I hope he can help," Aunt Vivian said, her tone kind.

"I feel confident he will."

She followed her aunt from the room and up the staircase. It was time to change for dinner, then she would need to ready herself for the reception they'd all be attending tonight. Mr. Hanbury would be there, and Gwen was determined to see if he acted any differently toward her after the events of this afternoon.

Her hopes for her and Avery may have been uprooted again today. But that didn't mean she was without purpose or something to offer. Once Dr. Smithfield fixed her foot and Gwen left England, she hoped to be free at last to follow her true aspirations.

⁄౦ᴎᴎᴎᴎᴎ

He'd done something wrong. But other than having Gwen join him in following Hanbury and nearly getting them caught by armed assailants, Avery couldn't think of what it might be. He didn't regret kissing Gwen, though he still wished he'd had time first to ask her permission.

As the carriage navigated the streets toward home, Avery couldn't stop thinking of those moments in the alley. Kissing Gwen while semiconscious at the opera had been nothing short of wonderful. However, kissing her while he was fully conscious had been extraordinary. Not only had their impassioned kiss saved them from harm, but it had tumbled the walls around Avery's heart too, revealing hopes and longings he'd barricaded long ago.

In that moment of sheer delight and vulnerability, he'd nearly confessed to Gwen that he was the man whose identity she'd hoped to learn. The commotion from the street had jerked him back to reality, though. A reality where he'd nearly witnessed Gwen getting hurt for her involvement in his spy activities. As long as he continued his work with Captain Kell, danger would be inevitable for any woman who chose to align her life with his.

Was that the reason Gwen had acted aloof during the long walk back to his carriage and on the return drive to the Rodmills' house? Had she realized what risks came with spending time with Avery?

Resting his elbows on his knees, he raked his hands through his hair and hung his chin. He'd made a mess of things, regardless of Gwen's reassurances that they were still friends. The hesitation on her face when he'd asked if he might see her again had cut straight through his chest. As had her honest reply that she didn't know.

His mind had shouted at him to begin at once to rebuild his inner fortress, but his heart hadn't listened, urging him instead to at least see if he could send her a note. Though what he'd say in his message, Avery had no idea.

The closeness he'd experienced with Gwen as they'd toured the orphanage had disappeared as quickly as Hanbury had. Even the information Gwen had gathered on the man and the triumph of catching Hanbury in the act of studying ships along the river failed to bring Avery the usual sense of satisfaction. In its place, he felt only confused and burdened.

He glanced up to see he was nearly home. The thought of being by himself for the rest of the day held no appeal for him. However, he didn't wish to divulge his inner struggle to his best friend within the public arena of the club either.

"Will you take me to my uncle's home?" he asked his driver.

The look of surprise on the older man's face probably mirrored that on Avery's. He rarely visited the duke's home. But something inside was nudging him to go see the only family he had in London.

When his driver stopped before the duke's residence, Avery found the front steps busy with foot traffic as servants carried items from the house to a waiting carriage. He climbed from his own vehicle and maneuvered his way up the stairs to the front door.

"Is His Grace at home?" Avery inquired of the harried-looking butler.

The butler frowned. "He is, Mr. Winfield. But as you can see, His Grace is—"

"It's all right, Tobias." The duke entered the foyer. "I can spare a few minutes to speak with my only nephew. Especially since such a visit is an unprecedented surprise."

Avery cringed with embarrassment as he followed his uncle into the study. "I apologize for coming unannounced."

With a wordless nod, Moorleigh moved to the book-shelves behind the desk. He selected a stack of books and turned back to the desk to place them in a crate.

"Are you going on holiday?" Avery asked when he noticed more boxes scattered about the room.

His uncle didn't pause in his work. "No. I'm retiring to Exeter."

"You mean you're quitting London for good?"

Moorleigh nodded again, his gaze moving from the books he held to the window. "Perhaps I should have left sooner, but I'd hoped to see as much of the season as I could."

No part of their conversation was making any sense. "I'm sorry, Uncle, I don't understand."

"I lingered here to see if you would finally make yourself a match, nephew." The duke's eyes flashed with irritation and something that very much resembled sorrow. "But since such an announcement has not been forthcoming, I find I've grown weary of London. I long for the quiet and peace of Beech-wood."

Chagrined, Avery stepped closer to the desk. "I know the estate needs help, Moorleigh, but there's still time to work out a solution."

"One that doesn't involve you choosing a wife, I take it?"

It wasn't stated as a question, though Avery felt the need to respond with honesty. "Most likely not."

"For what reason, Winfield?" The books smacked against the desk. "As far as I can tell, you are not out sowing wild oats as other young men are. Nor do you imbibe or gamble away your inheritance as your father did. So what, pray tell, is the cause of your reluctance to enter into the honorable institution of marriage?"

Annoyance created heat beneath Avery's collar. Who was the duke to lecture him on marriage, once again, when the man himself had never been married?

"Perhaps I like being a bachelor," Avery countered in a voice too tight to sound casual.

Moorleigh shook his head, his expression almost disappointed. "I used to tell myself the same."

The bitterness of the man's tone surprised Avery and eroded some of his irritation. "Is that why you chose not to marry in your younger years?"

"I cannot recall my reasons anymore." The duke's shoulders sank as if he were suddenly too tired to hold them up. "Though I will say whatever they were, they were likely foolish and driven by unfounded fears of my own making. I'd like to think if I were in your shoes, Avery, I would choose differently."

His earnestness and regret couldn't have been more tangible, even if his uncle hadn't resorted to using Avery's given name. Avery swallowed hard, unsure what to say next. "I know Gran will be pleased to see you."

"Yes." Moorleigh returned to the task of packing his books. "But she also understands what my return to Beechwood signifies."

"And what is that?"

He gave Avery a piercing look, all traces of fatigue now gone. "I'm dying, nephew. I've known for some time, and each day I wake up, I thank God that I'm still alive."

The shock of such a revelation sent Avery dropping into the nearest chair. His uncle was dying, and yet this was the first Avery had heard the news. No wonder the man had pushed hard for him to marry this season.

"Uncle Leo . . . I'm so sorry."

The duke added several trinkets to the crate. "I appreciate your sympathies, but more than anything, I hope you'll learn from my poor example, Winfield."

"Your poor example? I disagree. You've worked tirelessly to keep Beechwood running."

Moorleigh's chuckle held no merriment. "That estate, with its good memories and poor ones, means the world to me. But no matter how much you love them, land and legacy can never adore you in return, nephew. In the end, they'll not remember you or cherish you or prize all that you have shared of yourself. Only people can do that."

His uncle's quiet declaration left Avery shaken to his core, though he still managed to rise to his feet. "Is there anything I might help with, Uncle?"

"No. But your grandmother may wish for company . . . when my time comes."

Avery offered a solemn nod of understanding. "I'll come to Beechwood the instant someone sends for me."

"Good. Now I must finish overseeing the packing of the house."

His dismissal was clear as was the return to their usual formalities. Still, Avery paused on his way to the door to say, "I wish you a safe and pleasant journey."

"Thank you, Winfield. You'll see yourself out, won't you?"

"I will."

Avery was barely aware of the commotion in and out of the house as he returned to his carriage outside. He wasn't sure why he'd felt the need to visit his uncle today, but it had been the right thing to do. Avery's only grief was in not coming sooner and not being someone his uncle could confide in.

What of Moorleigh's allusion to his regrets in his younger life? Avery ran his hands down his face in weariness. Did they apply to him too? And what about the duke's words regarding the emptiness of land and legacies?

Instead of lightening, the load pressing down on him had increased, along with a greater sense of loss and confusion. He'd made a mess of things with Gwen, and in some ways, with his uncle too. But how could he rectify his relationships with both these people who were important to him? Where could he find the help he was beginning to see he desperately needed? The lonely clatter of the carriage wheels against the street was his only answer.

Chapter 16

"Shall I wait for you out here?" Gwen's aunt waved her hand to encompass the small foyer outside Dr. Smithfield's office.

Gwen nodded, one hand pressed against her middle where flutters of eagerness had been quivering all morning. "Thank you for coming with me, Aunt Vivian."

"You're most welcome, my dear."

Dr. Smithfield opened his door. "Miss Barton, a pleasure to see you again. Come in."

Her aunt offered her an encouraging smile as Gwen crossed the threshold into the office. Surely this was her real purpose in coming to London. After today, she'd be on a path to regaining full mobility in her foot and in her life. Then, once she returned to Heartwell House, she would be able to provide them with more physical labor in addition to her money. She would have a useful and valuable life, and she could content herself with that.

"If you'll take a seat and remove your shoe and stocking, Miss Barton."

As she did so, Gwen felt a flicker of awkwardness. No one had seen her injured foot for years now, except for herself and various maids. But the doctor didn't act aghast at the sight, which brought her some relief.

Dr. Smithfield helped her to sit on the examination table located to one side of the room, then he instructed her to extend both legs in front of her. For several long minutes, the only sound in the room came from the ticking of the wall clock and the occasional murmur from the doctor as he felt the bones in her foot and rotated the limb in different directions. Then he asked her to bend and straighten her leg as well as do the same with her foot. Gwen tried her best, but she couldn't keep her foot completely aligned with her leg without wincing with dull pain.

"Does that hurt?" the doctor asked, though not unkindly.

Gwen nodded. "Somewhat, yes. But I'm sure that's to be expected." She offered him an optimistic smile, but the doctor didn't return the gesture. If anything, his expression grew more somber as he slowly rotated her foot again.

Her excitement began to bleed into concern even before Dr. Smithfield straightened beside the table and looked directly at her. "How long were you in bed after the accident?"

"A few weeks." Gwen couldn't remember exactly. "Our doctor informed us that getting rest was the best thing for me."

Dr. Smithfield glanced down at her foot. "Yes, but you also should have been exercising your foot. Kneading the muscles, flexing the limb, bearing weight on it—all of those things would have been far more beneficial than bed rest."

"Wh-what are you saying? Is there nothing to be done?"

He blew out a sigh, his expression pained with compassion. "There's no harm in trying such exercises now, Miss Barton."

Her heart thudded at his hesitant tone. "Will they give me more mobility?"

"You can loosen the muscles that way, which will likely mean less pain and tightness. However . . ." The doctor gave a sad shake of his head. "I'm afraid the damage to your foot in terms of mobility is not likely to ever be restored, not after so many years."

A faint roar filled Gwen's ears. She gripped the edges of the examination table with her gloved hands. It was too late. That's what he was telling her. She'd never be able to do the things she had once done before the accident. Things like run and dance and stand in one place for longer than thirty minutes without extreme pain. Instead she'd remain as she was—partly broken and largely useless at helping her beloved Heartwell House outside of her money.

"Thank you for your time, Dr. Smithfield." She managed to keep her tone decorous and sincere. After all, it wasn't his fault he couldn't fix her foot. Everything inside Gwen begged her to slip to the floor and give into the tears rising in her throat. But she wouldn't cry here. Pressing her lips together, she climbed off the table and limped to the chair to put on her stocking and shoe.

"I'm sorry I am unable to do more."

Gwen attempted a smile, but her mouth refused to turn up fully. "That's why we need more doctors like you. Those who can help children in their youth while they are still healing, before the consequences of their illnesses and mishaps can no longer be changed."

"I hope you'll contact my colleagues in America, Miss Barton," Dr. Smithfield said as he accompanied her to the door. "I feel confident one, if not both of them, would be eager to help your cousin in his work."

She nodded, then stepped from the office into the foyer. Her aunt stood and gave Gwen a searching look. "Goodbye,

Dr. Smithfield," Gwen said. "Again, thank you for all of your help."

"I wish you the very best in your endeavors, Miss Barton."

Aunt Vivian led the way out of the building. The driver assisted both them inside the waiting carriage. "It didn't go as you wished, did it?" her aunt asked in a soft voice as they sat facing forward.

"No, it didn't." She coughed to dislodge the lump of suppressed tears from her throat. "Had we done more after the accident, it might be different. But there's nothing to do now to reverse the damage or regain full mobility."

Her aunt clasped Gwen's hand between both of hers. "I'm so sorry, Gwen. What upsetting news, especially after having such high hopes."

Gwen squeezed her eyes shut as several tears broke free and slid down her cheeks. "I really thought he could do something, but I'll stay just the way I am."

"And there's nothing wrong with that, my dear." Aunt Vivian tightened her grasp. "You have grown into a compassionate, beautiful, strong woman, Gwen. Your limp is of no consequence to your character."

Arguments settled on her tongue, but Gwen swallowed them back. How could she explain? How could anyone understand that the last of her expectations and plans had been shattered with Dr. Smithfield's prognosis? Regardless of what others thought of her, she had little to offer the world or Heartwell House, and no amount of admirable characteristics would change that.

⁓⟡⟡⟡⁓

Avery clapped his best friend on the shoulder as the two

of them regarded the crowded ballroom. "I appreciate you securing an invitation for me this evening, Linwood. I'm in your debt."

"The only debt I want you repaying is one of explanation." Linwood arched an eyebrow at him. "Why did you need to be here tonight?"

Avery's reason for being here was to talk with Gwen. She'd been avoiding him for nearly a week. He had sent her several notes, asking her to go riding or to visit another orphanage. But she'd declined them all. When he'd learned she would be in attendance at tonight's ball, his growing desperation to see her, to figure out what had happened between them, had driven him to beg his best friend for a last-minute invitation.

"I'd like to speak with Gw—with Miss Barton," he answered honestly.

Linwood nodded, then glanced to where his wife stood talking with several other women. "Love requires a great deal of effort, doesn't it? It's not the smooth course we often believe it to be."

"What do you mean?" Avery shifted his weight. "I said nothing about love."

His best friend slapped a hand on Avery's shoulder this time. "You didn't have to, Winfield. I've never known you to willingly attend a ball, let alone beg for an invitation. You're not here simply because you have nothing else to do tonight." He twisted Avery around, so they were both facing the spot where Gwen sat along the wall. "You're here because of her."

"Precisely," he grumbled. "Because she and I need to speak."

He started across the room in Gwen's direction. Still, Linwood's annoyingly amused chuckle reached his ears, in spite of the rise and fall of conversation and the tuning of the orchestra's instruments. He glared in annoyance at no one in particular as he continued working his way through the crowd.

His best friend was wrong. Avery wasn't in love. If he were, then he'd have some rather difficult decisions to make regarding his future—and Gwen's. No, they were nothing more than friends . . . or at least they had been, and he hoped very much that before the night was out they would be friends again.

As usual, Gwen exuded grace and beauty. Tonight she wore a purple ball gown with jet-black beading that attractively set off her dark hair. But her gaze, when she caught sight of Avery approaching, held none of its normal eagerness. If anything, she appeared sad.

"Mr. Winfield," she murmured. She looked away as he sat in the seat next to hers.

Thankfully, Gwen's mother and ardent suitors were absent at the moment. "Miss Barton, how are you?"

"I'm rather tired." She waved her hand, which was encased in a long glove. "Tired of everything here."

The note of finality in her voice brought a flicker of panic. "Are you leaving, then?"

"No, not yet. Not until the season ends." His relief was instant, especially when she finally turned to face him. "You'll be pleased to know I saw Mr. Hanbury several times this week."

Avery narrowed his gaze in frustration—and more than a little jealousy. "I told you not to see him alone, Gwen."

"I didn't." Her chin lifted a notch. "We've simply attended the same social events, including one last Friday after our . . . outing . . . along the Thames. Each time, he acted as if nothing had happened. I would say he's even spoken more to me than he did before."

Settling back in his chair, Avery surveyed the couples making their way onto the dance floor as the first song began. "That's exactly what someone in that profession is trained to do. To hide their real intentions and secrets."

"They certainly do."

This time she leveled him with a piercing look that made him swallow, hard. "Are you angry with me?"

"Why should I be angry with you?" But she twisted slightly away from him as she said it. "You've been nothing but honest with me, *haven't you*, Avery?"

Something in her tone sent alarm snaking through him again. "I've tried to be, yes."

"Except with yourself," he thought he heard her whisper.

This was not the conversation he'd been hoping to have with her. Perhaps sharing how much he'd missed her would help. "I was sorry you weren't able to come riding again. Or to see another orphanage." He boldly reached out and rested his hand on hers. "I've missed our outings."

"I returned to Dr. Smithfield's office." Gwen glanced down at their hands. "He looked at my foot."

He couldn't deny a sliver of disappointment that she hadn't asked him to accompany her again, but Avery also understood the private nature of such a visit. "What did he say?"

"He can't help me." Her words were barely audible. "I waited too long to do something."

The pain her admission stirred inside him was surely as keen as if the news had been about himself. "You were only a child at the time. How could you have known?"

She slipped her hand from beneath his and swiveled her knees, forcing Avery to lower his arm. "If I had exercised the muscles in my foot all those years ago, I would have likely gained back full mobility. As it stands, I can only hope to ease

some of the pain, but I'll never be able to do what I used to."
Her chin dropped. "What's worse is that I have nothing to
offer Heartwell House now, aside from my money."

The despair in her expression tugged deeply at him.
Avery wished he could comfort her by holding her hand again
or taking her into his arms. If only they weren't in a crowded
ballroom. Instead he'd have to satisfy himself with words and
hope she sensed he shared her sorrow.

"Gwen . . ." He waited for her to peer over at him again
before he went on. "I'm so very sorry. I know how much you
hoped and planned for a different answer. You still have
plenty to offer the orphanage, though. You have your passion
for kindness, your intellect, your beliefs. Those are surely
worth as much as any donation of money or physical labor."

There was an unmistakable glimmer of tears in her lovely
hazel eyes, which still looked clouded with doubt. Avery had
to fight the desire to caress her cheek as he'd done the other
day in the alley. "What will you tell your cousin?"

"The truth." The hopelessness that settled onto her pretty
face cut like a knife through him. "Perhaps I can increase the
amount of money I can give them if I do marry and convince
my husband to lend support from his own funds, as well."

Her response bowled him over as if she'd struck him.
"Who would you marry?"

"I still have suitors," she said, blushing.

Avery shook his head with confused irritation. "You
mean Lord Whitson or the infamous Mr. Hanbury? You can't
be serious, Gwen."

"I'm quite serious. Not that it's any concern of yours."

He hadn't come here tonight to argue with her, but he
also couldn't sit by and let her throw her life away. A loveless
society marriage might be enough to make some women
happy, but not her—not his Gwen. "So you'd risk a lifetime of

unhappiness in a loveless marriage in order to gift these orphans a larger pot of money?"

"Yes. I mean, no. Oh, I don't know," she countered in a choked voice. "Anything worthwhile requires risk. We can't keep our hearts walled off from everything and everyone, including God, and hope to still have the love and happiness we all yearn for."

Avery instinctively recognized she was no longer talking about herself—she was talking about him. The realization sent a sharpening ache through him, one Avery wanted desperately to escape. "I've risked a great deal to do what I do, Gwen. I've risked my safety and my chance to marry and have a family."

"That isn't risk, Avery. Your profession has let you hide, let you run away." Gwen peered down at her lap, where her hands were gripped together. "Tell me, when was the last time you let anyone see or know the real you? When was the last time you risked letting someone else see you for who you really are?"

His thoughts fell from his mouth before he could think to check them. "With you."

The smile she gave him held nothing but sadness. "I know, and yet you still kept back a part of yourself, didn't you?"

He didn't know what to say. Not when she was right. "I—"

"It's all right, Avery." Gwen stood, resignation rolling off her like waves. "I'm grateful I could help you, and I appreciate your help in return."

Avery hurried to his feet as well. Why did this feel like goodbye? "What are you saying?"

"That our partnership has come to an end." She offered

him her hand, which he took in his. "Goodbye, Mr. Winfield. I'll remember with fondness every moment we shared."

Before he could think of a reply, she released his hand and limped away. Avery watched her go, too stunned to move or think. At last, he sank back down into his chair. His chest felt tight, his lungs unable to drag in a full breath in the smothering heat of the ballroom. He gulped in a harried breath and hung his head.

He'd lost her. Somehow he'd lost his dearest friend, the woman he cared deeply for. The woman he'd even come to . . . Anguish rushed over him, bringing cutting clarity. Linwood had been right. Avery had fallen in love with Gwen. But his realization had come too late. She didn't love him in return—or at least she didn't anymore.

Avery stared at the floor, his thoughts spiraling in so many directions. Gwen had accused him of not risking his heart, and she'd been right. But he could change, couldn't he? *Can't I, God?*

It was the closest thing to a prayer that he'd voiced in almost twenty-two years. And yet he felt something shift inside. He might have lost Gwen, but he didn't have to lose everyone in his life. Standing, he strode purposely toward the open doors of the ballroom. After what had happened last week with Hanbury, Avery had already recognized the need to appear to back away from the investigation. To let Hanbury, and the man's superiors, think Avery had given up. Only he wouldn't spend his temporary reprieve from spy work by staying here and brooding over Gwen. No, he was going home—for a much overdue visit.

⁕⁕⁕

Another ride in Hyde Park with Lord Whitson the next

morning left Gwen with a pounding headache and serious doubts about her rash plan to marry either the earl or Mr. Hanbury. Lord Whitson had been his usual arrogant self. Only this time, it wasn't the exclusive invitations he'd received that brought out his irritating pride. It had been a conversation about Avery. How well did Gwen know him? Was he one of her suitors? And finally, in a boastful tone that made it clear the earl thought the advantage was all on his side, what did Mr. Winfield have to recommend himself beyond a future title?

Gwen had denied that Avery was her suitor, since he wasn't. They were simply good friends. But she hadn't been able to resist defending his character to the earl. Avery might not have chosen to risk in love, but that didn't make his many admirable qualities obsolete either. Thankfully Lord Whitson had dropped the topic after that.

Massaging her forehead, Gwen peered out the rain-soaked window in the library. She had a rare afternoon to herself, one free of social obligations. But even reading held no appeal for her today. All she could think of doing, all she wanted to do, was go on an outing with Avery. Such a thing would be pointless, however, since she'd told him goodbye last night. It was going to take time for her heart to align with her head in believing that Avery Winfield was no longer a part of her life.

A smothering sense of grief threatened to overwhelm her, driving Gwen from the room. She needed time alone, she decided as she ascended the stairs, away from her mother's constant questions about which beau Gwen admired the most. She'd already changed out of her riding habit, so all that was required for an outing were her hat and gloves, plus the use of the carriage and a footman to accompany her.

Gwen readied herself and made the appropriate arrangements with the butler. "I'm taking the carriage," she informed her mother, who was sewing in the drawing room.

"You're going out alone?" Cornelia's eyebrows jumped toward her hairline.

Suppressing a sigh, Gwen shook her head. "No. One of the footmen is coming with me."

"Fine, then. See that you're back in time to change for dinner."

"I will."

She started from the room, but a niggling thought had her turning back to face her mother. "Why do want me to marry someone with a title, Mother? I'd like the real answer. Not the one about being admitted into the upper echelons of society."

"Why?" Cornelia echoed as she set down her sewing. "Because I want you happy, Gwenyth. That's all I've ever wanted for you."

Her answer echoed what Aunt Vivian had shared the other day. Gwen considered saying nothing more. Yet what good had holding back done her in the past? Maybe things would be different between her and her mother if she had tried harder to understand and was more forthcoming about her thoughts and feelings.

"What if I'm happy as I am," she said gently, "spending my days helping Cousin Dean with his orphanage? Would that be so bad?"

Gwen expected a sharp retort from her mother, but instead Cornelia's tone was softened by sorrow. "Happy, maybe, but every day would be a struggle."

Her mother ran a fingertip over the stitches she'd sewn. "I so wanted the doors that were shut to me to swing wide open for you, Gwen. Then you had your accident." A visible shudder ran through her. "I feared all of my hopes and plans would be for naught, that you would be unable to enter society or even leave your bed at all, but you adapted. You still had something to offer the world by way of your beauty and your fortune, so all wasn't lost."

"I remember you sat in a chair right by my bed for days after the accident." Gwen hadn't recalled that particular memory in a very long time. Her mother had even missed several large social events to stay near her.

"There wasn't anywhere else I needed to be," her mother replied in a quiet tone. The vulnerability on her face was something Gwen had never seen before. "Just remember that happiness is largely what we make of it, Gwen. That being said, I expect you not to toss away what you've been given, what you could achieve, for the sake of independence or some romanticized idea of freedom."

A mixture of sadness and compassion prompted Gwen to cross the room to Cornelia's side. She didn't agree with everything her mother had voiced, but for the first time, she felt as if she understood the woman's hidden hopes and fears.

"Thank you for caring for me back then, Mother." She bent and placed a kiss on Cornelia's cheek. "And for bringing me to London."

For one brief moment, a tender look filled her mother's eyes. Then Cornelia took up her sewing again, and all traces of raw emotion disappeared. "Does this mean you've made a decision about which suitor you intend to encourage?"

Gwen shook her head. "I've made no decisions yet, but I will think on it."

"That's all I ask, though you will need to hurry. The season will be over in a month."

Stepping from the room, Gwen followed the assigned footman out of the house. He held an umbrella over her as she moved to the carriage. "Where to, miss?" the driver asked after helping her inside.

"St. Paul's Cathedral," she answered. She hadn't thought of it until that moment, but Gwen felt the rightness of the destination.

She settled against her seat, her back damp from the weather, as the carriage got under way. It felt strange to have another man besides Avery seated across from her, especially one who ignored her. Her own gaze flitted to the window to stare at the rainy street beyond as the conversation with her mother repeated in her thoughts.

In one regard, she and her mother were not so different—they both still held to the belief that Gwen had little to offer the world, other than perhaps her fortune. The awareness of that pinched at her yearning for peace like a shoe that didn't fit. And yet wasn't that what heiresses, especially ones with a disability, could contribute to society? Their money and, hopefully, in time heirs and heiresses of their own? Everyone around her believed that notion.

Everyone, that is, except Avery.

Leaning her forehead against the window, Gwen shut her eyes at the recollection of his words from last night. *You still have plenty to offer the orphanage. You have your passion for kindness, your intellect, your beliefs. Those are surely worth as much as any donation of money or physical labor.*

Could Avery be right? The possibility settled like a balm over her troubled heart.

She'd longed to do more for Dean and Amie's endeavor with the orphan children and had believed providing substantial funding was the answer. It wasn't the only one, though, was it? After all, while Dean had used nearly all of his inheritance to open the orphanage, the funding wasn't ultimately what had continued to make Heartwell House a success. That accomplishment was the result of her cousin's, and later his wife's, strong desire to assist and champion the helpless, the innocent, and the suffering of the city's children.

That same passion burned brightly in Gwen, especially after her own childhood experience. And as Avery had wisely shared, that was worth as much as a donation. Dean wouldn't want her to commit to a loveless marriage in order for her to give him more money. He would want her to be happy in a marriage with a man she loved and who loved her as Dean and Amie did.

The carriage stopped and Gwen opened her eyes to see the grand steps of the cathedral out the window. After assisting her from the vehicle, the footman led the way into the majestic building. Once inside, though, he indicated he'd wait for her near the entrance until she was ready to leave.

Gwen walked slowly across the checkered floor. She was unsure of where she meant to go until she came upon the spot where Avery had asked if he could call her by her Christian name. Locating a nearby chair, she lowered herself into the seat.

Her first visit here with Avery was not so long ago, and yet she could hardly believe she hadn't known him before coming to London. Of all the men she'd met, he was the one who'd accepted her exactly as she was from the beginning and had championed what she could be. Not by regaining the use of her foot but by shoring up her confidence in what she'd already had to offer the world.

It no longer seemed improbable that he'd been the injured man in the opera box. Gwen had experienced a feeling she never had known before as they'd kissed, and that feeling had only grown the more she had come to know Avery. Now she recognized it for what it was—love. She'd fallen in love with her man from the opera, with her sparring dinner partner, and her greatest friend and confidant. But, as wonderful and kind as Avery was, as open as he'd become about faith, he still didn't return her feelings.

Tears blurred the ornate ceiling above as Gwen lifted her gaze in that direction. "Why did we meet at all, God?" she whispered, her earlier ache filling her throat.

Was it simply to help her realize she needed to be herself, regardless if she married or not? Or was it so she could help him with his spy work? Perhaps their meeting had been required so Gwen would know what it felt like to be in love, to be seen for herself and not for her fortune or her limp, so she might recognize love in the future.

The latter thought brought her a little bit of comfort, but it didn't ease her sorrow for long. She couldn't imagine falling in love again or finding someone she wished to be with more than Avery.

Gwen lowered her chin, sending several tears dripping onto her lap. If only she'd told him what she felt last night, instead of allowing her anger-coated grief to have its say. It might not have changed anything, though she'd never seen Avery so miserable as he had looked as she'd bid him goodbye. What if she had given up too easily? He hadn't even told her the truth that he was the injured gentleman from the opera.

"I need to tell him how I feel." It was half-thought, half-prayer. But the murmured words brought a solace that didn't vanish after a moment or two.

Gwen brushed at her wet eyes and lifted her head. God had brought her and Avery together all those weeks ago—she knew it. Still, it made sense that Avery might not wish to risk his heart when Gwen hadn't yet voiced the feelings in hers. She stood and moved toward the exit, her pulse beating double-time with hope, determination, and fear. He might still choose a life without her, but she would never know what might have been if she left things as they were.

After she and the footman returned to the carriage, Gwen gave the driver the address for Avery's townhouse. She withdrew one of her calling cards from her purse, which also held a pencil. She scrawled a quick note on the back, then gave the message to the footman.

The young man hurried through the rain to the front door. Gwen watched from the carriage as the door opened. But the exchange between the footman and the butler took less than a minute. "I'm sorry, Miss Barton. Mr. Winfield is away from town," the footman explained as he dropped onto the seat across from her.

A curl of alarm unwound inside Gwen as she accepted her card back. "Do you know where he went?" Had his spy work taken him elsewhere? She didn't think so, given that Mr. Hanbury was still in London, but maybe Avery had been given another assignment.

"He's at the family's estate near Exeter."

She nodded acknowledgement, though the man's answer didn't squelch all of her concern. What if Avery didn't return until after the season, until after she'd left England for good? "Did the butler say when Mr. Winfield will be back?"

"No, miss."

Gwen swallowed her disappointment and instructed the driver to take them to the Rodmills' home. Avery might be gone for now, but she wasn't giving up on him yet, not after her realization in the cathedral. She would write him a letter, and then she would enlist the help of Lord and Lady Linwood to discover where to send it. Once he received her letter, he would need to take the initiative from there and decide if he was willing to risk his heart with Gwen. Either way, she wouldn't stop hoping and praying that he would do just that.

Chapter 17

"It's a blessing to have you home, Avery."

His grandmother smiled at him over her teacup, her hands holding the china piece steady despite her advanced age. Teatime was outside this afternoon, beneath the shade trees. The peace and quiet alone had been as much a comfort to Avery as seeing Rosalind Winfield and Uncle Leo again. They had both been shocked when he'd shown up in a rented carriage yesterday.

"However"—Rosalind lifted an imperious eyebrow—"you aren't here merely to see your grandmother and uncle, are you? Another reason has brought you back to Beechwood unannounced."

Avery chuckled as he set his cup onto the table covered in crisp linen. His grandmother's discernment and pointed looks, coupled with her unconditional love, had drawn out a great deal of private information from him during his boyhood and youth.

"You know me too well, Gran." When she made no reply, he shifted nervously in his chair, his gaze wandering to the pond. His uncle had finished his tea and now sat beside a fishing pole. Very few people had ever seen this relaxed side to the duke. "Yes, there are other reasons I'm home. One of them is Uncle Leo."

Sadness filled Rosalind's brown eyes, the same shade as Avery's, as she glanced at her oldest son. "He told you."

"Right before he left London," Avery answered. "I only wish he'd told me sooner."

His grandmother regarded him with a kind expression. "He wanted to tell you, my boy, but you weren't ready to hear it. I'm glad you finally were and that you came to spend some time with him too. It means a lot, though he likely won't say it."

Her gentle art of agreeing with his mistakes, while not making him feel judged or inferior, reminded Avery of Gwen. The ache that had taken up residence inside his chest since she'd bid him farewell surfaced again. "I'm also here because . . ." He pushed his next words from his mouth, knowing he needed to say them to someone. "I believe I've found the girl I love, Gran. The only trouble is, she told me goodbye."

"Oh, Avery." Her voice held unmistakable excitement and shared regret. "Who is she?"

"She's from America. Her name is Gwen."

Rosalind glared at him. "That's all you have to say about the woman who finally captured your heart?"

"Very well." He laughed again. "She's extraordinary. As a child, she suffered an accident that left her with a permanent limp. But it hasn't made her bitter at all. On the contrary, I've never met someone so compassionate or strong. Or so honest." He sent his grandmother a playful look. "She reminds me a great deal of you, actually."

Her nod of approval accompanied her warm smile. "I should like to meet this girl."

"I told you, Gran, she wants nothing more to do with

me." Avery studied the crumbs on his plate, his grief at Gwen's goodbye cutting anew. "She bravely confronted me about not risking my heart and about running away from myself and others . . . and she was right."

Leaning forward, Rosalind extended her hand and rested it on top of Avery's. "Did you tell her why?"

"Why I haven't risked myself?" He shook his head. "I only discovered the answer myself a short time ago."

Her thin, lined fingers squeezed his strong ones. "You fear becoming like your father."

He lifted his head and stared at her in amazement. "How did you know?"

"I've sensed that worry in you since your father died."

"Then you understand why I have to accept that Gwen is lost to me."

Rosalind drew her hand back and straightened in her chair. "Fiddlesticks. Where is that intelligence and drive that earned you top marks at university?" She didn't wait for him to reply. "When will you learn you aren't your father, Avery? You are your own man, with your own set of strengths, talents, and weaknesses." She waved her hand in the air. "However, you are very likely to end up in as much pain as he was if you keep love at a distance."

"Is that what you think I've done with you?"

Her tone gentled as she said, "No, my boy. But that is because I was determined you would know I wouldn't leave you as your mother had—and, in his way, your father too. You came to trust my love, Avery. So my question to you is, do you trust Gwen?"

"With my life."

"What about with your heart?"

Avery ran his hand over his jaw, trying to see through the dread such a question still prompted deep inside him. What if his grandmother was right? What if he was in danger of having his greatest fears fulfilled because he wouldn't risk himself with others, particularly with Gwen? He loved her, of that he no longer had any doubt. But did he trust her as he did his grandmother?

His thoughts went to his first meeting with Gwen, when she'd been an unknown young lady bending over his injured form in the dark. He'd been in no position to bandage himself, which meant putting his trust in the hands of a kind stranger. And yet what had prompted him to kiss her back that night? It hadn't just been the emotions her kiss had elicited inside him. A part of him had responded because he *had* trusted her—a young woman who was willing to do all she could to aid a man she didn't even know. And she'd been quietly aiding him ever since.

"Yes, I trust her," he answered at last, his voice choked with emotion. "I've been more myself with her than with any other person, save for you and Mack and Linwood."

Avery couldn't share with his grandmother all the details of first meeting Gwen at the opera, but he could tell her a piece of it. A piece he hadn't yet admitted aloud to anyone. "I had the thought after we met that God might have had something to do with it."

"Do you still feel that way?" The hopefulness in her tone was evident as was the glitter of tears in her eyes.

He remembered his short but heartfelt petition to Heaven after Gwen's goodbye. Since then, he'd offered several more prayers, longer ones, even. He couldn't deny that he felt Someone was listening. Someone knew him and his triumphs and failures, his worries and hopes. God hadn't condemned him as his father often had, nor had God disappeared from him as his mother had. He'd been waiting all this time for Avery to finally reach out.

"Yes, I believe God had a hand in bringing Gwen into my life."

His grandmother blinked rapidly, then pinned him with a determined glance. "Then what are you going to do?"

"I may have squandered my chance with her, Gran." He spread his arms wide.

But she didn't soften. "Is she still in London?"

"Until the end of the season, yes."

"What about shortening your visit here to less than a week?" Her eyebrows arched again, prompting another laugh from him.

"You don't mind? I promise I'll return and stay for longer once the season is over."

Rosalind picked up her teacup, her lips twitching once more with a smile. "If it's to bring this Gwen to come and meet me, I shan't mind at all."

Grinning himself, Avery pushed back his chair and stood. He no longer felt defeated or burdened by fear. "Seeing as it's Sunday tomorrow, would you mind if I accompany you to services in the old Beechwood chapel?"

"I would love that, my boy."

So would he. "I'll take the train back to London on Wednesday." He tipped his head in the direction of his uncle. "Do you mind if I discuss something with Uncle Leo?"

"Not at all." His grandmother took a sip of tea. "Just know that you have gladdened my heart, Avery. Today and every day since you came into this world."

A lump in his throat prevented him from speaking, so he settled for a nod. Then he strode across the grass to his uncle's side. "How are the fish today?"

"As lazy as I feel," the duke replied, but his gaze twinkled with mirth. "Want to join me?"

Avery sat with his back to the same tree his uncle lounged beneath. "I have a confession, Moorleigh."

"That sounds serious."

"It is." He stared at the ripples the fish made in the still water. "I haven't wanted to inherit the title or even the estate." He lowered his head as fresh remorse washed over him. "I even hoped I could find another way to save the place without marrying."

Moorleigh nodded slowly. "I see."

"That's the trouble, Uncle. You don't see, because I was too much of a coward to tell you any of this sooner." Avery pushed out his breath. "But I've changed my mind. I want to be someone you can trust to carry on the legacy of the Moorleigh title and of Beechwood Manor. I've met a young lady, and if I can convince her to have me, I hope to marry her. Her fortune would certainly help the estate, though I would only be marrying her for love and no other reason."

His uncle didn't speak for a long moment. "What of your work with Captain Kell?"

"My . . ." The air left his lungs in a choked gasp. "H-how do you know about that?"

A rare smile appeared on the duke's mouth. "The captain came to speak with me first, nephew. I'm a longtime friend of the Kells, and he wanted to be sure I was in agreement with his plan to recruit you." Moorleigh turned to face Avery. "I told him that he would not find a finer candidate for whatever work he needed done for Britain."

"All this time, you knew." Avery let out a startled chuckle. "Why did you encourage me to marry, then?"

His uncle looked genuinely surprised by the question. "Why shouldn't you marry? If a wife supports you in your work, that's all that matters."

And Gwen would, Avery knew that now. "You're right."

"Well, I can't say I've heard that admission from you before."

Avery chuckled. "Only because I've been as stubborn as we Winfield men are prone to be."

"Ah, now it's you who is right," the duke said in an amused tone.

Delight and sadness mingled inside him. The two of them might have enjoyed more of this rapport years ago if Avery had been more willing to try to understand his uncle.

"I appreciate your faith in my abilities," Avery continued, "but after I finish up my present mission, I've decided to resign." He'd made the decision on the train ride to Exeter, and thankfully, he still felt good about it. "I want to spend my time with the people and places that matter most, not hidden away in the shadows, searching for secrets."

The recognition in his uncle's eyes told him Moorleigh understood the reference to their last conversation back in London. "You've become a wise man, Avery."

"Only because God has placed wise people in my path."

If the mention of God was a surprise to his uncle, the duke didn't show it. Instead he asked as he adjusted the angle of his fishing pole, "Can you afford to share any details about your current assignment? I'll admit I have wondered since Kell approached me what he's had you doing."

Avery suddenly wished he'd known of the duke's involvement sooner. The man would have been as welcome and wise an ally as Mack had been. Though maybe it wasn't too late. His uncle might be able to provide a new perspective or additional information on Avery's present mission.

"If you promise not to share any of what I tell you with anyone," Avery said with a grin, "I'll give you all the details, Uncle."

The duke bent close, a resolute and excited glint in his gaze. "Your secret is still safe with me, nephew."

⁓ᴏᴏᴅᴅᴅᴅ⁓

Gwen had barely finished breakfast when the butler announced she had a visitor. Her gaze went to the mantel clock. Who would be coming here so early? Her mother had already gone upstairs to change into a different dress to go shopping, so she was downstairs alone.

Maybe it was Avery here to see her. Perhaps he'd received the letter she'd sent him two days ago and had rushed back to London. However foolish an idea, Gwen couldn't surrender the hopeful notion until the butler spoke again.

"Shall I have her wait in the parlor, miss?"

"Oh . . . yes." So it wasn't Avery. "Thank you. I'll be along in a minute."

After the butler disappeared out the door, Gwen allowed herself a moment of disappointment. Then she smoothed the front of her skirt, straightened her shoulders, and proceeded slowly toward the parlor. Inside, she found Syble pacing the rug.

"Syble!" Gwen exclaimed with a smile. "What are you doing here?"

Her best friend rushed forward and grasped both of Gwen's hands in hers. "I know it's early, Gwenie. But this is the first I could slip away to see you since the ball last week, and I couldn't share everything in a note."

"What do you mean?" Up close she noticed the paleness of Syble's face. "What happened? Is it something with Mr. Kirk?"

Syble shook her head as she led Gwen to the settee. Only after sinking onto the cushions and tugging Gwen down beside her did Syble release her hands. "It's that unbearable Lord Whitson," she said, her tone full of annoyance. "He arrived at the ball after you left and asked me to dance."

Gwen nodded for Syble to continue. She'd been relieved that neither he nor Mr. Hanbury had shown up before she'd convinced her mother to leave.

"He wanted to know where you'd gone, and I told him you had gone home. Then he started his typical boasting."

"About his special social invitations?"

Syble frowned. "No, he was boasting about you."

"Me?" Gwen gave a confused shake of her head. "Why would he boast about me?"

Her best friend glared across the room as if the earl himself were standing there. "He's convinced you're more interested in him than Mr. Hanbury. He sounded so sure of himself that I couldn't stay silent."

"What did you say, Syble?" Shots of alarm moved through Gwen as though her consciousness suspected what was coming, even if her head didn't.

Syble glanced down at her hands. "I told him you hadn't made any decisions yet, and that there were at least two other men who had captured your interest."

Gwen's dread increased, along with the thudding of her heart. "Which men did you name?"

"Mr. Winfield," Syble half whispered, "and the gentleman you helped at the opera."

"Oh, Syble."

Gwen hadn't yet told her best friend about kissing Avery in the alleyway or about her theory that he was the man from the opera. But that didn't mean she wanted others hearing about that night. "Do you say the gentleman was hurt?"

"Yes." Syble lowered her chin in a look of pure dejection. "I didn't tell him about the kiss, though. Just that the stranger was injured, that you helped him, and that in the process, the two of you developed a special bond. Lord Whitson asked who the man was, and I informed him that you didn't know but were eager to find out."

She stifled a groan of frustration. Other than Mr. Hanbury, Lord Whitson was the last person she wanted knowing about her involvement in aiding the injured gentleman at the opera. Gwen considered telling Syble her discovery now, but she dismissed the notion. What if, in another moment of heated annoyance, Syble told the earl that the injured man and Avery were one and the same? Lord Whitson didn't need another reason to throw aspersions against Avery's character.

"I'm so sorry, Gwen." Her friend raised her head, revealing tear-filled eyes. "I shouldn't have let him irritate me so much."

Compassion prompted Gwen to give Syble's arm a gentle squeeze. "He irritates me too."

"Which is saying a lot," Syble said with a shaky laugh. "I know I shouldn't have told him all of that. Will you forgive me for being so impetuous?"

Gwen offered her a genuine smile. "Of course. You were only trying to defend me."

"I'd better get back." Syble darted a glance at the clock and rose to her feet. "I hope the man isn't even more unbearable now."

It was Gwen's turn to chuckle. "I hope so too. He's accompanying Mother and me to the opera tomorrow night. I only agreed because Avery is out of town."

"So it's Avery now?" Her best friend arched her eyebrows, her blue eyes twinkling. "When did this happen?"

"I'll tell you everything soon," she said as she stood.

Syble cast another look at the clock. "Fair enough,

especially since I really have to go. But I want to hear every little detail!" They started toward the door, but Syble paused at the threshold and turned back around. "Are you all right, Gwen?"

"I am, truly." Even if Avery didn't return her feelings, she knew she would be all right.

Her friend embraced her. "I'm glad to hear it. Good luck tomorrow night. I wish I was going, so I could give you a moment's reprieve from the earl at intermission."

"I wish you were too." Gwen walked with her into the foyer.

Syble waved and hurried out the door. Turning for the stairs, Gwen blew out a low sigh. She hadn't been looking forward to going to tomorrow's event with Lord Whitson anyway, but now, her reluctance had increased tenfold. Maybe it was finally time for her to inform the earl that she did not envision a life with him.

Her future was hopefully reserved for Avery, if he was willing. With that reminder, she climbed the stairs.

⟡

"Two missives for you, sir."

Avery picked up the envelopes from off the salver. He'd just returned to the house after a morning of fishing with Uncle Leo. As he headed to his room, he examined the letters. The first was a telegram. Could it be from Captain Kell? Avery broke the seal and removed the notice. He glanced at the name of the sender. It read *Gwen Barton*.

His heart sped up even as his steps down the corridor slowed. Avery read through the short message. *Meet me tonight at the opera. There's something I need to tell you. I'll be waiting in our opera box during intermission.*

Avery dropped into the nearest chair. His surprise gave way to relief and excitement as he read through the telegram a second time. Gwen wanted to see him! But what did she mean by *our opera box*? He wrestled with different possibilities, but the only one that made sense was the opera box where she'd helped him when he'd been injured. Which meant Gwen knew the truth about that night. Did she want to talk because she was angry? Or for some other reason?

Blowing out his breath, he studied the other envelope. Gwen's full name and her aunt's London address were listed there. Why had she written him and sent a telegram too? Avery furrowed his brow as he tore open the envelope, but he felt more curious than confused. Perhaps this missive would better explain the first.

Dear Avery,

I visited St. Paul's Cathedral again. And though it was as magnificent as before, it felt empty because you were not there to enjoy it with me. I've done a great deal of thinking about our last conversation. I was angry and hurt, but those feelings were as much about what I'd learned about my foot as they were about you.

Today, I feel differently in regards to both matters. You were right—I do have more to offer Heartwell House and the world than my fortune. Thank you for helping me see that. As far as you and I, there are things I need to tell you. And not in a letter. A very wise and dear friend has encouraged me from the beginning to keep being honest and brave and strong, so I will wait and share what I have to say to you in person.

For now, I want you to know that while I said goodbye, I wish I hadn't. I'm not ready for our friendship to end. Besides, I still need the information you promised to gather on the identity of the man I helped at the opera. I believe I know who *he is, but I would like it confirmed by you. If my guess is correct, I would very much like to share a <u>third kiss</u> with this extraordinary gentleman.*

> *Sincerely,*
> *Gwen*

A joyous laugh fell from Avery's mouth and echoed in the stillness of the hallway. His gaze returned to the two words she'd underlined. She knew the truth—somehow, she'd correctly guessed his identity. What was more, she'd called him a dear friend, one with whom she didn't want things to end. And she wanted to kiss him again!

Only he still didn't understand why she had sent the telegram. He examined both missives again, hoping for an explanation. There was definitely a sense of urgency in the shorter communication. Perhaps Gwen had written the letter first, then decided she didn't want to wait any longer to see him.

Well, he could certainly accommodate that desire.

He grinned as he stood. Avery found his grandmother seated at her writing desk in her sitting room. "Gran, I've decided to return to London today instead of waiting until tomorrow." He checked the time on the clock. "If I hurry, I can make the next train."

"Oh?" She set down her pen.

He lifted the envelopes. "Gwen wrote and sent a telegram."

"Does she still wish to have nothing to do with you?" Her eyes hinted at the smile she held back.

Striding toward her, Avery bent and pressed a kiss to her lined cheek. "No," he said, easing back. "She's decided to give me a second chance. In fact, she would like me to meet her where we first met—at the opera."

"Then you must get yourself to the opera." Her smile broke through as she gave his cheek an affectionate pat. "When you return, I hope it will be with your intended."

Avery straightened. "I hope so too."

After asking Mack to arrange for the carriage to convey them to the station, he raced up the stairs with an exuberance he hadn't felt in a long time. "Thank You, God," he whispered. "And please help me make it to the opera on time."

He had a second chance with Gwen, and he didn't plan to miss it.

Chapter 18

He was much later than he'd hoped. Avery tapped his fingers against his knee as the cab turned onto the Rodmills' street. He'd debated going straight from the station to his own townhouse to change into evening clothes, since the opera had already started. But Mack suggested Avery might want to be certain Gwen had gone to the performance as planned.

The cab had hardly come to a stop before Avery jumped out and rushed up the front steps. He knocked at the door. Several long moments later, the butler answered.

"Is Miss Barton at home?"

The man shook his head. "No, sir."

Then she'd gone to the opera after all. "Thank—"

"Winfield." Bert Rodmill appeared in the doorway. "Looking for Gwen?"

Avery nodded. "I didn't actually expect to find her here, though. I was told she'd be attending the opera this evening."

"She is, with Whitson, no less," Rodmill said with a sly smile. "You may need to make your move soon, old chap, before he does."

Not wanting to hint at his plans and hopes without

speaking to Gwen first, Avery sent the other man a confident smile. "Good night, Rodmill."

He returned to the cab, but as he climbed inside, an unexpected feeling of uneasiness settled into his gut, as though some instinct had been triggered. Perhaps it was only jealousy over Lord Whitson accompanying the woman Avery loved to the opera. Though he did find it rather odd that Gwen would orchestrate a meeting with him while in the company of another gentleman.

"Do you think it strange, Mack, that Gwen would go to the opera with the earl when she intends to meet me at intermission?" He'd already shared the general content of her letter and telegram with Mack before they departed Exeter.

Mack shrugged. "Maybe she planned to meet you first, then when the earl asked to escort her, she figured she'd already be there and that it might be awkward to tell him *no*."

"That's a fair point."

Avery attempted to brush off his disquiet during the ride to his townhouse. If he hurried, he could still make it to the opera in time for intermission. His and Mack's sudden arrival caused a stir among his household staff, but Mack took charge. Before long, Avery had exchanged his wrinkled travelling suit for a pair of neatly pressed evening clothes. He still felt on edge, though—much as he had the last time he'd attended the opera.

Would Hanbury attempt to harm him tonight? It wasn't likely. No one knew Avery was back from Exeter, unless they'd managed to sneak past his watchmen. Even then, Avery's plans to go to the opera weren't common knowledge to anyone save for himself and Gwen.

"Did you hear if anything suspicious happened around here while I was gone?" he asked Mack.

His valet shook his head. "Sounds as though things have been quiet."

Avery felt a measure of relief. Perhaps Hanbury had realized his error in sending his thugs after Avery, and as a result, the man had backed off. Although, the duke had voiced his skepticism that Hanbury was actually a spy.

"Sometimes the real culprit is not the most obvious one," Avery's uncle had intoned in a thoughtful voice.

Avery did up his cufflinks, his mind turning the duke's words over and over. Was there someone else he'd dismissed as a real suspect? He mentally shook his head, but that only increased his foreboding, instead of lessening it.

What am I missing, Lord?

As Mack helped him into his coat, Avery reviewed the three attempts made on his life. The first had been at the opera. Hanbury had been there that night. The second time had been in Hyde Park. Avery had seen Hanbury before his horse had been hurt. Lastly, the third had been along the Thames with Gwen when they'd been following after Hanbury. The quiet man was the only constant in each encounter.

Although . . .

Lord Whitson had been with Hanbury that day in the park and at the opera too. And hadn't Avery caught a glimpse of the earl's carriage right before he and Gwen had started to follow Hanbury?

He frowned at his reflection in the mirror. Could Lord Whitson be an accomplice? It was certainly plausible, given the longtime friendship between the earl and Hanbury. But he'd previously ruled out Lord Whitson as a suspect. The man had no obvious connection with Germany, besides speaking the language.

Still, something urged Avery to pursue the line of

thinking further. Hanbury and the earl had been together before each dangerous encounter Avery faced. The only exceptions were his and Gwen's ride in Hyde Park and the night Hanbury had accompanied Gwen and her mother to the theater. Both times the man had made no attempt to hurt Avery.

Was that because Gwen had been there too? Avery dismissed the idea after a moment. Gwen had been with him the day by the river, and that hadn't prevented anyone from sending assailants after both of them. The one person Avery hadn't seen during their ride and at the theater had been . . .

Icy fear filled his lungs as he whirled around. "It isn't Hanbury, Mack. The spy is Lord Whitson!"

"Wait. You mean the man who is with Miss Barton?"

"Yes." Avery wiped his hands down his face and tried to gather his muddled thoughts. "Gwen doesn't know it's him. I warned her away from Hanbury. But I didn't think to do the same with Lord Whitson. What have I done, Mack?"

His valet gripped him hard enough on the shoulder to break through his fear. "It was an honest mistake. You had greater reason to suspect the other man."

"I've got to warn Gwen." He strode toward the door, then stopped. "I need your help, though, Mack. How fast can you dress in a set of my evening clothes?"

The older man grinned. "Faster than you." He was already hurrying toward the dressing room. "What do you need me to do?" he asked as he exited, a pair of evening clothes in hand.

"You go for the constable, and I'll meet Gwen in the opera box. I'll bring her to you, then I'll find the earl." He leveled a somber look at his valet and trusted friend. "I need you to watch over Gwen."

Mack gave Avery a grim nod, all hint of amusement gone. "You can count on me, sir."

"I know." Avery swallowed hard and headed toward the door once more. "You'll have to go without a cravat, or tie it in the carriage, Mack. We've got to go."

He offered a silent prayer of gratitude as he hurried down the stairs, Mack right behind him. God had blessed him with insight beyond his own. Now Avery could only hope—and pray—Gwen would be protected and that between him, Mack, and God, everything would turn out right.

⁓⟫⟫⟫⟫⟫⟫⟫⟫⟫⟫

To Gwen's surprise, Lord Whitson had been anything but arrogant this evening. Before the performance had begun, he'd complimented her sincerely on her gown and had even asked her questions about her life back in New York with every indication of actual interest in her answers. Not once had he mentioned some exclusive social event or his dislike for Avery. Maybe tonight wouldn't be so tedious after all.

During one of the numbers, near intermission, he leaned close to whisper, "May I have a moment of your time—alone—during intermission?"

Did he wish to share his desire for her hand in marriage? If so, then she would need to tell him that she harbored no feelings for him in return. "Yes," she answered back.

When it was intermission, Gwen stood, along her mother and the earl. "Lord Whitson would like to speak with me alone, Mother."

Cornelia glanced between her and the earl and smiled. "I see. Then I'll proceed to the refreshment room ahead of you."

"Thank you."

Gwen followed Lord Whitson and her mother out of the

box. As Cornelia joined the crowd heading away from the boxes, the earl held out his arm to Gwen. She hesitated a moment, then slipped her arm through his.

"Your friend Miss Rinecroft told me all about the injured gentleman you helped the last time you were here."

"Oh?" This was a topic she hadn't expected him to bring up.

The lights in the corridor reflected off his smile. "What if I told you I knew the identity of your mystery man? That he's here tonight, in the same box where you met before?"

"He is?" Avery was here?

"Shall I escort you to him?"

Gwen nodded, her pulse sprinting with hope and excitement. "I'd be very grateful if you did." She hadn't expected Avery to return to London this soon, but she welcomed not having to wait any longer to know his reaction to her letter.

"I appreciate your help, Lord Whitson," she said as he guided her toward the famous opera box. She pressed her lips over adding how out of character it seemed for him. Though perhaps he was gallantly bowing out of the race for her hand and this was his way of showing that. Such courtesy might be unexpected, but it was certainly welcome. "I'm sure . . . *my mystery gentleman* . . . will appreciate it too."

Lord Whitson pushed through the box's curtains, tugging Gwen along behind him. "I'm counting on it."

The box was disappointingly empty, but that likely meant Avery was on his way. "Will you be joining my mother in the refreshment room?" Gwen asked. Instead of answering, the earl's grasp tightened on her arm. Gwen frowned. "You can release me now."

"Not yet." In the shadowed space, his face appeared almost sinister. "You must first understand your role, Miss Barton."

She frowned. Her arm was beginning to ache. "My role?"

"You will silently wait here for Winfield," he said as if she hadn't spoken. "When he arrives, you won't make a fuss or dare look in my direction. Is that clear?"

A glint of light reflected off the barrel of the pistol he suddenly produced. Gwen sucked in a sharp breath, her earlier enthusiasm turning to ash. Her heartbeat now raced for an entirely different reason than anticipation at being reunited with Avery.

"W-what's going on, Lord Whitson?"

The earl gave a bitter laugh. "You think Winfield could outsmart me? He escaped those other times, but he won't tonight. Not after he received your telegram, asking him to meet you here during intermission."

None of this was making any sense. The earl didn't seem to like Avery, but this went well beyond dislike. "You sent him a telegram claiming to be me?" Had Avery even received her letter?

"Clever, wasn't it? Your friend's slip of the tongue revealed your connection to Winfield, even if neither you nor Miss Rinecroft knew he was the man you'd helped."

Gwen looked away from the man's sneering gaze, but apparently not fast enough.

"Ah, I see," Lord Whitson said with a note of triumph. "You've already discovered the identity of your mysterious man. Then you know why I must succeed in disposing of him tonight. No mistakes this time."

The bewildering conversation at last came together inside Gwen's mind, crystallizing into clarity. "You're spying for the Germans."

The earl arched an appreciative eyebrow. "Winfield has been sharing secrets."

Their suspect hadn't been Mr. Hanbury after all. "Is that

why you've courted me?" she countered, anger pushing at her fear. "To get at Avery?"

"Not at all, my dear." As Lord Whitson leaned toward her, Gwen backed up as far as she could with her arm still in his grasp. "My interest in you has been genuine."

She glared at him. "Genuine enough that you'd send your miscreants after me to do me harm?"

"You were there by the river that day?" The man sounded openly surprised. "My apologies, Miss Barton. I didn't know. However, you managed to escape unharmed."

"Only to end up here tonight."

His expression hardened. "Precisely. And if you value your life and that of your mother's, you'll not reveal my presence to Winfield when he arrives. Which should be at any moment."

Finally, he released her arm. He turned a chair around and thrust Gwen into it. "Do you understand what I've said?" He brandished the pistol near her face.

"Yes," Gwen whispered through her dry throat. She understood perfectly.

The man she adored was now the fish, and she the bait.

⁂

Avery rushed down the nearly empty corridor of the opera house. Outside his and Gwen's box, he paused to catch his breath. Still, his heart continued to pound with equal parts dread and anticipation. Was Gwen here? Was she safe?

He pushed through the curtains and stilled at the sight of her. Had it really been mere days since he'd last seen her? It felt like a lifetime. Gwen sat facing the entrance to the box, her chin lowered. Her pale blue dress glowed in contrast to the slight dimness around her, reminding him of how she herself had brought welcome light into his world.

"Gwen," he said softly.

She lifted her head. "Avery, you came."

"I got your missives." He was about to rush forward, to sweep her into his arms, but something in her expression stopped him from moving closer.

"I sent the one . . ." A long pause followed her words before Gwen added, "first."

Avery furrowed his brow. Something wasn't right. He knew by her demeanor—Gwen appeared determined but also alarmed. She hadn't stood and hurried toward him either as he'd expected. Instead she continued to sit primly, her gloved hands clasped tightly in her lap.

"I came as soon as I received them."

She peered directly at him. "We . . ." Gwen cleared her throat. "I . . . hoped you would."

What did she mean by *we*? Her and her mother? No, that couldn't be right. She seemed to be trying to communicate a different message within her words. But what was it?

Was she upset with him for leaving town with matters so strained between them? "I'm sorry I didn't tell you I was leaving for Exeter."

Her tone remained calm, though there was an edge to it. "I understand, but I think your absence became common knowledge to some."

To some . . .

He fought an audible groan of frustration. Gwen was telling him that someone else had learned that he'd left town. And that someone, not Gwen, had sent him a telegram about meeting here tonight. Someone who knew Avery would come to the opera—just as he had all those weeks ago.

There was only one person who would have cause to trap him. He glanced at the shadowed corners of the box, fully certain now that he and Gwen were not alone.

"I find I'm rather tired this evening." Avery fell backward a step while throwing Gwen a meaningful look he hoped she could see and understand. "Shall we continue this conversation later?"

"Enough!" a hard voice snarled as Lord Whitson came forward. "The game is up, Winfield."

Avery forced his lips into a casual smile, in spite of the horror he experienced at seeing the man standing beside Gwen, a gun in his hand. "Lord Whitson. To what do I owe this pleasure?"

The earl wrenched Gwen onto her feet, causing her to wince in pain. Angered, Avery took a step forward.

"Stop right there or I shoot her." Lord Whitson aimed the gun at Gwen.

Avery froze at once, the panic from earlier chilling his veins again.

"You know why I'm here," the earl barked.

"To finish the job your thugs couldn't?"

Lord Whitson waved the gun. "You know what they say, don't you? If you want a job done right, you have to do it yourself."

"Is that why you've been spying for Germany? They couldn't manage their efforts without you?"

The other man's cold laugh rankled him. Gwen remained silent and still, but Avery could tell her shoulders were trembling. "Not everyone is as altruistic as you, Winfield."

"What do you mean?" If he could just keep the earl talking, Avery would have a greater chance of coming up with a plan to keep Gwen out of harm's way. He hadn't come all this way to lose her now.

Lord Whitson shrugged. "When my father cut off my spending last year, I naturally sought another source of revenue. Unfortunately for Captain Kell and Britain, the

Germans were willing to pay a higher price for my services—enough to tide me over until a well-placed marriage could bring in the real capital."

"You said your interest in me was genuine," Gwen remarked, her voice full of sarcasm.

"Oh, it was." The earl glanced down at her. "I was genuinely interested in your fortune."

With the man's attention momentarily off him, Avery hazarded another step toward him and Gwen. "How much will you get for disposing of me?"

"Not nearly enough for all my trouble." Lord Whitson shot him an ominous smile as he pointed the gun at Avery. "Though the satisfaction of besting you as I never could at university almost makes up for it."

Avery lifted his arms in the air in a show of submission. "You need to let Gwen go first."

"No, Avery. I won't leave without you."

Lord Whitson made a tsking noise. "I'm not as foolish as you think, Winfield. Miss Barton here has heard and seen far too much to escape now. *You* sealed her fate when you allowed her to become involved with you."

The earl's words slammed like a fist into Avery's chest, resurrecting his dormant fears and tearing at his confidence. Would any woman ever be safe with him? He swallowed hard. His mind was spiraling out of control, making it difficult for him to think clearly.

"Avery?"

Gwen's whisper reached his ears, though it seemed to come from the far side of a long tunnel. He lifted his head. What he could see of her expression conveyed more tenderness than he'd ever seen. In it, he also read an unmistakable, though silent message. *The earl is wrong. I chose my involvement with you, and I would choose it again.*

Her belief in him renewed Avery's belief in himself and cleared his mind of everything but the need to ensure they both made it out of this alive. He assessed the earl's position to him and to Gwen. In that instant, he knew exactly what he needed to do.

Thank You, he silently prayed. Once again he'd been blessed with insight beyond his own abilities tonight—as Avery had at other times in his life, though he was just now beginning to see it. "May we have a moment to say goodbye?"

"You have to the count of three before I pull the trigger," the earl said with clear impatience. "One . . ." Lord Whitson kept the gun trained on Avery's chest as he took a slight step away from Gwen.

It was the exact opening Avery had been hoping for. "My dear Gwen . . ."

"Two."

Avery stepped forward, bringing himself almost directly in front of her. "Trust me," he mouthed, tipping his head to the side. With wide eyes, she inched in that direction.

"Three!"

Pushing Gwen farther out of the way, Avery drove his shoulder into the earl's chest, tipping him off balance. The arm with the gun flew upward. As the gunshot blasted loudly above their heads, Avery propelled the two of them backward over the banister and plunging toward the seats one floor below.

⌒☾◊〗◊⌒

Gwen scrambled to free her feet from her dress so she could stand. Pulling herself up, she leaned over the banister. Below, Avery and the earl lay unmoving atop the theater seats.

"Avery!"

He'd risked his life to save hers. Snatching up her dress hem in one hand, Gwen turned and hurried as quickly as she could out of the box. People were already returning from the refreshment room. Or maybe the gunshot had roused them back to the theater.

She elbowed her way through the throng in the corridor. "Let me through. Please let me through."

"Where are you going?" her mother demanded as she approached Gwen.

Gwen hurried past her. "Avery's hurt. I have to see him."

"What are you talking about?" The rest of Cornelia's protests became muffled by the crowd as Gwen was finally able to work her way through.

When she reached the ground floor of the opera house, Gwen could hardly bear to put weight on her injured foot. Her harried pace had intensified her limp, along with the pain in her foot and leg. But she wouldn't allow her impediment to delay her in reaching Avery. The growing crowd downstairs was a different story. A mob of opera patrons stopped her progress at the doorway closest to where Avery and the earl had fallen.

"Please, I have to get through! I have to get inside." No one heeded her cries.

Tears of frustration temporarily blinded her. She had to reach Avery. Blinking rapidly, Gwen noticed a small opening in front of her. She seized it, forging her way through the swarm of bodies, heedless of the exclamations of annoyance around her.

At last she cleared the crowd of onlookers. Her gaze went to where she'd last seen Avery, but he wasn't there. Had he been taken away?

"Avery?"

His hoarse reply from the side of the theater weakened her knees with relief. "Gwen!"

She rushed forward to find him lying on the floor, his eyes shut tight, his right arm at an odd angle. An older man knelt beside him. Farther up the aisle, Gwen could see the prone figure of Lord Whitson. Several other gentlemen stood staring down at the earl, along with a constable who held what she assumed must be Lord Whitson's gun inside a handkerchief.

"Are you all right?" She dropped to her knees beside Avery and clasped his hand.

He winced and she softened her grip. "Mack here says I dislocated my shoulder. He's my valet and the best medic Britain has ever seen."

"You must be Miss Barton," Mack said, his smile friendly and approving. "It's a pleasure to meet you."

Gwen smiled in return. "You as well." She turned back to Avery. "How did the constable know to come here?"

"I sent Mack for him," he said as he opened his eyes. "After I realized Lord Whitson was our spy."

Our spy. The words filled her with a relieving sense of happiness. Avery still thought of them as a team. "Will the earl be arrested, then?"

"Sure enough." Avery's valet threw a glare at the other man. "Attempted murder and conspiring against Britain are serious charges."

As if Lord Whitson knew they'd been discussing him, he let out a bellowing howl. "My leg! It must be broken. How am I supposed to ride now?"

Avery chuckled. "I wish I could have seen his face when I sent us sprawling over the balcony."

"I was terrified." Gwen brought her hand to rest alongside his cheek. "I thought you might have been killed."

His gaze gentled in a way that made her pulse trip. Thankfully, Mack promptly rose and went over to talk to the constable, leaving them to themselves. "Not without first telling you that I got your letter. *Yours*, not Whitson's telegram."

"You already told me that," she said with a laugh.

"Yes, but I didn't tell you all that I had planned to say tonight." His fingers threaded through hers. "You were right, Gwen, in what you said at the ball. I've been afraid to risk my heart. However, unbeknownst to me until this week, you have gently and courageously claimed it little by little, piece by piece, ever since that night in the opera box."

Gwen's breath caught as much at his declaration as at his touch when he lifted their hands to his mouth and kissed her knuckle. "Are you saying that . . . that you're ready to risk your heart?"

"Indeed, my love, I am."

She leaned over him, mindful of his injury, and brought her lips near his. "We really need to stop meeting under such precarious circumstances, Avery Winfield."

"Oh, we shall," he whispered back, his grin sending tingles of feeling through her middle. "I'm resigning from my post with Kell. I'd rather spend my days with the people I love."

Surprised, Gwen inched backward. "You mean that?"

"I do." He released her hand to cup the back of her neck and drew her toward him again. "I love you, Gwen."

"And I love you."

She brought her mouth to his and kissed him ardently, unaware of anything and anyone until a sharp voice from behind disrupted the joyous moment. "Gwenyth Barton! What are you doing? What happened with the earl?"

Drawing back slightly, she glanced up to see that her

mother had successfully followed her to the first floor. "I turned down the earl, Mother, and have thrown myself at Mr. Winfield instead."

"What?" At her mother's shocked exclamation, Gwen and Avery shared a laugh.

"I'm afraid that means my reputation is now in shambles, Mr. Winfield," she said, smiling down at him.

He caressed the side of her face. "Fortunately, that's something I believe we can rectify at once." Twisting his head, he glanced at Cornelia. "Mrs. Barton, I would like to marry your daughter. I love her fully and completely and would like to start marriage negotiations immediately."

"Well . . ." Cornelia lowered her hand from where she'd pressed it against her bosom. "I suppose that can be arranged." She flicked her fan open and waved it before her flushed face. "After all, I knew my Gwen could make a more suitable match than the son of a marquess. The nephew of a duke is so much more dignified. My friends back home will be green with envy . . ."

Gwen looked at Avery and they started laughing again. When they stopped, he tugged her forward once more. Then despite her mother's crowing and the bedlam inside the opera house, they shared another long kiss.

Chapter 19

London, November 1908

"Here's your tea, Grandmama." Gwen passed the teacup to Rosalind Winfield, seated beside her inside Avery's uncle's townhouse.

Rosalind smiled warmly. "Thank you, Gwen."

The two of them had taken an instant liking to one another when Avery had brought Gwen and her mother to Beechwood Manor in August. She and Avery were engaged by then. Gwen had fallen as much in love with the country estate as she had with Rosalind and Uncle Leo. Even Cornelia had vocally approved of the house and grounds as entirely suitable for an American heiress, to Gwen and Avery's amusement.

Their wedding in the old Beechwood chapel had taken place in September, following which she and Avery had gone on a honeymoon trip to France. They'd returned to Beechood for his uncle's funeral later that month, then to London to put their philanthropy plans into action.

"Your Grace," a reporter said, his pen poised over his notepad. "May I ask you a few questions?"

Rosalind followed Gwen's gaze to where Avery stood

with a group of men, among them the reporter and a number of interested patrons. "It's still strange to hear him called by his title."

"I agree," Gwen said, filling her own teacup.

She'd never imagined herself being a duchess, living in England and married to a man of such honor and kindness and growing faith. But she couldn't be happier. Her husband caught her eye and winked. She gave him a secretive smile, then hid her amusement behind the rim of her cup.

"I can't believe before the month is out, this house will echo with children's voices." Gwen glanced around them. There was still furniture to purchase and most of the staff to hire for the new orphanage. But Mack had recommended a friend of his to serve as director, and Dr. Smithfield himself would be on call for emergencies as well as scheduled visits to the orphanage twice a month.

Avery's grandmother set her cup into its saucer. "I'm most impressed with what you and Avery have accomplished so far, my dear." Her lips twisted in a wry smile. "And in spite of my dislike of London, I'm grateful I chose not to miss your reception today so I might see all of this for myself."

"We're very glad you're here."

The only other people Gwen wished could have been here too were Dean and Amie. But understandably, they didn't feel they could leave Heartwell House for such a long trip. Her cousin had sent Gwen a wonderful letter, though, thanking her for her generous donation to the orphanage in New York and expressing his pride in continuing her work of compassion across the Pond.

"My love," Avery said, approaching them, his hand extended toward her. "The reporter is asking questions I've assured him you are far more capable of answering."

Smiling, Gwen set aside her tea and placed her hand in

his. He pulled her to her feet, pressed a kiss to her temple, and tucked her arm through his. Then he walked slowly with her across the room.

"Will you share with us, Your Grace, how you chose the name of the orphanage?" The reporter looked expectantly at Gwen.

She'd become more proficient at making speeches and answering questions since Avery had assumed the Moorleigh title, though it still made her nervous. However, Avery's free hand resting tenderly against the small of her back and their united vision never failed to give her courage, as they did in this moment.

"Certainly." Gwen lifted her chin. "My cousin runs an orphanage in New York City called Heartwell House. In choosing a name for our orphanage, I wanted to honor his work. And since the duke and I met one another at the opera . . ." She glanced at Avery, who grinned. Few people, save his grandmother and Mack, knew the full truth behind their first meeting. "We decided to name our orphanage Heartsong."

The men murmured approval. "Tell us again what sort of orphans you'll be accepting at Heartsong House," the reporter asked next.

"We'll accept any child," Gwen answered. "However, as my cousin has done, we hope to specialize in helping children who've suffered from childhood illness or injury."

The reporter nodded as he scribbled notes on his pad. "I heard you had a bout with injury yourself as a child, madam."

"You are correct." She smiled at the group. "When I was a young girl . . ."

✽✽✽✽

An hour later, the room stood devoid of everyone save

her and Avery. His grandmother had already been conveyed in the carriage back to the Winfield townhouse. Gwen followed Avery as he carried the tea things to the kitchen, where some of their regular staff were helping.

"I think it was a success," she said when they returned to the drawing room.

Avery nodded. "It was a brilliant idea to hold a tea reception, Gwen. You convinced those men to contribute quite generously."

"Thank you," she said, blushing at his praise and intent look. "I suppose the carriage will be back by now."

She moved toward the front door to double check, but Avery tugged her to a stop in the foyer. "You are extraordinary, my love."

"As are you." Gwen draped her arms around his neck. "I appreciate you sharing this endeavor with me, Avery."

He rested his forehead on hers. "We do work rather well together, don't we?"

"Yes, we do. Be it saving lives, spying, running orphanages." She kissed him, then whispered against his lips, "Or being a father and mother."

His eyes widened as he eased back to peer into her face. "You mean you're . . ."

"Yes." Gwen smiled fully at him. "That's where I went yesterday afternoon. To see the doctor."

Cupping her face, he kissed her until they were both out of breath. "Thank you, Gwen, for helping me see that love is worth the risk. As a husband, and as a future father."

"You're most welcome." Tears of joy slipped from her eyes and onto his fingers. "I feel grateful every day, Avery, that it was me who found you in that opera box."

His answering smile filled her heart to overflowing. "So am I, my love, so am I."

From the 1870s through the end of the Edwardian Era, more than a hundred heiresses travelled from America to England in search of husbands. These "dollar princesses" were searching for the two things they hadn't been able to claim back home—a title and superior social status. Many of the land-rich members of the English peerage were more than happy to accommodate these heiresses and their determined mothers. After all, large country estates took a great deal of money to maintain.

Most of these marriages were based on mutual benefit rather than on love or affection. However, there were couples who found love and happiness within their transatlantic marriages.

In 1909, Captain Vernon Kell, a linguist and a captain in the British army at that time, assisted in the formation of the Secret Service Bureau, which was the precursor to Britain's Security Service or MI5 and the Secret Intelligence Service or MI6. For the purposes of this story, though, I have the bureau already in existence two years prior to its inception.

Even before the start of the first World War, there were tensions between Germany and England as the two countries raced to build up their navies. There was great concern in 1909 that a large network of German spies was operating in Britain. A newspaper article really did encourage the public to ask to see a passport if a waiter claimed to be Swiss. Most of these fears proved unfounded, though. However, Kell eventually did discover a network of spies who were working for German Naval Intelligence.

ABOUT STACY HENRIE

Stacy Henrie graduated from Brigham Young University with a degree in public relations. Not long after, she switched from writing press releases and newsletters to writing inspirational historical romances. Born and raised in the West, where she currently resides with her family, she loves the chance to live out history through her characters. In addition to writing, she enjoys reading, road trips, interior decorating, chocolate, and most of all, laughing with her husband and kids. You can learn more about Stacy and her books by visiting her website.

Find Stacy online:

Website: www.stacyhenrie.com

Facebook: Stacy Henrie

Twitter: @StacyHenrie

Made in the USA
Monee, IL
22 May 2020